D0297172

Honeydew

ALSO BY EDITH PEARLMAN

Binocular Vision

How to Fall

Love Among the Greats

Vaquita

Honeydew

Stories

Edith Pearlman

JOHN MURRAY

First published in Great Britain in 2015 by John Murray (Publishers)
An Hachette UK Company

1

© Edith Pearlman 2015

A CIP catalogue record for this title is
available from the British Library

Hardback ISBN 978-1-444-79701-5
Trade Paperback ISBN 978-1-444-79702-2
Ebook ISBN 978-1-444-79703-9

Printed and bound by Clays Ltd, St Ives plc

John Murray policy is to use papers that are natural, renewable
and recyclable products and made from wood grown in sustainable forests.
The logging and manufacturing processes are expected to conform to the
environmental regulations of the country of origin.

John Murray (Publishers)
338 Euston Road
London NW1 3BH

www.johnmurray.co.uk

To Sandy Siler

Contents

Contents

Contents

Honeydew

Tenderfoot

Tenderfoot was a pedicure parlor on Main Street near Channing. Two reclining chairs—usually only one was in use—faced the street through a large plate-glass window. And so customers, alone with Paige, got a kind of public privacy—anybody could see them, no one but Paige could hear them. Paige was an expert listener—rarely commenting on what she heard, never repeating it.

She was a widow, forty-nine and childless. She lived behind and above her store. She played poker with five other women every Saturday night. They called one another by their last names and smoked cigars. She had lost her husband, a talented mechanic, to the war. Carl was in favor of the war, more or less; but he'd joined up mainly to get further mechanical training at the military's expense. She'd objected to his risking their joint future, their happiness...but she'd let the argument drop. The Marines took him despite his age. And then, three days into the desert, the tank he was riding met a mine. Each of his parts was severed from the others, and his whole—his former whole—was severed from Paige.

Paige's practice expanded. She had always been popular with faculty wives and local lawyers and dentists, who appreciated that a footbath administered by a discreet attendant squatting on a stool could become a kind of secular confessional. Now, perhaps because of her recent sad history, she caught on with booksellers and high school teachers and nurses. They discovered how easy she was to talk to. Doctors sent patients to her, elderly women who could no longer bend down to clean their feet, could no longer clip their own toenails. Elderly men too—their joints were as stiff as their wives'.

That fall—the fall of Bobby Farraday's arrival at the college to teach art history—other male clients began to appear, not sent by their doctors. A professor emeritus of physics was the first. Then another professor, not emeritus. The high school principal, in a fit of bravado, had his toenails painted raspberry sherbet, chattering all the while.

Bobby had rented rooms ideal for someone newly separated with no interest in changing his circumstances. He hung the engravings that had been his, not Renée's, in the living room and the narrow one-bedded bedroom. The tiny kitchen was just big enough for him and an unseen resident mouse. These rooms and kitchen were on the second floor of a Victorian, and the bathroom occupied the whole of the third-floor turret. The house happened to be located on Channing Street near its intersection with Main, which put it more or less diagonally opposite Tenderfoot. Bobby and Paige often ran into each other in the early evening—at the vegetarian market, at the newspaper and tobacco kiosk, at the bookstore. Sometimes they talked, as neighbors do.

Secretly he considered himself more than her neighbor. He

was her invisible housemate, as the mouse was his. His high bathroom had a broad curtainless window next to the toilet. The window gave him an angled view of the work space of the pedicure shop and a bit of Paige's living area. He took advantage of his situation. Sometimes he stood to watch the pedicures, but usually he sat on the lidded toilet, like a peep-show connoisseur. He liked to see the customers relax on the chair, as if this quasi-biblical experience transported them to some soapy heaven; as if, briefly dead, they could call their sins forgiven. Or maybe they were just happy to have a chance to kick off their shoes and talk about their troubles.

He conducted his classes, showed his slides, met with students during his office hours. He found the teaching and the kids distracting. One of the blond young women reminded him of Renée—knowledgeable on the outside, unsure on the inside. But even inviting a student to take in a movie was forbidden; and so he hurried away from his office hours to watch, alone, the blameless performance on Main Street.

The days got shorter. Paige's last customers walked under dim streetlights and entered a brightly lit shop. One dark afternoon Bobby saw the red-cheeked chemistry professor and his wife side by side on the chairs as if driving to the movies. Paige, gently kicking her stool, moved from one to the other.

Down in his study Bobby took off his own shoes and then his right sock. He had stopped attending to his feet after the accident. Now, how appalling the linty corned toes, how distressing the jagged toenails. No wonder all his socks had holes. He took off his left sock and rested the left foot on his right knee. His heel was scored with lines, as if it could reveal his fortune. Still barefoot, he returned to his unlit turret and looked out of the window. Bent over the chemistry professor's tootsies,

Paige personified hard work, like Renée bent over her briefs. Back in New York, Renée had moved inflexibly toward her goal—she wanted to be made partner—whereas Bobby had practiced indifference and inattention, writing careless reviews for short-lived arts magazines, making off-the-cuff attributions for the galleries he consulted for. This difference in attitude had led to arguments.

After her last customer left Paige often came out and sat on the store's single broad step and lit a narrow cigar. Bobby used the toilet, reading by flashlight. He turned off the flashlight and watched her smoke. Around midnight she went to bed. He did too.

This went on for a while. He thought of buying binoculars, but she wasn't a bird. He thought of dragging out his opera glasses, but she wasn't a soprano. He thought of employing his loupe, but she wasn't a work of art, and even if she had been a painting he was too far away to examine brushstrokes. After the first snowfall she wore a parka outdoors, and a fuzzy hat. She needed a fur coat—otter, maybe, like Renée's—but the animal-rights students would put her in the stocks. Anyway, she probably couldn't afford a fur coat. How much did you collect for a dead Marine? And even a flourishing pedicure business couldn't make a big profit. She could always go to work in the local pharmacy, he supposed. She'd studied pharmacy, she told him once; but she preferred this work—she was her own boss, and she ministered directly to people.

Spring at last moistened the town. Impasto leaves replaced pastel buds. He considered self-improvement. He might become a vegan. Let the mouse have his cheese. "So how much does it cost?" he blurted one afternoon. They'd met in the health store, he holding a jar of prune extract plucked in a hurry from the shelf, she examining something in a bottle.

"This is a dollar an ounce. But for efficacy it has to be mixed with—"

"Not the snake oil. A pedicure."

She looked up. Her eyes in her lightly wrinkled face were the blue of a Veronese sky. "Fifty dollars. Ten more for polishing. Tipping not allowed."

"Oh. Can I have one?"

"Sure."

"When?"

"Friday at eight."

"Eight? My cubism seminar is at eight thirty..."

She smiled. "Eight in the evening."

"Oh...I'll see you then?"

"See you," she assured him.

Friday night he scrubbed his feet. He put on clean socks. He snatched up a book he wasn't reading, *The Later Roman Empire*.

He took the left-hand chair. When he tipped his head sideways and raised his eyes he could see the window to his bathroom, its light carelessly left on, wasting his landlady's electricity.

While Paige was filling an oblong wooden tub with hot water and a swirl of thick white stuff, he took off his shoes. She herself removed his socks, folding them onto the top of the table between the chairs. In the old days Renée had picked them up from the floor, stuck out her tongue at him.

"White, red, or tea?" Paige asked.

"...White."

She moved to the back of the room and a refrigerator door opened and closed. She put a goblet of wine on the table next to the socks. "You can recline further. Just push the little button on the side of the arm." He reclined further. A ledge rose with his bare feet on it. She dragged over her stool and sat down. He covered his erection with *The Later Roman Empire*. She rolled up each leg of his jeans to the middle of the calf.

Then she contemplated her new customers. "Have they ever had a pedicure?"

"Nope. Ten little virgins."

"Some men find the process effeminizing."

"Well...no polish, please."

"Not a drop. And some find it decadent, like your Romans. We'll see how you feel."

Wearing surgical gloves she examined his dreadful feet—the corns, the ragged nails, the discoloration, the beginning of a bunion, the heels that seemed made of animal horn. Then she fetched the tub of water. Cradling his ankles in one arm, she bent back the foot ledge of his chair and moved the tub a little and slid his feet into the warm liquid.

The stuff that resembled crème fraîche turned out to be a lightly foaming soap and the water glimpsed beneath it a smoky gray. He closed his eyes, imagined a future filled with princely attentions.

After a while he opened them. He saw that she was continuing to sit on her stool, a thick towel on her lap, and that his now clean but still unsightly feet were on the towel. They seemed detached from his body, from his rolled-up jeans; they were a pair of unnecessary footnotes. "Ibid and Sic," he named them aloud.

"Exfoliation is the next task," she told him.

"Exfoliation?" He knew what it meant, but her voice was a lyre.

"To exfoliate is to cast off or separate in scales, flakes, sheets, or layers. Flakes is what your feet will yield."

She began to scrape his soles and heels with an elfin scalpel. He glanced at her. The dark head was bent, and she offered no small talk. So he closed his eyes again, thinking of his mother and tender bathtimes. But a different memory muscled in.

They were driving in a snowstorm. They wanted to get home. Everyone on the highway, coming and going, wanted to get home. Twelve inches were expected. The storm forbade speed. Whiter and whiter became their medium, and all the cars within it a pastier white, white spread with a knife. Suddenly, on the other side of the median strip, a bit of humped purple spun like a dancer, lifted itself like an animal, groped in the air with its four round feet, and fell back onto its roof. It lay in the highway. Other automobiles edged slowly past it.

"Did you see?" Renée gasped.

"Yes."

"Go back."

"No."

"There'll be a turnaround ahead. We *must* go back."

"And do our own somersault? There are state police. There are other people traveling in the same direction as that Volkswagen."

"Other people? Nobody is stopping. Only us."

"Not us, darling."

He heard the click of her seat belt and she fell onto his feet and tried to pry his boot off the accelerator.

"Stop that, Renée. I'll have to kick you."

"Kick me."

He didn't kick her; his instep sternly lifted her hands. The buckle of his boot met her face and entered it, though he didn't know that until later. She gave up then, and hunched in her seat, crying, crying.

"Put your seat belt back on."

Click. She stopped crying, stopped speaking. They got home after a few more perilous hours. She slept on the couch. And the next day, a Band-Aid on her cheek, and a little rosy streak making its infected way toward her chin, she went silently to work.

And then she transformed the episode into an argument about moral responsibility. It was what she did best, and so she did it—night after night, then once a week, then once a month. He argued back to show he cared about ethical behavior, though what tormented him was the vision. He saw the spin and the overturn again and again. Then he elaborated: onto a white shirred background came a splash of purple; it bounced; broken stick figures slid from the half-open door. Or he saw, within the upended machine, soft sculptures sinking into their own mashed heads. Or he saw the windows shatter and the white surround become splattered and splotched with red, ecru, gray—blood, flesh, brains. Porcelain bits landed on the canvas: bones and teeth.

When the letter came from the college inviting him to teach he presented it to her. She said no.

He wrote *Yes;* and shipped the etchings; and boarded a plane.

"Exfoliation completed," said Paige's soft voice. He opened his eyes. She held the folded towel aloft. He beheld a mountain of translucent flakes of skin with here and there a toenail poking out and, on top of the mountain, a large bit of callus she had removed without his feeling a thing. He marveled at this exuda like a small boy proud of his poop. "A second soaking now," and she brought new, clear, warm water.

He soaked without assistance.

She sat down next to him. She sighed: a rather happy sound. Perhaps fate, working through the rental agent who showed him his place, had delivered him to her. She could learn to like paintings, even cut down on poker. He sighed too; and with his nearer hand he picked up the wine from the table between them and transferred it to his other hand. She put her palm on top of his folded socks. He fingered her fingers.

Together they watched a cab roll down Channing Street toward them, bright eyes shining. It stopped at his house. Out stepped a blonde in a belted raincoat. The April thaw was too warm for the otter. Her hair was more disheveled than he'd ever seen it outside of the bedroom. A stocky cabwoman removed a large wheeled suitcase.

"That's Finnegan's cab," Paige said. "She's a poker friend of mine."

Finnegan received her money and drove away, though the house was dark except for the turret. Renée left the suitcase on the sidewalk and went up the steps to the door. Bobby could see her, could feel her, pushing the bell.

Renée stood in front of the door for a while, then with bowed head descended the stairs and trundled her suitcase across Channing and headed toward Main. He could see her pretty face and the expression of anxiety it never quite lost. It was the face that had approached him as she walked down the aisle. He could see, or thought he could, the scar he'd created. He could guess that she had at last forgiven him for not turning around and driving back and extracting corpses from the Volkswagen. He had long ago forgiven her those saintly reproofs. She crossed Main and stood in front of Tenderfoot, peering in.

Should he let her in? Her presence or nonpresence, her forgiveness or dismay, his occasional indulgence in exfoliation, or in psychoanalysis, meditation, religion, drugs, coffee enemas— nothing would scrub from his mind's eye the purple machine leaping upward into the falling snow and returning head-down to asphalt. He had to live with the memory. He might as well live with Renée too.

Still he sat.

Still she peered.

With an irritated shrug Paige walked to the door, opened it, nodded at the after-hours guest, motioned her inside.

"This is Renée, my wife, former," said Bobby. "This is Paige, my pedi... my aesthetologist."

"Pleased."

"Pleased."

"Perhaps we could have some more wine," Bobby said.

"Perhaps you could dry your feet," Paige said, "and take the lady home."

He was slow about foot drying, shoelace tying, looking in vain for the book on Rome, paying. He forgot not to tip; Paige took the extra money. At last they were gone, Renée still wheeling the suitcase. Paige turned to the welcome chores of throwing towels into the washing machine and boiling instruments. Then she turned out the lamps in the shop.

His turret was still bright. She knew that he spied on her from its obliging window. She had seen him plain, doing it at twilight; she had seen him at night, when the mild light from the streetlamps entered the turret and was modestly strengthened by porcelain and mirror, creating a complicated chiaroscuro background against which his seated form was an opaque cutout. Maybe the comings and goings at Tenderfoot raised his spirits; maybe he needed to transcend difficult moments on the can. She'd sympathized with his aloneness; she'd considered it promising. Now—for he had talked unaware during his reverie, people often did—she knew that he was not alone, that he lived in the crushing embrace of an unforgettable incident.

Even when miserable after Carl's death she had endured no such haunting. When she thought of Carl she remembered with pleasure the soft brown hair of his thick eyebrows, and the reflective way he examined any broken-down appliance before deciding how to fix it, and Sunday football, and the disappointing fact of his sterility, though it had troubled him more than it did her: she played the hand she was dealt. And anyway, he wasn't impotent. Oh, his feet. He liked her to wash his feet and clip his nails, and she liked to do it, and they always made love afterward, first lowering the shop's blinds, then lying flat on the floor, sole to sole. Edging forward, he stroked her inner thighs with his heel and then he put his big toe in her keyhole and worried it for a while, and that was all she needed. After her ecstasy they progressed to conventional positions and a second pleasure.

She sat down in Bobby's chair and kicked off her clogs. She picked up *The Later Roman Empire*—it was hiding under a towel. She let her bare feet slide into his tray of water, now cold. She felt the calm disinhibition that liquid provided. She thought: Bobby and his wife, former, had been selected to witness a disaster and had failed to act. Another thought, heavy and treaded like a tank, rolled up to her; Carl gazed out of it with disappointment. She too had failed to act. She had not refused to let Carl enlist. She might have stopped him. She *could* have held him home. "Who knew there wasn't a child in that car?" Bobby had inquired half an hour ago, eyes closed, Ibid and Sic on her lap, not knowing or caring that he was thinking aloud, not knowing or caring that his unmoving feet had kicked a hole in her smooth innocence. "An infant, maybe."

An infant, an ancient, a mature U.S. Marine...what matter who. Whoever they were they had been flipped into lifelessness and had abandoned the future. They had turned their dead backs on survivors now doomed to mourn until the end of their own days.

Dream Children

Willa found the first portrait on a July evening while she was straightening her room. She had invited the two older boys to play there before bedtime, and the floor was strewn with chessmen and Othello counters. She picked up these fragments and put them where they belonged: in the next-to-lowest drawer of a scarred, ivory-knobbed chest—an architect's chest, the mother had told her—that stood under the window. Willa's own blouses and underwear lay in the shallow upper drawers. The chest and a lamp and a bed—a bed not quite long enough; she often slept on the floor—were the only furnishings in this narrow room behind the kitchen. But the other rooms didn't have much in them either. In her country there was a TV in every village bar, and in the island's capital city even the poorest family owned a set. But in this New York apartment—none.

"We don't like to watch, we don't want the children to watch," the mother said that first day, looking up anxiously at tall Willa. "But if you wish..."

"No, ma'am."

"No *ma'am*, please," the mother cried.

"No, ma'am, please," Willa repeated.

"No, no, I mean, do call us by our first names: Sylvie—"

"Yes, ma'am," Willa said.

"—and Jack."

The bottom drawer in the architect's chest was stuck. Every night she caressed the knobs as if to fool them, dark fingers soothing the ivory, and then gave a single sudden yank. Tonight the thing slid out at last. In the drawer were some large, deckled drawing papers, facedown. She picked up the top one and turned it over.

It was a pencil-and-watercolor portrait of a little boy. The left side of the child's face bulged like a potato, a blue and purple potato. It wasn't swollen because someone had smacked him, wasn't bruised either, the worst smack couldn't do that, he had been born that way. The eye above the bulging cheek seemed okay. The right side of the face was ordinary. The lower lip was a rubbery ledge, bigger on the left than the right. The upper lip almost met the lower lip on the big side of the face and didn't meet it at all on the other side. Spittle, she could see it, a few curly lines.

Boy's costume was like Pinocchio's: shorts, a honey-colored vest, a shirt, kneesocks. The black hair was thick and neatly parted. Somebody was taking care of him. He carried a toy boat. There was a friendly dog at his feet, exactly the color of the vest.

The portrait was signed with a date—five years ago—and the initials *J.L.* The father's imagining, then.

Willa put Boy back in the drawer. She went into the living room. They liked her to join them there, just as they liked her to eat with them. They worried about everything—traffic, poisons in food, mosquitoes, whether she was happy.

Dr. Gurevich from across the street was talking, her eyes huge in her square face. "I will bar the door," she rasped. "I will lie down in front of the bulldozer." She leaned forward. "I will drill their evil skulls."

Then she leaned back, as if to get away from her own popping eyes. Maybe she had the goiter. She wore her gray hair in a bun.

The father said, "I heard of a group practice, three men on East Twelfth Street. They're looking for a fourth, and they'd prefer a woman."

"East Twelfth Street?" Dr. Gurevich sat up straight again. "I belong here, on West Eighty-Fourth Street. The city has given me no satisfaction," she added.

"The firm who owns your building hasn't broken any laws," the father said. "I looked into it, remember?"

Dr. Gurevich was being evicted from her narrow building across the street. She was a dentist, and lived and worked in her second-floor apartment. Willa had been brought to see it one day in June by the ten-year-old, who planned to be a dentist himself. Patients sat on a chair in a bay window. "See, Willa, this would be a dining room for a regular person," the boy had explained. He climbed into the chair. "Dr. Gurevich doesn't require a dining room," he said, opening his mouth and baring his teeth. Then he said, "Wider, please. She eats her soups wherever she likes—sometimes on the fire escape. Spit, please."

A firm had bought Dr. Gurevich's house and the one next door, and sent notices that condominiums were to be built. The current occupants must leave by July 1.

Willa had watched July 1 come. She'd watched it go. The other tenants left. The dentist remained, along with the janitor, who lived in the basement. There wasn't much work for him in the building, so he planted vegetables and fruits in the deserted back garden. Raspberries were just emerging.

"You could plant squash," Willa said.

"We won't last until squash," he told her.

But tonight, Dr. Gurevich, raging in their living room, looked as if she would last forever.

There was a *cheep* from the end of the hall. The *cheep* came again; then again; then a rapid twittering of sounds.

Willa got up and walked down the long hall and went into the darkened bedroom. The five-year-old slumbered spread-eagled on his parents' bed. She rested her palm briefly on his back. His bony face lay in profile on the pillow. The three older boys resembled the mother—sharp features, long mouths, narrow intelligent eyes. The little fat fourth looked like the father. "Each one starts out looking like Jack," the mother had mentioned; and the father laughed: "All babies look like me."

Willa bent down to the cradle and slid her hands under the newest soul. Her fingers found a place beneath his head and her thumbs hooked around his moist armpits and she swung him up onto her shoulder. This always satisfied him for a while; he slept again, his nose against her neck, pressing the pulse there, life to life.

She brought him to the changing table that was wedged between sink and tub in the apartment's bathroom. The floor tiles were chipped but there was a stained-glass window featuring a tall, robed redheaded figure. "After Burne-Jones," the mother had bewilderingly said when she was showing Willa around. The mother was a part-time professor. The father was an engineer.

Willa changed the baby. He opened his eyes and stared at her. She carried him into the living room and handed him first to the dentist, who pressed him against her dress; and then to the father, who laid the child on his own wide thighs and stared at him as if to memorize the eyelids, the lips, the damp folds on the neck; and then to the mother, who said, "Thank you, Willa." The mother released her firm little breast from her shirt; milk was already spurting.

"What a warm night," the dentist said.

"Warm," said the father serenely. "Warm?" he repeated with a nervous twitch of his cheek, as if he sensed a hurricane.

"Warm, sir," said Willa. That nightmare child in the bottom drawer—it was like having a secret family.

The baby suckled. The father and the dentist and Willa silently watched. They might have been underwater; they might have been floating on the surface of a pond; they might have been sitting on lily pads like the illustrations in the favorite book of the second boy, the eight-year-old—a textbook about frogs.

The mother shifted the baby to the other breast. "Good night," said Dr. Gurevich. She let herself out and walked down the three flights and crossed the street.

A week later, at five in the afternoon, Willa opened the drawer and looked at another picture.

Its subject seemed to be female—at least, the figure was wearing a smocked dress. There was trimming on the puffed sleeve; she could tell from the swift little circles that the trimming was lace. Fine lines on the slender hands represented wiry hairs; broader lines on cheeks and chin were hair too. There was fur on the scalp. This creature's eyes were dull. Her nose was all nostrils. The upper lip was long, and the mouth stretched widely in a smile without happiness.

The date on Monkey Girl's portrait was eight years ago, and

the paper was initialed with the father's two letters. If he were hers, Willa thought, she'd insist that he purge his bowels with bark, once a week if need be.

Willa came out of her room to find Dr. Gurevich in the kitchen, heating some of her own soup. "My electricity has been turned off," said the dentist. "The janitor is hooking it up again, to somebody else's line, please don't ask me how."

"All right," Willa said.

"Willa, Willa, what is to become of me?"

Back home this old woman would have been respected. She would not have been forced to work. People would have brought her stew and beer and smokes, and she would have sat on her porch and looked at the sea. "I have a...leaf," Willa said.

Dr. Gurevich was silent. Then: "Something I could roll?"

Willa nodded. "I can show you how."

The woman sniffed. "And will it find me a new apartment and a new office?"

"It will ease your spirits."

They exchanged a long look. "Please," said Dr. Gurevich.

All of Willa's herbs were in the third drawer from the bottom, above the chess pieces. Rolling took a few minutes. She left Dr. Gurevich smoking in the kitchen. She picked up the baby without waking him and went down to the curb to meet the day-camp bus. How tanned they had become. The five-year-old buried his face in her belly—it was a long day for him. The ten-year-old trudged into the building, the eight-year-old at his heels.

Upstairs the boys crowded into the kitchen to help prepare the evening's baked rice and salad. Dr. Gurevich took her weed into the living room. There, dark and featureless against the window, she looked like Aunt Leona, who'd told the future. "You will be useful to the family in New York," Leona had promised Willa. "They will be kind to you, in their way."

The father came home. The mother came home. The janitor rang the bell and called up through the intercom that Dr. Gurevich's electricity was on again. Dr. Gurevich, throwing Willa a sweet glance, left the apartment to join him.

Dr. Gurevich's water got turned off early one August morning. The janitor—no longer on salary, but still occupying a room in the basement—said he could attach their pipes to another main, but not before nightfall. The dentist canceled that day's patients. She had fewer patients now than formerly, and those who came urged her to find new premises. "They think it's easy to pull up roots," she said. "You understand how hard it is, Willa."

Willa nodded. She was holding the five-year-old on her lap. He had begged to stay home from camp that day. So the dentist, the mother, the baby, Willa, and the five-year-old all sat on the stoop of the family's apartment house and watched the empty brownstone next to Dr. Gurevich's house get wrecked. Neighborhood children who didn't go to day camp watched too, and some of their mothers. The wrecking ball swung forward and backward, attacking the façade like a boxer. Stone and glass and wood and plaster crumpled at its touch. Debris piled up. Meanwhile an earthmover in back picked up the junk and deposited it into an enormous dumpster. A few scavengers hung around.

Willa, abruptly homesick, thought of her aunt's little house on stilts, and the foaming sea, and her own three daughters in their school uniforms, there without her.

The building gradually collapsed. The debris mounted in its stead. By midafternoon the wrecking truck had driven off, leaving the busy earthmover to its work. The ice cream truck jingled down the street.

The mother took the baby upstairs for a bath. The five-year-old dozed in Willa's lap. The street got more crowded: cars, teenagers on skates, the knife grinder, a bicycle whose wide basket carried stacks of straw boaters. "Hats! Hats!" the cyclist shouted. When the camp bus came, it couldn't pull up against the right curb and so it parked on the left. The children would have to step out into the street, Willa saw. The bus had its flashers on but who knew? "Hold him, please," said Willa to Dr. Gurevich, transferring the five-year-old to the dentist. Willa went out into the middle of the street and stood beside the bus, staring down the impatient cars. She heard the children behind her, crossing the street—her two, and some others from the building. The father rounded the corner from the subway, and he started to run, though it couldn't have been easy, he was so fat. "Where's Paul! I don't see Paul!" he yelled, and Willa pointed to the child on the dentist's lap, and the father stopped running and took off his seersucker jacket and mopped his face with it, though she had ironed all his handkerchiefs just yesterday.

That night she looked at the third picture. This one was a baby dressed only in a diaper, a baby of about a year, the age of toddling. This child would never toddle. Instead of legs, he had flippers; instead of arms, flippers. His eyes had no pupils. His bare chest was like any white baby's: pink, the nipples suggested by rosy dots, so sweet she wanted to kiss them.

The date on Seal Baby was ten years ago. There were no more drawings: just the three.

When the youngest started to run a fever, the mother gave him some liquid medicine, not aspirin. "We don't give aspirin to babies, Willa."

"We don't either, ma'am."

"*Ma'am* again—oh, oh, oh."

"...Sylvie," Willa managed.

When the fever continued—down in the morning, up again in the afternoon, higher still at night—the parents brought him to the pediatrician's office. Willa and the boys did a jigsaw puzzle at home. Virus, not bacteria, the pediatrician said; it will run its course.

"But how long is its course?" the father moaned on the fourth day. "*You* never had such a high fever," he accused the eight-year-old, who burst into tears. "I am sorry, I am sorry," the father said, and he hugged his son.

At night the adults took turns tending the infant, sitting in the living-room rocking chair. While the mother was rocking him, Willa slid into the kitchen. She carried a packet of the reddish powder Aunt Leona had pounded from various nuts. She boiled water and let the powder steep. By the time it was her turn to rock the baby, the tea had cooled. She poured it into a bottle and slipped the bottle into the pocket of her apron. She took the baby and sat down on the rocker. Exhausted from fretting, he fell asleep on her shoulder. She heard the mother stumble into the bedroom. The father came out; she heard him in the kitchen opening some contraption, a folding chair maybe...There was a full moon. Through the living-room window Willa saw Dr. Gurevich and the janitor walking down the street, arm in arm.

Willa took the bottle from her apron. She shifted the baby to her lap and cradled him and stroked first his left cheek and then his right, and at last he opened his eyes and then his mouth and she inserted the nipple. Looking at her, he drank about two-thirds of the bottle. She could feel the heat draining from his body, feel his breathing become slower, feel the rasp in his chest grow still. He slept again. He smiled in his comfortable sleep. She got up and carried him into the kitchen. The contraption she had heard was an easel. The father was working at a drawing, intently using the side of his pencil to create shadows...

"Jack."

He turned. "What! What!"

"The fever has broken."

He took the baby from her. He was not ashamed to cry. But when she stared at the drawing—only a head this time, pointed ears and one eye missing and an open mouth, lipless—he gave an embarrassed snort. "It's like an amulet; it's to prevent catast—"

She touched his shoulder to show she understood. Then she moved to the sink and took the bottle from her pocket and unscrewed the nipple and tipped the thing, and the rest of the amber-colored potion poured out in front of his eyes and hers.

Castle 4

The hospital—red-brick High Victorian Gothic—had been built atop a low hill just after the Civil War. It was named Memorial Hospital but was soon referred to as the Castle. The structure had been modernized inside, many times, but the balustrades and turrets and long thin windows from which you could shoot arrows at your enemies—all these remained.

And, like a true medieval fortress, it cast its formidable shadow on the surrounding area. Everyone who worked in it or lived near it or occupied its rooms felt its spirit: benign maybe, malign maybe, maybe neither, at least for now. The place harbored secrets—electronic information, sneaky bacteria—and it was peopled by creatures who had wandered in or maybe had lived there since birth, like the AIDS babies, the short-gut babies, the babies lacking brain stems: all abandoned to the Castle by horrified parents who sometimes even fled the state. There were beautiful ladies-in-waiting—waiting to die; and crones whose futures were no happier; and tremulous knights; and bakers with envelopes of magical spices. There was an ugly guard with a kind heart.

* * *

Zeph Finn had lived for the past year and a half in the Castle's domain, first in the residents' quarters and now in the top flat of one of the nearby three-deckers. He rarely went anywhere: he shuffled from Castle to flat, flat to Castle. He had ventured forth tonight, however, to a potluck party. And now a pretty girl had asked him something, but for God's sake what, he hadn't heard—oh, what do they always ask. "I do regional anesthesia," he guessed.

"Oooh, do you. What region—the Boston area? Do you move from one hospital to another hospital?"

Silent, Zeph moved from this guest to another guest. Most of the potluck people here were doctors and knew that a regional anesthesiologist specialized in nerve blocks. Many knew Zeph. Because of this familiarity he'd agreed to drop in, a box of cheese straws under his arm. The host, chief of the emergency room, was one of his few friends—his dogwalkers, he called them; they dragged him outside whenever he'd been noticeably unresponsive for a while.

He had no girlfriend at present. He never had a girlfriend for long. But there were some women who saw in his numbed silence, his reluctance to meet the eye, something to work with. They hoped to rescue him. Rescuing the rescuer, ha! A doomed enterprise.

"He's married to his specialty," somebody once said to somebody.

"Oh, no," said the other somebody. "He's engaged to his cart."

Zeph had heard this joke and was not offended. Who wouldn't feel an abiding affection for that cart of scrupulously ordered drawers with a disposal container attached to one side. Needles, syringes, label tapes, and IV catheters in the top drawer. More needles and ampoules in the second. Continuous-nerve-block sets in the third. Emergency stuff in the fourth, along with drugs whose names scanned like poetry, according to a would-be girlfriend who had memorized them as an aid to seduction. "Lidocaine, ephedrine, phenylephrine, epinephrine," she began, and then got stuck on *atropine*, poor puppet.

When he left the party he walked home along half of the perimeter of the hospital grounds, looking up at the edifice every so often. A huge parking lot floated from the rear. Some old-timers—that is, docs who had been young in World War II—remembered the year-by-year expansion of the lot.

But long before that brutal felling of trees, neighborhoods were forming just beyond the fringe. At the beginning of the last century a subway station had been constructed near the Castle and the three-deckers were built. They became—they were expected to become—dwelling places for the poor. Birthed together like litters, block after block, the houses were clapboard, and each floor had a porch. There was a plot of land in the back of each to be shared by all three tenant families; Irish then, now folks from more faraway places: there were the Filipino blocks, the Venezuelan area, Little Brazil...Many adults worked in the Castle; others took the subway to jobs in town. Each neighborhood had a few restaurants, a bar, a grocery, a couple of day-care centers.

The area had one unexpected feature, discovered when the three-deckers were erected. This was a stream, mostly underground, but running for a while through a little wood. The earth was more swamp than soil; strange bushes and spindly, widely spaced trees thrived in it; nothing could be built on its softness, you couldn't even hide there. The city, acknowledging the piece of land unprofitable, might have embellished it a bit, put up markers to identify the vegetation, made a sanctuary of it for people and birds. But the city left it alone. The two public schools among the neighborhoods of the Castle each had a playground and a basketball court, and one had a baseball field. And so kids ignored the little forest. The only people to visit it during the day were peculiar children, perhaps shunned by their boisterous fellows, perhaps preferring isolation. Zeph went there occasionally to smoke and very occasionally to snort.

This summer the woods were being explored by two sixth-graders from the Filipino community, Joe and Acelle, Joe because he liked plants and insects, Acelle because she liked Joe. Every afternoon Joe tolerated Acelle's almost wordless presence. Her chief occupation when school was out was helping her only sister—their mother was dead. When not busy with that task she followed Joe, obeyed him, adopted his ideas. Sometimes, though, she just lay down and listened to the birds.

"My house is too quiet," she explained.

"Mine isn't."

Acelle's flat held three people at its most crowded; Joe's was occupied always by a festival of relatives. Even the basement had been taken over. The only real silence was in the doc's place on the third floor. Joe could go there anytime, even when it was empty; and when Zeph was there it was as good as empty.

For a few hours each day these children waded, climbed trees, chased rabbits, dissected worms, and built a kind of teepee, which they called Castle 2.

There were three entrances to Castle 1. The wide one, designed for horse-drawn wagons, was now used by ambulances.

Another served the parking lot, and had become willy-nilly the main entrance. The former main entrance, with its five arches—four windows and a door—welcomed people who came on foot or by bus, who walked up the numerous stairs to the door or were wheeled up a winding ramp by a feeble relative or, if their arrivals coincided with his, by Zeph.

This was the access that Zeph preferred. At dawn the morning after the party, he climbed the stairs, carrying a knobby walking stick, his legacy—his only legacy—from his father. He went through the big doorway into the old beamed hall and then into an old-fashioned elevator like a cage, and then down to the surgical suites, thoroughly up-to-date. He began the ritual of changing his clothes and scrubbing up. Zeph had a limited wardrobe—he was still paying off college and medical-school debts, would be doing so for years—but he always wore a jacket and tie to work. You would expect these garments to smarten him up. In fact they made him seem more shambling and unaware: a tall loose-limbed guy carrying a stick for no apparent purpose.

"Your stick—maybe there's a sword hidden inside," a resident had suggested.

"I've never looked," he fibbed.

As for his head: he had brown hair, too much of it, a blunt nose and chin, and a habit, during conversation, of fastening his gaze on one side of your neck or the other. "Make contact," his preceptors had urged. "Look at me," pleaded women of all types. *Contact? Look?* Not in his repertoire. He had been self-sufficient all his life. He'd gotten through medical school by virtue of a good memory and deft fingers. And despite that continuing interest in the sides of patients' necks, he didn't flunk bedside manner; the soft voice and the thoughtful answers to their questions told patients he was in their corner even if he didn't meet their eyes. Some patients may have even preferred the averted glance.

Zeph's eyes, if you did get a glimpse of them, were dark blue. When he was giving general anesthesia—he occasionally got nonregional assignments—he leaned over the patient and asked him to count backward from ten and there was a kind of cobalt flash just before seven. But mostly Zeph's job was regional, continually administering exactly the right amount of blocking drugs to exactly the right nerves, and delivering a little sedation too. The less stuff given, the better, but there must be enough of it to keep pain at a safe distance. Zeph considered all pain his mortal enemy, all patients of either gender his suffering mother, all surgeons dragons indifferent to the cruelties they were practicing. The patients' conversation during this partially sedated state included long sleepy pauses between phrases and sometimes between words, but the talk only occasionally turned into jabberwocky. The dialogue began in a confidential mode and soon acquired a tone of intimacy, though the topics were unromantic. Bird-watching. Jazz. Immigrants, too goddamn many. Zeph's responses were invitations to say more, continuing the palaver while his hands and eyes kept busy. *What color is the bobolink? You prefer Bird to Coltrane? Yes, many people here were born elsewhere; have you traveled yourself?*—a reply intended to blur insult if anyone had heard it; often the entire surgical team was made up of fellows from the Asian rim or the subcontinent, though the surgeon in charge was usually Yankee. Or Jewish. Sometimes Irish. Zeph was Irish on both sides, though his father had not been a surgeon, not any kind of doctor, just a feckless hippie who named his one child Zephyr and willed him a walking stick and did talk jabberwocky.

When Zeph paid his postoperative visits a few hours after the surgery, the patients did not seem to remember these conversations, and sometimes they did not even remember the man now standing beside their bed with his eyes on their neck. Being forgotten didn't trouble him. He'd learned also to tolerate the next string of visits to the next day's batch of surgical patients, though he always entered the room as if he were metal and had neglected to oil himself. He swiveled his eyes until they briefly met the eyes of the person in the bed. He said his silly name. He shook hands if the patient seemed so inclined. He was here to answer questions no matter how trivial they seemed. He sat down, preferably on a chair, on a stool if necessary, indicating that he was in no hurry. He answered the queries and he wrote a note or two on his clipboard, and when the questions were done (though some were repeated and repeated) he took over the conversation, explaining in the simplest lay terms possible the nature of the dope, its duration, its possible side effects, the probability of nasal intubation, and the unavoidable necessity of tethering the patient's wrists to the side rails. "I'll be taking care of you," he said. And then, with a little less effort than earlier, he met the patient's eyes again. And shook hands, maybe, and said good-bye.

Now, at 6:30 in the morning, he walked in his paper slippers to the OR anteroom, where he was the first doctor to arrive but the second member of the team there; the scrub nurse was always waiting. She helped him into his mask and gloves and he entered the pearl and silver sanctuary. He checked the treasures in his beloved cart. The other docs padded in. Then the first patient, supine on wheels. Things began.

This patient was an overweight man of fifty-seven with diabetes and a raging need for a knee replacement.

"I'm going to insert the needle now, just as I explained," Zeph said, and even as he spoke, the needle was reaching the necessary nerve. Zeph lowered his head toward the patient's head so they could speak and Zeph could meanwhile watch the monitors and not get in the way of the surgeons, already clustered at the knee like jackals. "Are you feeling anything in your left foot?" Zeph said, and a nurse scratched its sole. "No," the man replied. The nurse pinched his thigh. "Do you feel anything in your left thigh?" Zeph said. Another "No." Zeph announced, "Ready," in a firm voice never yet heard outside of the operating room.

The patient told Zeph about sailing: "Nothing like it, you are master, you are jubilant, you yourself are the…are the…"

"Wind?" Zeph suggested.

"Out of body…out of mind…you are made of air and sky."

"Water?"

"Marshmallow…peanut butter."

Zeph reduced the Versed.

"Come out with me sometime, Doc."

"Love to."

The next patient was so talkative that Zeph added diazepam to her IV, then joined in her complaints about children and grandchildren; you would think, if you heard his responses, that dealing with recalcitrant offspring was his life's interest. The third, a boy with a supposedly operable tumor in his abdomen, was a general. Zeph, unable to communicate with this child sunk in artificial sleep, noted that the tumor was extensive and not completely excisable. The final surgery was a lumpectomy, nice and clean. The woman on the table flirted with him and he flirted right back, kept her as close to full awareness as possible. "Have you ever been in love, Blue Eyes?" she giggled.

Afterward, a mute shower, his second of the day, while the chatter that had clung to him drained into the hospital's sewer.

One day, shortly after a rain, something unfortunate happened. While sliding on her backside down the bank toward the stream, Acelle was stabbed by what felt like a dagger. It was in fact only a bit of narrow branch. It would have done little damage had she been wearing jeans, but today she'd worn last year's party dress. Below the striped mini her legs were bare and her upper thigh and even part of her buttock were vulnerable to the miniature weapon; worse yet, the thing had its own pointed twiglet, which had entered the flesh easily enough but, Joe saw, would be a bitch to dislodge.

"It's like a fishhook, pointing backward," Joe explained to Acelle. "They make fishhooks that way on purpose...so they can't be pulled out the way they came in, and the fish can't get loose."

She was lying on her stomach. "Pull it out anyway."

He bent and looked closely at the little bit of tree that seemed to be feeding on her tenderness. "No, the fishhook will rip you. It went in slanted, like a splinter. It's very near the...skin, the surface. Maybe I could cut your skin and lift it out."

"Maybe you could stop talking and do it."

He took out his imitation Swiss Army knife. The two of them had been enjoying it all summer. It was his birthday present. Even this knockoff was so expensive that all his relatives had to chip in. "I should sterilize the blade."

"Spit on it."

Instead he turned around and urinated on it and on his hands. Then he gave her his wadded-up and filthy handkerchief to hold between her teeth. He stretched the affected area between his forefinger and middle finger, and made a swift cut with the point of the blade, just deep and long enough to flip the twig out with the flat of the blade. The nasty twiglet came out too. The thing lay on her thigh; he brushed it off. The bleeding narrowed to a trickle.

"It hurts a lot but not as much as before," Acelle said. "I'm sorry I snapped at you."

Near the main entrance—the de facto main entrance, not the original one that Zeph entered every day with his stick under his arm—was the gift shop that had recently become Victoria Tarnapol's to manage. Victoria had been born in the Castle but had rarely been back since that uncomplicated event nearly six decades earlier. Returning now, even to run the silly gift shop, seemed momentous.

The gift shop was a place where an empty-handed visitor could pick up a box of scented soaps or an embroidered handkerchief or a glass candy dish to delight a moribund patient. A rotating rack of paperbacks was useful, as were the games and puzzles for children. And since Victoria's ascendancy, two round café tables and little chairs had appeared, and she served coffee and tea and slices of the pastry she baked at home early in the morning. Her mini-café became popular—many visitors did not like the hospital cafeteria, where you could overhear conversations between doctors about conditions you'd prefer not to know existed.

Mr. Bahande, a security officer, was posted near the glass-walled gift shop. In those first days he merely nodded to the new manager. But one morning he had to skip breakfast because his older daughter—she had a face like a goddess, she had a spinal deformity—had trouble settling herself at her workbench, and the younger one, who usually helped out, was late for school, and so he had to make all three bologna sandwiches: his, Camilla's, Acelle's. On his midmorning break, when he would normally be walking in the hospital garden, he headed hungrily for the cafeteria instead. But he stopped to look at a ship in a bottle in the gift-shop window—he'd like to try making one of those things—and then, looking up, looking farther in, he saw the café tables, one of them occupied by a man slumped with worry, and behind him, in a little recess, the manager. Her gray hair was cut close to her narrow head. The slide of her nose was interrupted by a bump, adding beauty to a face which was already distinguished. She was slicing something and the sight of that something pulled him right in. It was linzer torte. It turned out to taste better even than Marie's, God rest her soul.

Thereafter he came in every morning at 10:15. He ate various breads, various coffee cakes, various pies; also citron gâteau and baklava and a puff inside which seemed to float not chocolate but its divine essence. He liked them all but he preferred the less sweet pastries. She began to make more of those, fewer of the sugary ones.

Since the gift shop was rarely busy before eleven, they were able lightly to pass the time of day. One morning—the treat was gingerbread with pieces of ginger in it—he asked her to join him at his table. After a moment of confusion, during which her palms reached for her sculpted hair, she washed her hands again and cut a slice for herself and sat down opposite him.

Without discussion Joe and Acelle went to the Castle, using the old entrance, the one Zeph favored. In the emergency room Acelle gave her name and the family's insurance number. She knew it by heart because of her sister's frequent visits. The doctor thought Joe was Acelle's brother and allowed him to remain in the cubicle, but when he examined Acelle he pulled the curtain.

"I'm going to give you a shot of Novocain and then wash this out for you. Have your mother change the dressing every day and put on this ointment, and don't take a bath tonight. I'll give you a tetanus shot for good measure." After doing exactly what he said he'd do, he rolled her onto her back and lifted her easily—she was a small girl—and stood her up. "Dizzy?" he asked. His hand on her shoulder steadied her for a couple of necessary minutes. "Sitting will be painful for a few days." He flicked open the curtain to reveal Joe, waiting on a stool, and on his lap a plastic bag holding Acelle's bloody underpants. "Did you make that incision, dude?"

"Yes," Joe said.

"Good job."

"Good job," Acelle echoed as they left, and she attempted to take his hand, and after a few moments he allowed it to be taken.

And now Zeph prepared to visit patients scheduled for surgery tomorrow. He put on fresh scrubs because people like to see their doctors in costume.

The first was an old childless widow with cancer of the tongue. It was advanced—she had ignored it, had skipped appointments with dentist and doctor, had worn a kerchief whatever the weather, had invented excuses not to visit her few friends still living, all incapacitated anyway. But yesterday, fate in the form of a fissure in the sidewalk had tripped her. The ambulance attendants, placing her swelling hand on her thigh, gently removed the telltale babushka. The lesion bulged like an apricot. The emergency-room doc splinted her broken fingers and she was whisked to Head and Neck, and examined, and talked to, and scheduled for surgery.

Of course the mutilated tongue slurred her speech. But Zeph understood it all, giving her the occasional gift of a direct gaze.

"I taut...go way," she fabricated.

He knew she had not thought it would go away; she had thought instead that discovery would mean instant yanking out of the organ and death shortly afterward, whereas secrecy would mean prolonged if solitary life.

She wanted to know—she had resorted to a pad of paper now, managing the pencil with her less damaged hand—how much of her tongue they would leave. Her surgeon wouldn't say.

"She *can't* say, Mrs. Flaherty. Neither can I. But I can tell you that there are many ways therapists can restore some patients' speech." She had to be content with that, and also with his now averted gaze, though he did press her hand.

"U eye oy" were her parting syllables.

He didn't feel like a nice boy. In two days, when he made his post-op visit, she wouldn't be able to manage even those vowels, and if therapy could help this half-tongued woman it would be a miracle. But he hadn't lied.

He looked at the next patient's chart. An unsingular history. White female; thirty-six years old; unmarried; healthy; one pregnancy, terminated. No immediate family. Complaint: back pain lasting several months, recent inability to walk without severe pain. X-rays and an MRI of the vertebrae showed a mass obscuring L4 and L5 but revealed nothing more about this secret. A needle biopsy had told more. Stage 4.

Her name was Catherine Adrian. Faint lines fanned from the

corners of her eyes. Shallow vertical grooves, one on each cheek, enclosed her sculpted mouth in loving parentheses. Her jaw was long and slender. He could make these observations freely because she was asleep and he could comfortably look at her face.

He glanced at his clipboard. He had three more patients to visit, to reassure about tomorrow, to convince that they were in good hands, or at least that their pain from the knife would be managed to their satisfaction. He'd come back to Ms. Adrian later.

As if on cue, she opened her eyes. They were blue, almost as dark as the ones he avoided in his mirror.

"Hello, Ms. Adrian. I'm Zephyr Finn, your anesthesiologist."

"How nice."

In Ms. Adrian's room there was both a chair and a stool. Zeph chose to sit on the side of her bed. "Are you worried about tomorrow?" he asked.

"Say that I'm curious."

"About...?"

"I want to see what it looks like, this alien that's wrapped itself around my spine. I'd like to watch on a screen while they disappear it."

"Some back operations are done with regional anesthetic," he said as if reading from a script. "Patients on the table can watch a monitor. Most close their eyes. But we don't know the depth of your growth and we can't risk touching an organ while you're awake."

"Can you preserve the thing in alcohol?"

"I can ask the surgeon."

She sighed. "Whatever they find, there will be an end to my pain."

She would soon be paralyzed, he guessed. "Yes," he said with assurance.

And then—as if she were under his care already, as if he had administered a nerve block and a sedative and was keeping her lightly awake—he talked. The volumes by the side of the bed were children's books—*The House at Pooh Corner,* the novels of Peter Dickinson, the Grimms. "I read those too," he said. "My only genre. That small amount of magic."

"Chaste pleasures."

"Endings never final . . ."

She taught mathematics at a local junior college, not a very good one. "I do mainly remediation, I try to make things interesting; some of them fall asleep anyway. I'm a soporific— perhaps I'm really in your game."

Game took them to chess and Scrabble and the Red Sox—he avoided mentioning participatory sports; she probably had played tennis, poor thing. An hour went by. More time would have passed had the surgeon not entered the room to find his best anesthesiologist sitting on a patient's bed.

Robotic again, Zeph got to his feet. "Good afternoon, Dr. Schapiro."

Dr. Schapiro nodded and took Ms. Adrian's hand in his. "How are you feeling today?" he began.

Zeph walked toward the door, turned, flashed his eyes at hers. She flashed back.

The mass, as she was about to learn, had wangled its way inward from its claw hold on L4. A frozen section done in the OR confirmed that the tumor was a ferocious beast; it had already eaten bone; bits of it must be all over the place.

Hector Bahande and Victoria Tarnapol gradually exchanged life stories. Hector spoke of his hopes when he'd come to this country and of the things that had bedeviled him one after another—

his child's affliction, his wife's death, rest her soul, the necessity of finding a job near home. Victoria told him that she had been a youngest daughter persuaded by her sisters to quit art school and take care of their ailing mother. Mama kept ordering her to find a husband who could install all three in a better flat. *Maybe if you cooked better...*

"She won't last forever," Victoria's sisters had falsely assured her. Well, Mama was dead at last. Victoria was not sure she would ask God to rest her soul. "How does your older daughter occupy her time?" she said to Hector.

His face shone. He was short, he had a little paunch (helped along by his recent indulgences), a lumpy nose, not much of a neck, a noticeable mole on one cheek. "She carves," he said, his homely face continuing to beam. "She carves animals and small human figures."

Oh Lord, sweet little lambs, darling odalisques. She was sorry she'd asked.

"Shall I show you?" His hand was already in his pocket. "Most are bigger; this is a mini."

It was the figure of a dog—a puppy, really—peeking in solemn distress, with no cuteness at all, from the jacket of a man. You knew it was a man because the buttons were on the right side and he was wearing a tie, its stripes delicately incised. He had no head and his torso ended just below the frayed jacket.

"Are there more of these?" she asked sharply.

"Many, many, but bigger."

"Does she sell them?"

He shrugged. "There's a man comes to look, takes one or two, comes back with a little money."

A pimp, she thought... "Perhaps I could do the same, and give you a bigger percentage."

He carefully wiped his mouth. "Miss Tarnapol—"

"Victoria."

"Hector is my given name. Victoria, forgive me, who buys a carving here? People want tissue boxes decorated with shells."

"Yes, of course...but I still have friends in the art world. I was also a sought-after window dresser for a time. Hector... may I come and see the others?"

"I will bring you two tomorrow."

He brought a unicorn and a round figure that looked at first like an unpainted Russian doll. The unicorn was smiling. The Russian doll's carved face was not smiling, and her arms in relief, pressing themselves to her stomach, suggested that this would not be an easy labor, that she would perish from it, that the nine or ten dolls nested within her bulk would crumble there.

"Your dealer probably gives you ten percent of what he actually gets for these. Let me try to sell them, and *I* will retain the ten percent and give the rest to you. I'll peddle the unicorn first and put the doll in the gift-shop window as advertisement. 'Not for Sale,' the card will read...intriguing."

"Nobody will be intrigued by a woman about to die in childbirth."

"We'll see."

She placed the unicorn in a gallery about to open in her own town of Godolphin, just over the Boston line. Then she persuaded the owner of a flourishing dress shop in fashionable downtown to display the next piece Hector brought her, a mynah bird with a stocking cap, each stitch visible. An environmentalist bought it, perhaps making sense of its ambiguous message. Victoria split her own commission with the dress-shop proprietor and from then on one of Camilla's pieces always occupied a place of honor there. Some people began to come in not for the clothing, primarily, but to see what was on display, though everyone usually bought at least a skirt and sometimes a whole outfit.

As the weather grew colder and school began, Joe and Acelle abandoned the woods for Joe's house. They had to be quiet during this one shared afternoon hour. Neither of their families would approve of their blameless activity: reading Zeph's anatomy book in Zeph's monkish bedroom. They called the room Castle 3.

Anatomy wasn't altogether strange to them. In sex education, they had seen a coy diagram of a sperm shooting up toward his partner, the ovum; and they knew there were times he would fail to reach her—because of her monthly, maybe, or fate, maybe. "But fate may be against you," the teacher warned. In the anatomy book they had seen artists' renditions of various tumors, some like sacks of vermicelli, some like furry fungi. And when a popular football player injured his knee, the television anchor informed them—separately, for each was at home, though they conferred about it later—that the knee was one of the most complicated joints in the body. Certainly it seemed loaded with ligaments, menisci, tendons, and cartilage. The whole apparatus looked untrustworthy, Acelle told Joe.

"Interdependent," he corrected.

Her father's knee gave him a shitload of trouble. She'd wanted to borrow the book for a night and bring it home to Camilla, who could have looked at the various two-dimensional drawings and carved a knee in her own peculiar style. But Joe would never permit the book to leave the room. So one day Acelle herself tried to draw versions of the joint. Joe was muttering the names of the facial nerves, probably memorizing them. Zeph's book was open on the bed, and they were kneeling before it. Joe kept repeating his sequence, and she kept drawing. Then he turned toward her. "Lacrimal, lingual, mandibular. Aren't you through yet? Ophthalmic."

"Yes," she said. She would come back to the knee.

They turned a few pages, and found the circulatory system.

And there it was, just what she'd been waiting for: a lumpy device with chambers and ventricles and arteries and atriums—atria—looking nothing at all like a valentine. Yet in one of those ventricles love got born, and then leaped to somebody else's ventricle, from one heart to another, that's how it was, it happened in every story she'd read. It happened in palaces and cities and farms and in the neighborhoods. You could be a princess lying in a Castle bed, you could be stuck in a wheelchair, you could be a security guard, you could be a woman with hair like a boy's. The anatomy book did not identify which chamber was the seat of love, but the anatomy book was shy, like Zeph, like Joe...

"It's getting dark," Joe said.

"I'd better go home."

"Tiptoe," he warned.

Catherine would receive her useless chemical infusions as an inpatient—fetching her with an ambulance every day, meanwhile trying to slow the failure of the other organs, was too impractical even for the nitpicking insurance company.

"So I'll die here," she said, "of one thing or another."

It was their five o'clock visit—the only one of the day. This was her most alert half hour. By the end of the first week they knew everything about each other—her long deteriorating love affair; his compliant mother, who followed Old Walking Stick from commune to commune, Zeph in tow, until she died of exhaustion; his difficulty talking to anyone who wasn't on the table; her disappointment with the trajectory of her life. He described special places in the Castle. There was a memorial tomb containing a Civil War soldier in the basement, so big you could sleep on it yourself—he sometimes had done so. The residents' crash room, where anyone with a free quarter of an hour could lie undisturbed on the bed. ("I kept *Treasure Island* under the pillow," he confided.) The hospital chapel, so plain and undenominational that, when empty of sobbing people, it seemed like the waiting area of a railroad station at two in the morning.

He always brought pastry from Victoria, who saved it for him. Catherine managed a bite; after a while Zeph ate the rest. One afternoon, after leaving Catherine, he went into the gift shop and bought the suffering doll. "Preeclampsia," he diagnosed. Victoria quietly took down the Not for Sale sign and wrapped the thing. Zeph put it on a shelf in his room.

The time came when Catherine's organs insisted on failing—kidneys, liver. "Without the chemo I might feel less sick," she said.

"You might."

"I think I'll order it stopped."

He didn't reply.

"What would you do if you were me?"

"If I were you? If I were you I'd marry me."

IV poles were their best men. Zeph had invited Joe and Joe had invited Acelle. The justice of the peace ignored the ages of these witnesses—they could write their names, couldn't they. Through the three narrow archers' windows a pale sun illuminated Catherine's pale face. The groom had remembered to supply the bride with flowers, and he had bought rings for both of them. His "I do" was firm, surprising everyone but Catherine. He leaned over and kissed her on the lips. Her breath was bitter.

He had signed up for vacation beginning that day, and as a family member he was permitted to sleep on a folding cot beside her bed. The walking stick stood aslant in the corner. It did conceal a sword, as Zeph knew. One night Zeph drew the sword from its sheath and swished at the air, back, forth. Catherine laughed a little. He reinserted it.

From the cot he held her hand as both pretended to sleep.

She died a week later of renal failure—more or less peacefully, as such things go.

Camilla didn't become the rage, but she acquired a small reputation in the city, and she banished the crook who called himself a dealer. Victoria persuaded her to entrust her work to a small respectable agency with a good publicist. Camilla agreed, on the condition that her own photograph never appear and her disability not be mentioned. Pride, Victoria expected, could be overcome as time went on. Money came in. The Bahande flat was gradually improved until it looked like a home.

"But what about *your* ten percent?" Hector argued one day after dinner.

He and Victoria were now sitting on the porch, Hector's painful knee elevated on a wicker stool. Victoria had cooked the meal for everyone in the Bahande kitchen—fish, a salad, fruit, walnut bread. Joe had spent the rest of the evening reading Richard Dawkins; Acelle, working on her knitting: a scarf for someone. Zeph watched Camilla carve a cat's head for his walking stick; one feline eye had a congenital droop. Only Camilla knew that Zeph was planning to give the stick to her father. When Joe said he was going home, Zeph had interrupted his silent concentration to keep the boy company on the walk. The girls had gone to bed.

"Your ten percent," Hector said again.

"I'm aging, not an agent. I'm glad someone else is doing that hard work. I'm suited to a gift shop."

"You have been a gift to us," he said softly.

How handsome he looked in his new shirt—though no more handsome than in the security officer's uniform he put on every day.

"As for old—you are not much older than me," he said, leaning forward but not yet touching her.

"I'm sixty."

He nodded without surprise. "I'm forty-five, and my bad joints make me fifty. Come live with us."

She considered this suggestion. Her sisters would never speak to her again—that would be a blessing. She was an experienced caretaker. The family's nutrition would improve. She could keep an eye on the romances developing in the neighborhood.

"Together we can walk to the Castle," she said. And he took that as the acceptance it was.

Stone

She had come south from New York City to live with a small family in a stone house in a flat town. There was lots of wildlife too. She wasn't much of a naturalist, or someone who craved companionship, or a gifted cook. She must, then, be something of a fool.

The flat town was surrounded by low mountains and contained a small college and a river and a single movie house. The family was a decorous threesome. And she, Ingrid? A woman of a certain age, twice widowed, made rich by the second spouse. Member of several boards; at home, always a telephone call away from any one of her interesting friends if she wanted a brief spurt of company; possessed of a little den lined with books when she wanted to be alone. Admired for the arresting angularity of her face; and for her height (she was very tall and her extra-long neck added a few inches); and for the melancholy curve of her smile; and for her golden eyes, halved by bifocals, turning their gaze nowadays toward distant hills, though their usual view was the row of brownstones across the street from her Upper West Side apartment. She lived on Sixty-Third Street.

She *had* lived on Sixty-Third Street. Now, in this town of no account, she was employed by her first dead husband's dead sister's son. During the past decades he'd grown from a rangy quiet boy into a tall taciturn man with thighs as strong as the trunks of pecan trees. Now she engaged in not-quite-confidential conversations with his underweight wife, Lynne. Lynne was exactly the age—thirty-six—of Ingrid's own daughter, a photographer out in Seattle with a wife who was also a photographer. Strung with equipment, the two women came to New York every so often. Eager, bold greyhounds—next to them Lynne could be taken for a rabbit. Now Ingrid played Sorry! with her nephew's five-year-old daughter, Chloe, exactly the age that her own son had been when disease snatched him from her...well, wouldn't that be synchronous. In fact, her little boy had been only four.

Ingrid missed her favorite lunch place on Broadway. She missed those interesting friends; they would do anything for each other, see each other through sicknesses and crises and losses, supply a word that had fallen through a crevice in the brain and try to patch the other cracks of their shared aging. They wanted her to come home; so said their letters (she had taken a vacation from e-mail). Also she missed her dressmaker, a genius whose designs did not attempt to conceal Ingrid's long, long neck with collars or scarves but instead advertised it with long, long necklines, making it seem something that you might want for yourself.

Here she was, and not a dressmaker for miles.

The house was at the end of a dirt road. Its gray stones glinted, and a fecund trumpet vine ran all over the walls. There was a gable roof of slate and a chimney and a pale garden tended by Lynne. The dense woods pressed on the backyard; it seemed as if the two apple trees in front had pushed themselves forward without permission. The house had an old black stove in its kitchen—an inconvenient appliance you had to light with a sparker. Someday, Chris swore, he would provide his family with a house of his own making—wooden, of course, for wood was his business; porched, the better to admire the flowers outside; a second floor as wide as the first; and, in back, a shed for his tools, now rammed behind the furnace. And a real downstairs bathroom, not just a toilet on the other side of the little room off the kitchen, a room called Useless. Useless had a single high window and a sink in one corner. You could wash one handkerchief in that useless sink. Someday, yes, a new house. Meanwhile, Ingrid thought, the small deep-set windows with their lashes of vines gave the old house a knowing air, as if it heard your thoughts.

Ingrid's living there—it had happened in an accidental way. She had been visiting last June—she came every season for exactly four days. Chris was then completing the arrangements to enlarge his carpentry and woodworking business to include the manufacture of wood pellets. He was converting a small plant a few miles away from the shop. The lining up of suppliers and distributors and the hiring of staff—that work would soon take almost all his time. He needed someone to keep the business itself running. Ingrid and his uncle had run a small leather-brokerage company. And so, seemingly out of the blue, he invited her to be the temporary manager; to join his staff and his household as well. "For about three months, I'd say."

"Me? Why on earth me?"

"You are . . . wise."

She shook her head so violently that her glasses flew off—

very smart narrow ones, she hoped they hadn't broken—and her hair shook too, hair that had once been the color of an autumn maple leaf but had now faded to wood shavings. Here and there her expert hairdresser had striped it with the old maple color. "Wise," Chris repeated, with one of his rare smiles. "Worldly."

Did he mean *old?* She sucked in her stomach, and her bosom swelled slightly. She was wearing a V-necked jersey blouse. It had captivated a number of elderly suitors, but paired with these jeans she'd bought yesterday, it probably looked ridiculous. When Chris had first seen the blouse, he turned his face briefly away...Did he think she was too noticeably available? She was still interested in men at seventy-two; perhaps that offended him.

"And warm," he finished, pulled by alliteration. "Can I have you?"

"Oh, good Lord." And she produced an exaggerated and somewhat tactless groan. "I don't think so."

He picked up the fallen glasses and folded the earpieces inward without touching the lenses. Holding the bridge between thumb and third finger, like a ring, he handed them to her. Almost handed them to her, that is—she'd been told that her eyes without glasses gleamed like warning lights. And so, warned, he paused, and pressed his well-defined lips together into a grimace of disappointment—no, it wasn't a grimace, he was preventing himself from saying please. Then he gave her the spectacles. "Maybe?" he said.

Of course not, she thought. And then: *Why not? A stone house instead of a stone city. An underfunded public library instead of that pretentious den. Rabbits on the lawn instead of monkeys at the zoo...*

"Maybe?" he repeated.

"Maybe," she echoed. But it turned out she meant yes.

To slip away from her New York life...it was as easy as stepping on an escalator. Board members would hardly notice her absence; real decisions were made by three or four people who met in a broom closet. She leased her apartment immediately—one of her friends had a cousin from New Jersey eager to spend a season in the city. She gave herself a farewell party on Labor Day.

The following morning, she visited Allegra. Allegra was not bedridden yet, but soon.

"Don't look mournful, Ingrid. You've seen me through a long illness. There are plenty left to help me die."

"I...should be one of them."

"Perhaps I'll hold on." They wetly embraced.

And just like that, Ingrid returned offhandedly to her relatives, as if the visit would be the usual strict four days, not a lax three months. She took a plane from New York to a southern hub with a moving walkway that kept falsely warning her it was about to stop, a mini-plane to an airport thirty-five miles from the town, a bus. At the depot, the driver pulled her single large scuffed suitcase from the bus's belly. "What an item!" Allegra had once said.

"Fido? My second-best friend."

Lynne had wanted to give Ingrid the guest room she occupied during her quarterly visits, one of the three charmed rooms under the slanted roof—she'd been able to hear Chloe cry when the child was an infant, she could hear Chloe's parents' soft lovemaking now. The room would have been perfect for a second child, but Lynne's hysterectomy precluded another child. Ingrid didn't want that room. "I am no longer a guest," she said. "I am an employee." And indeed she was; Chris was paying her a salary; she was quietly depositing it in the trusts she'd set up for her daughter and for Chloe. "An employee of the woodworks, with household and child-care duties at home. I will sleep in Useless. Let's find a bed, a bookcase, a dresser. Secondhand, please." The four of them went right out and bought those items. What more did she need? Well, a mirror would be nice. Chris supplied one he had made himself, probably intended to sell, could sell, after she left. It was oval, framed in cherry.

The woodworking shop was two miles away along a two-lane road. She could have hitched a ride with Chris in his pickup, but at six a.m.! Anyway she liked to walk through the woods. It took more time. She'd discovered she was interested not in saving time but in spending it. She chose a longer route along a path of old-growth trees and new saplings and spiders' webs and busy wasps. Brushwood guarded her way.

Then she turned off again, along a second path that led to a narrow river with a gentle decline. The water splashed swiftly through groups of pearly rocks, then leveled. She called this little plaything of nature the Falls. Alders by the side of the brook were dropping leaves thin as tin. Cylinders hung in tiny clusters from their branches, protecting the pollen of the spring to come. On the other side of the river the ground was green with tiny, ivy-leaved veronica boldly rising. They would straggle through the winter and in April greet the sun. And greet Ingrid too—she often visited in April, when the opera season was over. Nearby, unseen, caterpillars were spinning their cocoons.

She noticed one day that a black stone was awaiting her on the path. She picked it up. Partially smoothed and also jagged, veined with green, it seemed to throb on her palm. She slipped it into her back pocket.

From these private Falls, she returned to the main path and went on to the woodworking shop. There, as Chris had predicted, she deftly handled the business of the business. Her office was a little doorless room off the large shop floor. During her few idle minutes, she watched the men at work. She saw chests and dining tables and moldings in the making, and sometimes an artistic element—an elaborate architrave which would surround a simple window. She thought briefly of her own slatted Manhattan blinds. She admired the tools: drills and chisels and gouges and what seemed like hundreds of kinds of saws. She loved the planes that lifted a thin epidermis from a plank. There wasn't much conversation on the floor, although one man, Danny, older than the others, sometimes took his break at her desk and talked about his beekeeping. He lived alone in a cottage and grew vegetables. He told her that the black and green stone now resting on her desk was chromite. The rough part could be smoothed. "I know a silversmith who could set it, and you could wear it dangling from your neck."

My long, long neck... But she didn't say that. "I don't want to tamper with it" was what she did say.

At the end of the day she tramped back through the woods. At the familiar black stove she prepared dinner with Lynne and Chloe. Then came the eating of dinner, and the washing up, and then Sorry! or television or reading. They had no stereo. She wanted to give them a piano but they wouldn't accept it. She could will her own Steinway to them and then fling herself onto the Falls, but she'd just smash her kneecaps on the rocks.

Sometimes, in the late afternoon, if Chris had loaned his pickup to someone, that someone drove him from the pellet plant to the shop. From there, Chris offered to walk her home, grave as a suitor. He pointed out things that she was not yet clever enough to notice: the hunting spider, which does not build webs but instead spies her prey and chases it and pounces. He showed her a toad crawling to his death while nearby a generation of tadpoles, some of them his progeny, sped through the water. His fingers lifted a low branch and there bloomed a miniature plant with a tiny dark flower: a plant that lives its whole life under a leaf, hostage to its own nature, visible to no one except some expert winged pollinators. Its story would make a good opera, Ingrid thought; no, not an opera, a ballet, a ballet meant for children. She imagined lines of well-dressed kids and their grannies lining up to see *The Lonely Flower*. If she were in New York she'd be obliged to take Allegra's grandchildren... She was still squatting to peer at the flower. Getting up wasn't as easy as it had once been. Chris held out his hand.

In the evening Danny sometimes dropped in. His bees were swarming, he told her. The queen mates with a few lucky drones—they are her sons, if you want to be accurate, sometimes her grandsons. Nature is no respecter of seemliness.

Happiness lengthens time. Every day seemed as long as a novel. Every night a double feature. Every week a lifetime, a muted lifetime, a lifetime in which sadness, always wedged under her breast like a doorstop, lost some of its bite. When she went back to New York she would feel that a different person had occupied her body for a while, and a different wardrobe had taken over her closet—now she wore only tees and jeans. The stone had found a proper home in her back pocket. The

V-necked blouse had been shoved into Fido. Her hair was of course longer, its seemingly random stripes of chestnut—how clever her hairdresser was, how natural they'd looked—now surrendering to honest blond-gray. Brown, pale yellow, gray—she was coiffured in wood bark, wood pulp, and dust. Her glasses were permanently bent because Danny had sat on them. She could probably be mistaken for a displaced bag lady. Or a beaver, who lived among trees and water and other beavers, and feasted on cellulose.

In November she went back to New York for a few days. Allegra had died.

"I'm sorry for your loss," said the well-brought-up Chloe. "Come back right away," she then commanded. "It's more fun when you're home."

"Keep the chromite for me," said Ingrid. "Rub it once in a while."

In her ragged state, Ingrid attended the funeral and then went to Allegra's apartment. Everybody recognized her except for one woman she had never liked, who glared as if she were a hillbilly freeloader. But other friends asked eagerly when she would return to New York. "I'll be back soon," she promised. She visited a gallery she admired, and also the optician.

And again the big plane, and the talkative moving walkway, and the small plane, and the bus. She stepped down off the bus into tiny Chloe's arms; into Lynne's arms, not much bigger; into Chris's gentle, huge embrace. From the backseat of the car she saw the house over Lynne's shoulder. In the late afternoon of the late fall day, the stones looked mauve, a color borrowed from Odilon Redon. Should she mention that? She should not. A rabbit from the woods was chewing on a carrot that Danny must have dropped.

* * *

Sometimes the college hosted a quartet or a singer for an afternoon concert. One principal violinist rose up and down on his toes. A poorly modulated soprano projected into the next county. But there was a good second-rate pianist, and Chloe and Lynne listened attentively, and Ingrid, leaning forward, listened hungrily until the last almost-good arpeggio. She felt Chris's eyes on her. Afterward they went to their favorite restaurant. The waitresses were in their fifties and wore aqua dresses under white aprons. The lamps in the booths were pleated. There was always meat loaf on the menu, and crab, and a vegetarian special. The corn bread was the best she'd ever tasted. They ate from one another's plates like any family—two big people and two little ones.

When they ate at home, Chris served from the head of the table, handing Ingrid the first plate, his thumb flipping a stray string bean back among the others. After dinner, when Ingrid read to Chloe, she read fairy tales—they both had a taste for make-believe, especially if royalty was involved.

"You're our queen," Chloe said one night.

"Queen Giraffe?"

"Yes! Daddy is the Lion King and Mommy's one of those little princesses that gets stolen or put to sleep for a while."

Lynne was doing laundry and missed the exchange. "And what are you?" Ingrid asked.

"The nightingale the king can't live without."

Stones figured in many tales, inert minerals transformed into active participants. They induced love, they captured memories, they murdered ogres, they arranged themselves on the path so that Hansel could find his way home.

Some evenings, when Chris put his feet up on a particularly ugly brocaded ottoman and closed his eyes, Ingrid and Chloe and Lynne busied themselves in the kitchen making a pot of soup that would last a week. Lynne's garden supplied herbs. Chloe threw in the chromite. Ingrid muttered some syllables. "That's an incantation," she invented.

"Are you a witch?" Chloe giggled.

"No, just a crone."

"A glamour crone," said Lynne. "Always New York beautiful."

"Oh... it's the eyeglasses," said Ingrid hurriedly. "Here's a Chinese proverb that will make the soup even better. *Cutting stalks at noontime, perspiration drips to the earth. Know you that your bowl of rice, each grain from hardship comes?* I learned that from a healer on Mott Street." It was only a slight exaggeration. She had found the proverb in a fortune cookie; in Chinatown what she'd learned was that there were elderly men whose impassivity seemed like friendship. In narrow store after narrow store, she'd heard Allegra recite her symptoms. The men pulled out little drawers and scooped up powders and leaves and poured the stuff into sacks and handed the sacks to her friend. Allegra boiled them into a tea.

"How does it taste?" Ingrid asked.

"Rank. Nauseating, like the chemo."

Tonight's soup, unadulterated except for the stone, was perfect. Ingrid put the stone on the windowsill, ready for the next meal.

When Lynne came home exhausted from teaching fourth-graders, Ingrid ordered her into the guest-room daybed and tucked the quilt around her. Mostly, though, it was Chloe who needed time off, time off from being an only child, time off from the helpless scrutiny of her parents. Then Ingrid spirited her away into the woods.

They walked along various paths. Just yesterday they had followed a trail to a little pond. Ingrid pointed to the knobs on the willows. Each was a tightly curled leaf, saving itself for next spring. "What goes round comes round," Ingrid heard herself saying. "Death is the gate of life."

"Don't you ever die, Queen Giraffe," ordered Chloe.

"I'll die in my time, darling. Like everyone else."

The child shook her head. "You belong to *us*," she said, as if that conferred immortality.

And then in January the pellet plant was built and running, and Chris was free to return to the little office off the shop, and Ingrid was free to go back to her real life.

On one of their walks home together, they stopped to rest beside the Falls. "You'll be glad to return to New York—theater, friends, fabrics, museums."

"Fabrics?"

"I meant clothing. The walks in the neighborhoods, I know you love to do that, you've told me. Parties..."

She listened to him telling her what she was presumably feeling.

He said: "I spent a year in New York once, studying wood sculpture..."

"I remember. Your uncle was still alive."

He nodded. "I liked the fresh mornings, the sound of the garbage trucks. But there is so much more that you like. Maybe we've kept you here too long."

"Not at all," she said politely, telling the truth and not seeming to. Let him think she wanted to leave. Let him never know what she really wanted.

Let him never know that she—with the wisdom of crones, of Mott Street medicine men, of memory-laden stones—knew what *he* wanted. He did not look at her breasts, her abundant hair, her eyes kept safe these days behind newly broken glasses. They had been born thirty years apart, he was thinking, she was thinking; and they had known each other all his life. They stared at a tree which would outlive them both. He wanted to bury his nose in the cleavage she had learned to hide. He wanted to say sweet words.

Instead he pressed his lips together to let no words escape. *Stay with us* was all he would have said. *Stay in my sight.* To keep wanting, and not getting—it was a satisfaction of its own. She was another house he would never build.

I cannot stay, she might have said. *Oh, Chris. Oh, Lynne, oh, my Chloe, how sweet it sounds, how tender it might be. The four of us living a life, running two businesses, not getting in one another's way. Danny visiting. Bees swarming.*

But I see farther than you. I see myself weakening, getting querulous, not useless but not useful either. I see Chloe outgrowing Queen Giraffe. I see Lynne trying to conceal her boredom. I see you mourning the loss of your longing... And beyond that bearable future, there are less pleasant predictions; dirty pictures, you might call them. There's a stroke, and you attach yourselves to the nursing home—not giving money, for I can pay; giving attention you dare not withhold. You cannot leave me day after day, strapped to a chair, calling for my dead child. Or perhaps, mobile, I'll become a demented comic, wandering from floor to floor and stealing my neighbors' false teeth. The home will call you like an annoyed principal. And there are worse scenarios—the illness of organs, who cares which organ or what illness so long as it doesn't kill me as it should but instead keeps me in my room here, visited regularly by strong-armed nurses, the walls shaking with my strenuous attempt not to cry. I'll scream—too late—for the bedpan. I'll throw my stone at the laggard aide. Our dusty street will be invaded by the occasional ambulance. My body still alive but decaying visibly and audibly and odorously next to the kitchen will remind us to regret your invitation, my acceptance. The house will call us fools.

In a few days they drove her to the bus. Embraces all around, like other families. "I put the chromite in Fido," said Chloe.

Ingrid looked at her for a while. "Thank you," she said. "I'll use it. And on my spring visit I'll bring it back to you."

She boarded the bus. They waved and waved. She twisted her neck and watched them until the first curve took them out of her sight. Then, she guessed, Lynne and Chloe got into the car, while Chris kept his arm uselessly in the air.

Her Cousin Jamie

At their annual convention—they were both high school teachers—Fern and Barbara always got together at least once for coffee. Last year they had graduated to gin. Now, on the final night, they installed themselves at a little table in the hotel bar. They talked about this and that—about the decay of classroom decorum, of course; and about the tumblings that took place at this convention, once-a-year love affairs that saved many a marriage.

"Like emergency medication," Barbara suggested.

"Relieving the flatulence of wedlock," Fern expanded.

Fern in her fifties had a broad, unlined brow, clear gray eyes, a mobile mouth. She was fit, and her blondish hair was curly and short, and she wore expensive pants and sweaters in forest colors: moss, bark, mist...Really, she should have been considered handsome; she might even have been admired. But those athletic shoulders had a way of shrugging and those muscular lips a way of grimacing that said she expected to be overlooked. As for Barbara—wide face, wide lap—she was the kind of person people felt safe telling their stories to. Fine: she liked to listen.

No story had ever come from Fern, though. None seemed to be forthcoming tonight. The two women might have finished the evening in amiable silence—Earth Mother and Failed Beauty, drinking—if a certain colleague hadn't walked swiftly past the bar toward the elevators.

Fern leaned forward. "Jamie!" she called, apparently too late. She leaned back again. "Oh well."

"Jamie," Barbara repeated. "That Jamie is the most scrupulous-looking woman I have ever seen. Pulled-back hair. Round glasses. Pale lips. Every day a clean white blouse... You're related, aren't you?"

"We're cousins. She's my Cousin of Perpetual Penitence."

Barbara sipped. She sipped and sipped. "Does she have cause for penitence?" she asked at last.

Fern said, "Oh, I couldn't." And then she did.

Decades ago, Fern began.

Remember the fizz of those times? The era, they call it now. Women and blacks, upward and outward, not exactly hand in hand except for certain instances. Well, this was an instance. Jamie was just out of college, doing an assistantship in Lev Thompson's think tank. Fern had been in New York too, she said, student-teaching children who might as well have been orphans—whose parents noticed them only to knock them around. She and Jamie shared an apartment.

Lev Thompson. A figure. He'd passed his sixtieth year; he'd packed those six decades with admirable activity. He'd been a doctor, a civil rights leader, the head of one national organization and adviser to others. Now he spent most of his time on the lecture circuit. His voice wasn't one of those fudge-rich bassos, no; it was soft and grainy. His skin was the color of shortbread. His mother was a teacher, Fern said, like us.

Jamie's face was too thin and her shoulders too narrow. But her blue eyes were shot with golden glints; and then there was that head of hair: lots of it, mahogany. He liked to hold a thick strand of her hair between his fingers, she told me. She told me everything. He held her hair as if his fingers were tongs, and he slid the tongs down to the end, and then he started again from the scalp.

A flat chest; and her two front teeth overlapped. Some men were wild for such defects, who knew why. She and Jamie came from a certain sort of family, Fern said. You know, Connecticut—money so old that it's gone. Anyway, Jamie, no boobs, too aristocratic for orthodontia—she appealed to him. He was populist, he had more than a streak of the preacher; but there was nothing coarse about his tastes. The first woman, the one he'd married when he was a young doctor—she was a person of refinement. Their three kids were a credit to them both. The second wife was a Gabonese surgeon—they had a daughter he doted on. The third was a German tennis player—he was still married to her when he and Jamie got together. Class acts, the lot of them. Sure, he'd played around some, he told Jamie, who told Fern. But just a little: Jamie was only his second affair this marriage. Schmidt, the tennis player, was on the road a lot, and at his age he didn't like to be alone.

Fern stopped, ordered another drink. Barbara did too.

He needed company, Fern went on. He probably could have done without the sex. But Jamie was in love, just like her predecessors—in love with his voice, his skin, the way he had of shrugging and waiting in argument, palms turned outward, as if he had all of God's eternity to spend until the other person came around to his way of thinking. The kindly smile—you saw it across the room, stretching his tawny face, and you ached to see it hanging over you, and you on your back... The hair on his chest was silver, Jamie reported. Sometimes, before they happened upon licking, she was slow to come. "So what?" he whispered into her ear. "I'm a patient darky." Well, you know, only a man like that can say a thing like that.

His apartment was books and leather and wood, and there were pictures of his wives and children, including a life-size photograph of Schmidt returning a backhand. Jamie stayed there infrequently, and of course only when Schmidt was on tour. Schmidt liked other women, Lev told Jamie in that tolerant voice—liked men too, liked riding him as if she were a circus performer, her knees up around her ears, her arms stretched diagonally toward the heavens. "Want to try it that way—me the tired old horse, you the young rider?"

Sure: anything for him. But what she liked best was to lie beneath him, to let him envelop her, to raise her own knees only slightly, to listen to his labored grunts and at last his sharp intake and his final sigh and his heart thudding against her chest. His lips, so soft on hers, slid down the side of her cheek and kissed the white pillow.

Together they went to this function and that. Jamie, usually wearing a skinny red dress he admired, hung up his coat, held on to his briefcase, hunted up a can of ginger ale if the event's organizers had provided only water. "My Stepin Fetchit," he'd say later, licking the underside of her chin, her labia, the backs of her knees; and whenever he licked, wherever, her inner tumblers rolled helplessly until they locked one to the other in shuddering orgasm. He could lick her earlobe in a taxi with the same quick effect. Jamie said a year later it occurred to her that her own tongue might perform that useful office, and, alone in an elevator, she pressed the inside of her wrist against her open lips and knew her skin's salt and her stringy tendons, mm, oh.

He could give a speech on anything. "Filth as Thou Art" was the title of his lecture on Caliban and nature and the need to protect the damaged by a kind of enslavement. "Watch Him While He Sleeps" promoted the tithe over the progressive tax. His reputation had been made by a book that likened the underclass to the population of a late medieval city during the plague. But these later days he talked about a variety of unpopular things: about the right to be rescued—this at the time that mental hospitals were pouring their inmates into the streets; about God, the living God, not a forgiving deity or a righteous one, but a God you sat wrapped up in like an overcoat. He refused to appear on television, saying that the medium itself, no matter how high-minded its content, was a scourge. He returned letters to their senders—even letters of praise—with corrections of grammar in the margins. His enemies included Action for Children's Television and some noted psychiatrists. They allowed that he was a good man. His wives said the same. The first two marriages had ended because each wife in turn had wearied of the causes, not of the husband. As the Gabonese doctor put it in a farewell note: *Your attention, dear Lev, is forever elsewhere.*

And that summer night in his apartment, Fern said, his attention was certainly elsewhere. The grooves in his face had become furrows, Jamie had noticed during the lecture he'd given earlier. His voice was raspy. His amber eyes had retreated into their lined surround. The public was demanding too much of him. In the cab afterward she asked him: "Should I go on home? You seem tired." But she didn't mean the offer—Schmidt would soon be back in town.

"Perhaps that would be..." he began. Her fingers in his cold wet hand twitched. "No," he reversed. "Come up to my place."

He sat in his easy chair for a long time, looking over some papers and drinking several cans of ginger ale, belching uneasily. He took forever in the bathroom. She was dozing when he finally got into bed. He turned his back in what she suspected was a common marital maneuver.

Fern looked at Barbara. Barbara nodded at her to continue.

But Jamie would not be denied, Fern said. She touched Lev's shoulder, played a little tune on it, and, slowly, he turned toward her. That nimble hand of hers now entered his pajama shirt between the buttons and tweaked his nipple. With a sigh he heaved his body onto hers. He waited a few moments. She should excuse him tonight, she thought...but there it was, his erection, making its way through the fly of his pajama bottoms. He kneeled, still clothed, and entered her. A thrust, another thrust, and he fell—so quickly! And she not half begun; he had forgotten to apply his tongue. His face as usual kissed the pillow and his heart thudded against hers.

Only it wasn't thudding. She held her breath. Perhaps he was holding his breath too. She exhaled. He did not exhale.

Five minutes to midnight.

Staring at the ceiling, she remembered that he had had a heart attack in his fifties. His father had died young, and his uncles and his one brother, all of the same thing, he had told her. It ran in the family, sudden fatal infarctions. There were worse ways to go, he'd insisted. Those pills he sometimes took, waving away her concerned flutterings—they must be in his jacket. She leaped out of bed, found the vial, shook it at him. She could force the tablets into his mouth. She could force them into his rectum. What was the rhythm of CPR? She had taken a workshop in college, practicing on a puce dummy. She remembered almost nothing. Four minutes to midnight.

She rolled him onto his back. *Loosen clothing,* she recalled: she unsnapped his pajama bottoms. His penis lolled. She pressed her fingers to the side of his neck. Nothing. She knocked on his chest. Nobody home. She placed her mouth on his and blew, and raised her head, and lowered it and blew again. His mouth was foul—hadn't he brushed his teeth during that long stint in the bathroom? Still, there was something encouraging about the terrible smell and taste. His personal bacteria were still alive. She blew one more time, and then reached for the telephone and dialed 911. Three minutes to midnight.

By the time the police and the ambulance came she was again wearing her red dress. She had broken one of the straps in her haste to put it on. He was wearing his trousers. Flat on the bed, his bare brown feet below the pinstripes, his rumpled pajama top above, he looked like a melancholy minstrel.

The ambulance men were so deft, with their oxygen and their resuscitation attempts and their gurney. The police were so kind. One of them was female. What a fine career for a woman, Jamie thought. Yes, she told them, she was his assistant. Yes, he'd given a lecture. They had returned here to work on his next speech, it would be in Chicago...it would have been in Chicago. How had he seemed? Oh, preoccupied. "Infarctions run in his family," she confided.

They drove her home. Fern had been awake, she said, planning the next day's lesson for her wretched students, when the police delivered Jamie to her. *An unfortunate incident* was what they said. They left. Jamie threw herself onto her bed, still wearing that red dress, and gagged her story into the pillow.

"I turned her over," Fern said, "and got the unbroken strap

off her shoulder and rolled the dress down her body. I was sure that reporters would show up any minute and would seize on the dress, would call it scarlet. I slid an innocent nightgown over my cousin's head. I threw the red heap onto the floor of my own closet."

But the reporters didn't come. Except for one tabloid, the papers left Jamie out of the story. Lev's biography filled their articles; the work he might yet have done interested the pundits.

The staff went as a group to the calling hours at the funeral home. Jamie had planned to wear the red dress but Fern talked her out of it, she said. Jamie wore a black suit instead, with a very short skirt. In the coffin, she said later, he looked rested and handsome. Of course she could not give him a special good-bye, but her gaze traveled through the clothing and snuggled right next to his noble heart. And then she went into the next room to offer her condolences to the mourners.

They were sitting in a semicircle. The mother: that severe chignon, pewter tinged with bronze. "She grayed in an eccentric manner," Lev had told her. "She never did do things like other people." The first wife, queenly despite an unflattering beige outfit, and her sons and daughters-in-law and grandchildren, all solemn, sad—grief-stricken, you might say. One son looked just like him. Did he also have a heart that would fail too soon? Jamie wondered. The stunning second wife, wearing a silver pendant that resembled a stethoscope. Her teenage daughter, Thalia was her name, whose kneesocks and trashy novels Jamie had found here and there in the apartment. Schmidt, sobbing. Thalia was holding Schmidt's hand. Another older woman—who? Oh yes, the wife of the dead brother.

Jamie, her quick eye sliding from face to face, her fingers tapping her own thigh, her tongue thrumming behind her crossed teeth...she counted them. Nineteen. Nineteen broken hearts. Well, eighteen: the sister-in-law was perhaps unaffected. Eighteen people who had lost a loved man husband ex-husband father grandfather son; who had lost him to sudden death; who had lost him because of an assistant they were glad to tolerate, no one minded his little failing; who had lost him because the upstart assistant had fastened onto him, exhausted him with her demands, driven him over the brink; and then, scared out of her silly wits, had shaken pills as if they were castanets, and weakly punched his sternum, and breathed fecklessly into his mouth, and wriggled a pair of trousers onto his uncooperative legs for the sake of his earthly reputation, or hers. To cover their shame.

The sister-in-law burst into tears.

Nineteen people, then.

"Jamie left New York after that," Fern wound up. "She got a master of arts in education at a state university, and she married a good dull math teacher who gave her two good dull sons. She scraped her hair back, and renounced contact lenses, and bought a lifetime supply of white blouses."

Silence for a while. Then Barbara said, "So she's up in her room now, hair loose, glasses off, reliving it all, drenched in guilt."

"Yes," Fern said. She was staring at the olive in the bottom of her glass. "Some people have all the luck."

Blessed Harry

I.

On the first Monday in March Mr. Flaxbaum received the following e-mail:

Distinguished Myron Flaxbaum,

I am Professor Harry Worrell from King's College Campus Here in London, UK. We want you to be our guest Speaker at this Year's Unanticipated Seminar which will take place Here. We are writing to invite and confirm your booking. The Venue is as follows: King's College campus in Strand, London, UK. The expected audience is 850 people. The duration of the speech is one hour. The date is the 31st of May this year. The topic is "The Mystery of Life and Death." We came across references to you on the Internet, and we say you are up to standard. A formal letter of invitation

*and Contract agreement will be sent to you as soon as you
honor our Invitation. We are taking care of your travel and
hotel accommodation expenses and your speaking fee.*

Stay Blessed,

*Professor Harry Worrell
King's College Campus*

Mr. Flaxbaum reread this epistle, removing his glasses for the
second perusal. "I'm invited to give a lecture," he mentioned to
the three boys, who, though hurrying off to school, paused to
look at the invitation. "Fab," "Wicked," "Steamy," they agreed
one after the other; and, one after the other, backpack following backpack, left the flat, their departure as usual causing a
small conflagration in Flax's heart. "Awesome," added Felix
over his shoulder, revealing for a moment the abbreviated nose
and one of the blue eyes inherited from Bonnie. Bonnie had already been at work for several hours—she was a surgical nurse
at a Boston hospital—but she would affirm late that afternoon
that the Unanticipated Seminar would be elevated by the presence of her Myron. (No one except Bonnie called him by his
first name; even his sister called him Flax.) Bonnie would bend
her blond, large-chinned head toward the screen and review
the topic—"The Mystery of Life and Death"—and then stand
erect again, an oversize woman, authoritative as a Roman aedile
though she wore pants and sweater and sturdy shoes rather than
toga and sandals. "Darling, you could even do it in Latin."

Now, in Bonnie's absence, and after the noisy departure of the
boys—in the presence only of the Flaxbaums' peculiar house-
plant—Flax indulged in an unusual activity: he googled himself.

His name came up just once, as he had known it would: on the website of Caldicott Academy, Godolphin, Mass., the private girls' school where he worked. In a photograph, taken several years ago, Flax's hair was retreating but not yet fleeing. His upper lip had not yet put forth its slim mustache. His plump cheeks did not show the two vertical creases that appeared whenever he produced a smile, and his glasses concealed the considerate gaze that had made many a slipshod student called in for a conference feel suddenly worthy, though worthy of what she could not have easily said. Maybe worthy of a conference with Flax; maybe that was enough. Most students responded to their conversations with Flax by paying more attention to their Latin grammars, by finding something intriguing in the ablative absolute, by renouncing their trots—one girl actually burned hers in a little ceremony behind the gym.

Under the picture the legend read *Myron Flaxbaum, BA Brooklyn College, MA Columbia, MAT Harvard. Teaches first-, second-, and third-year Latin. Coaches the chess team.* It was a tribute to the electronic world that this mild entry had brought him to the attention of the director of Unanticipated Seminars at King's College on the Strand. What could he invent as a usual fee? More critically, what could he say in his lecture? *Let us think for a moment* (he thought). *Perhaps I can work up something about the history of life—the big bang, the primordial soup, the development of bacteria, the emergence of creatures with a sort of brain and a sort of eye and some locomotion. I will reread Darwin and Linnaeus and Mendel and Richard Dawkins; I will review the Bible. I might require an agent...*

And then, shaking his head violently (for him), he stopped considering this daunting task. He googled King's College on the Strand and discovered that it indeed existed but that no

Harry Worrell was named on its faculty. Perhaps Harry was blessedly modest. Flax then shrugged himself into his worn overcoat and checked his shabby briefcase, making sure it carried the books and papers necessary for today's lessons. He tested the loose button on his overcoat—yes, it would probably hang on another day. He lifted from its hook the beret his sons had given him for his recent birthday—an accessory they considered a sartorial improvement on his old tweed cap—and slipped it onto his semi-bald head. He picked up the half-full cup of coffee resting on the computer table and brought it to a familiar dark corner and dumped its contents into a pot of soil and mismatched pedicels, bracts, peduncles, and leaves. Then he abandoned the flat to this plant's caffeinated care.

II.

Nobody remembered where the plant had come from. It seemed to have been sitting forever in that ill-lit and (for a plant) unwholesome corner of the living room, on a little table whose provenance was also forgotten, protected by the scrolled arm of the brown plush sofa. The middle boy, Leo, suggested that the plant had been spawned by the sofa, which was called Jack, after Flax's dear uncle who had lived with them for some years. Uncle Jack had shared a room with the youngest boy, Felix, and never got in anybody's way, largely because he was usually occupying the sofa, sometimes flicking cigar ash in the direction of Plant. "A lovable schnorrer," said Mr. Flaxbaum of Jack, though not as part of the formal eulogy.

Young Felix suspected that he himself had brought Plant home from the garden shop during an annual giveaway of moribund merchandise. Flax, devotee of Ovid's *Metamorphoses,* entertained the fancy that Plant had once been a nymph changed like Daphne, although not into a laurel on a hill near Olympus but rather into an ill-favored thing rooted in a pot in their living room. Perhaps she had misbehaved when she still had legs and hips. Bonnie, who had received a classical education from the nuns, thought Plant was a household god responsible for luck, one of the Lares or one of the Penates. Why not? The family had been fortunate so far, unless you were silly enough to consider fat bank accounts and granite kitchen counters signs of luck. Even her Leo, who had a neurologic condition which might prove progressive but might not—even he was not unlucky, not yet, not yet, maybe not ever...Plant might be a succulent, Leo had speculated.

In a family discussion soon after Plant's appearance, Bonnie remarked that it might have been a variety of primrose emigrated from the railroad tracks. Sean, the eldest, taking charge of a one-volume *Encyclopedia of Botany* no one had known they owned ("Sort of like the plant," mentioned Uncle Jack), said that its pallor indicated that it might be mycotrophic, might "'obtain nutrients from the soil by means of the fungi that inhabit its roots,'" Sean read aloud. Its rosettes made it a cousin to *Anacampseros telephiastrum variegata,* "'also called Sunrise.'"

"*Telephiastrum,*" Flax repeated. "Greek, not Latin. 'Casting afar,' maybe. Go on, Sean."

"Like *Arsaenia,* the tip of its leaf is 'elongated, upturned, and coiled.'"

"Only one of its leaves," Leo said. "The striped one is flat."

"There's a hint of a caudex just above the soil," Sean said, and closed the book.

"What's a caudex?" Felix said.

"An early manuscript," Jack said.

After a while: "Taproot," said Sean.

"Our guest has lots of characteristics," Felix said. "Some growing out of others."

"Some mutually exclusive," Leo said.

Plant's supposed taproot had never been examined (they didn't want to kill the thing). Sometimes it produced tiny flowers in hues of lingerie. Sometimes it put out scramblers which crept to the edge of the pot and then disintegrated. It was probably a hybrid. "Who isn't?" Sean inquired (biology was one of his AP courses). It troubled no one, and it endeared itself to no one. In that way it was different from the little terrier the family had acquired from the pound some years ago. Buddy liked to chase cars. It was only a sometime habit; they hoped he'd outgrow it. Otherwise he was affectionate, recognized the boys by name and also Uncle Jack, who gave him candy in secret. He seemed numerate; Leo thought Buddy might learn to count, or at least to feign counting, like Clever Hans. But math lessons never got started, because one misty morning the fit was on him, and he came to grief with a Camry. Poor Buddy...Plant persisted, like the busy Flaxbaums themselves—like Flax, Bonnie, Sean, Leo, Felix, and the incarnation of Uncle Jack.

III.

The next morning, Tuesday: "Do you want me to print out Professor Harry Worrell's invitation?" Flax asked Felix.

"Thanks, no," Felix said. "Have you answered it?"

"Not yet."

"Well, maybe I'll take the next communication if it comes by mail."

Felix was a scrupulous collector, not a catch-as-catch-can hoarder. He didn't care for documents, though he did admire stamps. But his taste was mainly for odd items like fancy buttons and bicycle bells and orphaned circuit boards that might come in handy sometime; and he also liked things with a peculiar beauty, like the last garnet inch in a flask of cough medicine, or his own vermiform appendix, deftly removed from his cecum and preserved in a bottle of formaldehyde. He picked up crosses on chains in secondhand shops—they reminded him of his early childhood when he'd attended Masses with Grandma Reilly, his mama's sweet mama. Felix might never have indulged his scavenging habits—or might have been reduced to collecting Pokémon cards—if Uncle Jack hadn't died and abandoned his half of the shared bedroom. Over the next few years the boy built some shelves, bought a glass aquarium, discovered in a junkyard a small office safe and repaired its lock with Leo's help. There Felix kept his crosses. The aquarium now housed some goldfish, two, three, four, or five of them, their number depending on their own luck and on a larger fate which Felix didn't understand and which he guessed was a mystery also to his dependents. They conducted repetitive exercises under Felix's benign attention. He fed them flakes that looked like dried cilantro. He gave them the names of Latin poets in honor of his father, but whenever one of them was found floating without purpose, he retired the fish while recycling the name. He had thus been guardian of numerous Virgils and Juvenals. Mr. Flaxbaum was comfortable with the monikers but he thought the group as a whole ought to be called by its appropriate Linnaean taxon. So Felix posted a little sign: *C. auratus auratus.*

Felix played basketball and soccer, but his favorite sport was walking with his head down and stopping to look at a fallen leaf or worm cast that attracted him and sometimes picking it up, bringing it close to his frank Irish face—a physiognomy unusual in the Flaxbaum family but occurring often among the Reillys. He particularly admired a lifeless bug trapped between the two panes of stormproof glass in one of his parents' bedroom windows. Their bedroom was just off the living room.

"Can't we liberate him?" Felix had wondered. "How did he get there?"

"It's an adult longhorn beetle," said Flax after some research. "My guess is that its pupa was blown between two sheets of glass when the workmen in the yard of the glass factory were jamming them together. We have double panes on our windows to keep the cold out, Felix, and they can't be separated—they'd have to be broken. And for what purpose?—to extract the cadaver of a common insect. I know you'd like to add him to your curiosities, so please consider our room your annex."

"Thanks. What killed the dude?"

"Insufficient oxygen. In one way or another that's what kills us all. Uncle Jack..."

"He had a blood disease."

"Yes, in the end his blood couldn't carry oxygen to his heart and he died."

"Oh. The bug didn't disintegrate," said Felix. Flax guessed that the boy was thinking of Uncle decomposing in the earth. He treated himself to a measured look at his son's eyes. If sincerity had a color... "Lack of oxygen again," Flax explained. "He was preserved in an accidental vacuum."

Every morning Felix opened his safe and took out one of the crosses. Then he stashed it again, gave Plant a fish-flakes treat, and took a quick look at the beetle to see if it had been resurrected yet.

IV.

On Wednesdays, Leo's first class was at ten. Godolphin's progressive high school mandated attendance at classes but allowed freedom at other times. On Wednesdays Flax didn't teach at all. So at eight o'clock the two were home, alone with each other. And on this Wednesday, already afternoon in the UK, Professor Harry Worrell was probably alone in a pub booth, empty steins accumulating around his laptop, sending messages to distinguished Americans.

While thinking of the blessed professor, Flax was enjoying a lethal breakfast of pancakes and syrup and bacon, Leo a life-enhancing one of muesli and tea and several colorful capsules. There was a resemblance between these two—limp brown hair, abundant in the son and scanty in the father; gentle voice; slow smile; a talent and love for teaching. Leo at sixteen was already helping the ninth-grade teacher explain logarithms, in so modest a manner that his classmates were unoffended; and on late-afternoon visits to the local elementary school, he tutored some kids who were called intellectually challenged. He hated the term. It was mathematics itself that was challenged. There was something wrong with numbers, their incarnation on paper. They were flummoxing these dear children, preventing them from doing more than count. The children were good at counting when they used words, *one, two, three;* they also loved *gazillion.* But the shapes for numbers made their eyes fill. And the visual aids some sadistic pedagogue invented: handcuffs for 3, a hook for 5, an ax for 7; 4 was a cruel pitchfork... "I've come to hate number shapes," Leo said.

They washed the dishes. Leo did not feed Plant but he did stand looking down at it. "I wonder if Buddy could really have learned to count," he muttered. He was still thinking about numbers, Flax realized. Might Plant be numiverous? Leo slanted his head forward and Flax imagined ungainly symbols tumbling into the pot; good-bye, 2, 5, 17; good-bye, 9, you noose.

Then Leo picked up his backpack, father and son got their bikes out of the garage. Beneath the helmet Flax's beret flapped onto his forehead. In overcoat and headgear he looked stately on wheels, Leo noticed, though a button appeared to be missing from the coat. Flax noticed the angularity of his son and experienced that cold dread that someday Leo's dormant disease would dispatch tubers to his organs and turn him into wood. They rode, Flax first, into the empty street and bicycled side by side until at the second intersection Leo with a wave turned toward school and Flax with an arm raised in answer went straight ahead, toward today's job, selling shoes at Dactyl.

V.

Though Bonnie's days were packed with obligations, she nonetheless devoted an hour every Wednesday to minding her man. After work she took the underground as always from the hospital to the central metro station and then, instead of trolleying to the section of Godolphin where the Flaxbaums lived—firm wooden three-deckers, mostly firm families within—she trolleyed to Godolphin's commercial area, Jefferson Corner. Dactyl, where Myron worked Wednesdays and Saturday afternoons, was on the historically registered block that included Forget Me Not, an antiques shop; Roberta's Linens; Dunton's Tobacco; and the Local, a restaurant. This stretch of stores stood behind a brick colonnade. Each store had inner doors opening to its neighbors. Historians guessed that the whole arrangement had been part of the underground railway. The door between Forget Me Not and Dactyl had a square glass window. At three o'clock, Bonnie, wearing a bowler she kept at Forget Me Not and rimless glasses with no refraction, took possession of the window after first exchanging nods with Renata, Forget Me Not's proprietor. In her long years of store-keeping, Renata had seen far more peculiar things than a wife keeping an eye on a blameless husband.

Bonnie's habit had begun on a July Saturday. Coming out of the bookstore across the street, her arms full, she had glimpsed Myron inside Dactyl. She swiftly crossed the street and took a spy's position behind one of the columns and peeked out. She could see him better now. He was standing with his hands behind his back. His chin was slightly lowered as if he were looking down, but his glasses pinching the tip of his nose indicated that his eyes were raised in order to see over them. She watched for a while. And then, bending the rules of physics and physiology, she entered him. She burrowed between his ribs; she spread her sub-stantial self within his smaller periphery. The scraps and scrolls of his knowledge occupied their now-shared frontal cortex. His lively interest employed four optic nerves. His disappointments made four shoulders slump. She knew his shame at having to sell footwear in order to increase the family's comfort, and she knew the secondary shame that so respectable an extra job should cause that first shame. And so whenever she watched him on Wed-nesdays—watched only; she couldn't occupy him after that first exalted melding—she was able to feel again what was felt by this father brother husband nephew teacher protector salesman pa-tron of a botanical curiosity lover of Ovid...

So the practical, competent woman, every surgeon's favorite

nurse, calmness itself behind her mask and gown, ready always with the instrument needed, her pity always contained, this paragon of unflappability surrendered to her own soft interior every Wednesday and peeped at her husband from the window of Forget Me Not, saw pride and disappointment and shame and resignation, saw him kneeling like a knight—not like a servant, Myron!—in front of some woman shopping for pumps exactly the color of a certain Bordeaux, exactly the height of a certain stair rise, no, no, no, higher, lower, redder, less red, did I say I wanted a bow, a buckle, a golden chameleon climbing up my instep, amphibians give me the creeps...

"Reptiles," corrected Flax.

The woman bought the shoes.

"Can you read their lips?" Renata inquired.

"Not exactly," Bonnie said. "I supply."

"That's the how of communication, isn't it."

"Yes." It was the how of family too, but she didn't say that to the kindly spinster. All commensals supplied each other in one way or another—commensals, from *com mensa,* eating together. She loved mealtimes, preparing the dinner with help from everybody, using ingredients bought with the money she and Myron supplied. Dinner-table conversations were full of information, not always accurate, and full of earnest misquotations; the boys' manners if not perfect were adequate, and the dining-room mirror obediently reflected them all, her own fat self and Myron's balding self and Sean's and Leo's loved faces, and the back of Felix's loved head, although in his darting way he showed one profile and then the other. "Salt, please," he would say to his father. (Someday she must stop putting salt on the table.) Myron passed the salt; Myron, the fellow she had stumbled upon, literally, twenty years ago.

He'd been slumped in a chair in the surgical waiting room while his poor sick father died under the knife, it couldn't be helped, and returning from the sad conclusion of the operation, she had tripped over his legs sticking out into the room. A small woman slept in the next chair—his sister, it turned out. It was three in the morning.

"Oh, I'm sorry," she'd said to his feet.

His eyes flew open. His mouth flew open. He wanted to ask her. It was not up to her to tell him. But she broke protocol with a gesture: she put her hand on his shoulder, and then fled. The woman beside him stirred.

Later he sought her out to thank her for the care she had given. "Papa had a good life," wearily.

"And an unterrible end," she said, breaking protocol again.

He'd called her a month later and they were married a few months after that.

And now there were five Flaxbaums, moving every night within a silvered oblong, a group portrait, including a corner of the couch in the next room. This portrait would disappear when the last of them underwent the physiological necessity of individual extinction, when the last memory of the last of them was gone. Then these two generations of Flaxbaums would fade from history, taking with them all their supplying and rely-ing and self-denial and dissatisfaction and gratitude. Life and death? They were incidental, in her opinion, though of course she deplored suffering. But what counted was how you behaved while death let you live, and how you met death when life re-leased you. That was the long and short of it. Her honorable spouse could instruct those overeducated Brits, all 850 of them, just by his own example.

VI.

Very late Thursday night (Friday at four in the morning, to be exact), in the kitchen, Flax wearing pajamas encountered Sean wearing underwear. This was not an unusual occurrence.

"Which exam tomorrow?" Flax inquired, though he knew.

"Evolution. The origin of life will be inquired about. I'll respond that life was an accident, arising from the unexpected concentration of organic molecules in hydrothermal vents four million years ago. Then I'll expand on that."

He would get an A, Flax knew. He always got As. They sat down opposite each other, Flax sipping warmed milk, Sean ignoring a glass of some red stuff. Flax said, "Yes, life began like that. We were all there already—those molecules have drifted down through the millennia and become part of us. And the vents in fact are still in the ocean, and the giant tube worms that live near them."

"Will you mention that in your...London speech?"

"Maybe. Do you want to become a physicist?"

"I...No. I hope to become a poet."

"I thought so. And write epics?"

"No, sorry. I want to write compressed lyrics. 'Walk on air against your better judgment.'"

"'The beauty of innuendos,'" supplied Flax. "Felix will get baptized and become a priest," he predicted.

"'Guilt, justice, the desire to be good.' Our Felix."

Flax cleared his throat. "Poets eat, I'm told."

"Physics will be my day job." Sean grinned, softening the grandiosity.

"*Medio tutissimus ibis,*" the father said.

"'You will be safest in the middle,'" the son translated—remembered, really; all the boys knew Ovid. "Yes, I will."

His very dark eyes were inherited from Flax's own father, he who had arrested on the operating table and dispatched Bonnie to Flax. The boy's irises were almost indistinguishable from the pupils. Dark, dark brown, the distilled mixture of every shade in the world. If determination had a color...

"My son, I remember when our family was only you and your mother and I, Jack was still making a living somewhere. I remember when this refrigerator was hung with your nursery drawings. I remember when you put your child's hand so gently against Leo's infant cheek, silk touching silk, I remember so much, I would keep you here until morning telling you, beloved boy, but now I must go to bed." And he stretched his own hand across the table and with its hairy back stroked the cheek of his firstborn. "What on earth is that stuff you're not drinking?"

"Mouthwash. It's the last thing I take the night before an exam."

"Don't swallow, it'll poison you."

"I always spit." Sean stood up, took a swig, swished, and then, holding the liquid in his mouth, walked through the dining room into the living room and, one hand on Jack, awarded Plant a pinkish stream. The creature as usual stretched its stem toward him.

VII.

On Friday evenings the Flaxbaums attended the bar and grill down the street, and idly watched its television, and talked of this and that. That Friday Flax wore his beret and Bonnie introduced her bowler. Aunt Jan Flaxbaum met them there. She was Flax's diminutive sister, a busy dentist with crooked teeth.

"I googled King's College on the Strand today," Flax told his family. "I thought I'd ask for a more modest topic and more time to prepare it. On the site was a notice surrounded by a rectangle. 'It has come to our attention that persons are sending out invitations in our name. Unless the invitation has kc.uk at the end of its address, it is fraudulent.' There was in fact a banner of letters after the e-mail address of last Monday's invitation, but not the ones mentioned."

"There were some numbers too," Leo remembered.

"There was no *u*," Sean said.

"No *c*," Felix said sadly. "It disappeared, maybe." His treasured beetle was crumbling at last, would soon be invisible.

"No *k*," Flax said.

"Fuck King's College," Bonnie remarked, or so her three sons thought they heard. "Please, what are you all talking about?" Jan said.

Leo told her, while Bonnie imagined Myron enduring the collapse of a fancy he had perhaps only half believed. At some point he'd probably caught the aroma of scam that the rest of the family had sniffed—erroneously, they'd hoped—from the start. She saw him standing next to the computer, his head lowered, his glasses at the end of his nose, one stubby finger on DELETE.

"Well, they'd have been lucky if he'd accepted," Jan said, ignoring various irrelevancies. "Is that your coat on the first hook, Flax? What's that enormous jet-and-velvet thing—did you get an award?"

"It's a button from Felix's collection. Leo sewed it on."

"It was once Great-Aunt Hannah's," Jan recognized. "It decorated a mauve toque."

"I remember!" Flax said. "She had a shelf of fancy hats." And the conversation drifted away from Unanticipated Seminars and the Mystery of Life and Death and entered the comfortable area of family history.

VIII.

That Saturday morning, shapeless in her flannel robe, Bonnie tiptoed into the living room, not bothering to close the bedroom door. She took a brown bottle from her pocket. It held the extract of the *P. vulgaris* root, a variety of primrose. This liquid was the Czech preparation *solutan*—a nostrum against bronchial asthma and bronchitis. She poured some *solutan* into Plant, practicing a version of homeopathy. "Take some of your own medicine." Her cousin in Prague supplied the stuff to Reilly, the chemist, his shop not far from the Zizkov Tower. The Irish are as disseminated as the Jews; Flax had noted this. Concealed behind a half-closed door he had frequently watched Bonnie dose Plant. This morning he was watching from bed. "I love you," he whispered to his wife, who couldn't hear this unoriginal unbeatable declaration. Of necessity he whispered it also to *P. vulgaris flaxbaum,* who might be developing a rudimentary tympanum within that coiled leaf, who knew, Linnaeus and Darwin and Dawkins hadn't figured out everything; and Plant, like the rest of the family, was entitled to its secrets. He often wondered what unanticipated being Plant was destined to become. But he wondered even more frequently what kept the organism going—cilantro, mouthwash, slain numerals, coffee, a Mitteleuropean nutraceutical, the last ashes from Uncle Jack's cigar? A mystery, isn't it, Blessed Harry.

Puck

The statue—hollow, bronze, about three feet in height and about thirty pounds in weight—wasn't the sort of thing Rennie usually bought. And for an excellent reason: it wasn't the sort of thing she was able to sell. In the antiques business you couldn't just follow your whim; you'd go broke in a month. At Forget Me Not, Rennie's shop, she dealt in French clocks, and English silver, and pottery made a century earlier in a Boston settlement house—a set of those plain plates now fetched more money than the immigrant potters had made in a year. Forget Me Not was known for its Regency teapots and Victorian jewelry and hat pins from the 1940s, bought these days by collectors or—who knew?—murderers.

Rennie herself was known for discretion and restraint. She allowed certain customers to use the telephone to get in touch with a detective or a divorce lawyer—cell phone calls can be traced, the customers nervously confided; may I . . . ? Old ladies came in with valuable saltcellars; circumstances had forced them to part with the family silver. Men bought pendants for women not their wives. Elegant matrons wept over sons in jail.

Rennie kept such facts in her head like diplomatic secrets. And this caution had led, through the years, to a general prudence: she did not tell any customer anything whatsoever about any other customer. It was one of her two cardinal rules.

The other rule also involved keeping her mouth shut: she refused to give advice. "Advice is the province of psychiatrists and hairdressers," she said. "Me, I'm just a rag-and-bone woman."

The statue belonged in a chamber of oddities. Rotund, almost naked, male—at least, fig leaves hinted that the figure was male—with a little jacket over his shoulders and a top hat over his curls. He carried a spear in one hand and held a mirror aloft in the other. His face was round and merry.

Ophelia Vogelsang had staggered in three months ago with this fellow in her arms. "From Uncle Henry's apartment," she'd crowed, as if saying "from the Vanderbilt collection." She set the statue on the floor and sank onto the striped love seat.

Ophelia was also small and round. She wore her abundant hair—mostly beige but streaked with rust and pewter and old gold—in the confused whorl she must have adopted during her free-spirited days in New York's Greenwich Village. She had been in her twenties then, under the guidance, such as it was, of her uncle Henry. She was seventy-five now, and for the past half century she had lived here, in Godolphin, Massachusetts, with her dear husband, Lew. Lew had died six months ago.

The day Ophelia brought in the statue she was wearing her version of widow's weeds—black sneakers, a full black skirt, a black blouse open at the throat, and long earrings woven out of tiny beads. She bent to touch the statue's curls. "He's called Puck," she said, looking up at Rennie. "He guarded Uncle Henry's back parlor fifty years ago. Though *parlor* isn't the right word." And she sat up straight and shook her earrings. "The place was all carpets and cushions and fringes. Oh my! Not a chair or a respectable piece of furniture in sight. A room to frolic in." She poked her fingers into her unfashionable, immensely flattering coiffure, dislodging several gingery strands which then floated near her lined and lovely face. "Puck watched over my love and me." She didn't smile in a reminiscent fashion, as a less subtle person might have done. She didn't smile at all. Nevertheless, information was transmitted.

"The statue stood on a pedestal in the archway," she went on. "We could see it from our pillows on the floor."

Rennie had been running Forget Me Not for twenty-five years; very little could shock her. But even twenty-five years ago, the news that Ophelia had once conducted a love affair on the floor of Uncle Henry's back parlor would not have brought a lift to Rennie's eyebrows. Yet something did surprise her—a hot fizz that accompanied the little confession. The space between the two women seemed to have been sprayed with attar of sentiment.

"Are you selling the statue?" asked Rennie, high on romance.

"I am."

"Well, I'm buying," Rennie heard herself say.

"I'm so glad," Ophelia said. "I wanted to honor dear Lew's last wishes, and one of them was get rid of that goddamn Puck."

So apparently it was not husband Lew who had made love to Ophelia on the floor of Uncle Henry's parlor. But it was certainly Lew—a small, twinkling academic—who had made her happy for half a century. And it was Lew who had collected modern paintings—oblongs of gray overlapping other oblongs of gray. "Puck did look out of place in our living room," Ophelia admitted. "But Uncle Henry had left him to me—what could

I do? Now Lew's wishes trump Uncle Henry's. And I drop in here so often—I'll get to visit the boy. Until you sell him, of course."

Rennie figured she would die before unloading this impulsive purchase. Nevertheless, she installed Puck in the shop window. There he brandished his spear and waved his mirror for several weeks. Children passing by pointed at him and laughed. Dogs too seemed to laugh. Rennie moved him inside and put him next to an elaborate Chinese vase. It was a miserable pairing. Finally she put him on top of the safe. And so a customer entering Forget Me Not saw the usual old things: the striped love seat facing the waist-high jewelry case; within the jewelry case, brilliant adornments; behind the case, impassive Rennie; and behind Rennie, the safe, high on its table. And one new thing: cavorting on top of the safe, a plump bronze boy.

The man with the white mustache came in on a Monday. He was tall and somewhat awkward, but his suit was expensive. The tanned skin around his eyes was puckered and pleated, so that the eyes seemed on display.

"Good morning," he said. "I'm staying at Devlin's Hotel— they recommended your shop."

"Good morning," Rennie said.

His blue gaze traveled around on a preliminary excursion. It landed briefly on Puck. "That's a nice piece."

"Would you like a closer look?"

"No, thank you." And then he took his mild self around the store, looking at this and that. Eventually he chose one of the millefiori paperweights—for his sister, he said. He paid cash—his wallet delightfully bulged—and dropped the glass weight into his jacket pocket. "You have wonderful taste," he said, like everybody else. "I'm in town for the rest of the week, on business. I'll drop in again."

He didn't come on Tuesday—at least, Rennie didn't think he did. The store was particularly busy, and people often glided in and out without speaking. Cathy Lovell the artist did come in. Her sneakers, her jeans, her smock, and her hair were noticeably spattered with paint, as if she'd decorated herself before leaving her studio. As usual she tried on all the art nouveau jewelry. She bought a Lalique pin. She'd return it in a few days, again as usual. Yuri the fix-it man came in hunting for old radios; he wanted to scavenge their insides. Mr. Brown, who had a high, freckled dome, came in to buy a bracelet for a beautiful girlfriend and a similar but less expensive bracelet for a less favored one. Rennie suspected that neither of these women existed. Many of her customers were subject to harmless delusions. She wondered what Mr. Brown did with the jewelry he frequently bought—maybe sold it to a dealer at a loss. Mr. and Mrs. Yamamoto...Ophelia came in.

Ophelia had at last ended her period of mourning. She was wearing a red checked skirt, an orange dotted blouse, and her signature earrings. On Ophelia, hodgepodge looked like a style worth copying: every woman should go out and bedeck herself from the nearest dumpster. She settled on the love seat, and Rennie, helping the Yamamotos, felt her spirits rise several notches.

"Hello, Rennie," said Ophelia when the Yamamotos had gone. She raised her eyes above Rennie's head. "Hello, Puck." She picked up a paperweight from the table beside the love seat...one of the paperweights that the man with the white mustache *hadn't* bought. "He was king of the fairies, you know."

"Uncle Henry?"

"Oh, Uncle Henry was indeed gay, gay before being gay was even mentionable in polite circles. But Henry didn't give a damn for polite circles. He was a tender guardian. He liked Lew. He gave me away at my wedding." A tear traveled down her cheek. "Henry liked the other one too. The man I shared the pillows with, in the parlor."

And who was he? But Rennie didn't ask. She never had to ask. She just sat on her high stool behind her jewelry, her brow wide, her jaws wide, her red hair scraped into a topknot, her shoulders square in the inevitable jacket (she owned them in dozens of colors), her lapel adorned with a single splendid pin. She had none of the softness of a therapist, none of the forgivingness of a clergyperson, none of the piled-up wisdom of an old family friend. Still, calmed by her inexpressive face, people talked. She nodded, never commenting, never making suggestions, never breaking cardinal rule two. But they left comforted.

"Who was he?" said Ophelia, echoing the question Rennie hadn't asked. "Oh, not one of your sparkling personalities. Deep, didn't say much. Geology was his passion. He was getting an advanced degree in it. And then he was going out west...some desert in Colorado. So very far from New York. Lew, now, he came along later, he belonged to Uncle Henry's world—funny, irreverent." She paused. "The soul of a gentleman," she said, and Rennie knew she was referring to the other man.

Ophelia sighed, and slumped; and for a moment she was a wretched old woman in tatters. Then she collected herself and gazed up again at the statue. "Puck was king of the fairies, as I was saying. He put love potions in people's eyes. Brought about misalliances. A mischievous sprite. I have to go now, Rennie. Today is my grandson's ballet recital."

*   *   *

The man with the mustache came in again on Wednesday. This time he was interested in silver. His daughter-in-law collected pillboxes, he said. "In that way, she wards off illness." He was attracted not to the most expensive item in Rennie's collection but to the finest—Georgian, chased, with a tiny painted shepherdess enclosed in a glass oval. The pillbox had a little slide that revealed a hidden compartment. "What do you suppose that's for?" he wondered.

"Love potions."

"Oh, no, love potions, that's *his* business," said the man, raising his face to exchange a stare with Puck. "I'll buy this mysterious pillbox." Again he paid in cash, a wad of hundreds.

She watched him leave, as she watched everybody if she had the leisure. He wore a long brown suede trench coat. Hair as white as the mustache grazed the coat's collar. He had an outdoorsy stride for all that he appreciated indoor things like paperweights and pillboxes. He had purchased presents for a sister and a daughter-in-law, not a wife. Of course, he might have bought his wife a mink downtown. But Rennie didn't think so.

"A baby gift," Ophelia said breathlessly, on Thursday. "A very special baby, my next-door neighbor's granddaughter, four pounds and some ounces. In our day they didn't live at that weight. Now they grow up to play third base and the trumpet. Have you got a silver mug?"

Rennie had a silver mug; it lay on the very shelf in the cabinet where the pillbox had rested. Which reminded her: "Somebody's been admiring Puck," she recklessly revealed. "You might consider this tiny spoon," she said in a hurry; and together they bent their heads over an exquisite and useless utensil.

"I'll take them both," Ophelia said. She wrote a check, backed away with her purchases, gave Puck a little salute. "The arm holding the mirror," she said. "I used to hang my clothes on that. He hung his clothes on the spear." She was at the door now, but she didn't leave. "I had a necklace made out of campaign buttons—*Madly for Adlai,* each one said. He wore an *I Like Ike* hatband. Nineteen fifty-six."

It was a hard-fought election, the Stevenson-Eisenhower presidential race. Once at a flea market Rennie had found a cigarette case enameled with the message *Stevenson for President.* She sold it to a collector. The case now resided in a university library.

"Politics…politics drove us apart," Ophelia said. A pair of customers came in, sidling around her.

"Well," Rennie said.

And then Ophelia was gone, and someone wanted to examine the strange-looking Turkish lamp that had been part of an estate sale. "Does it work?"

"I've never tried it," Rennie confessed.

A dreadfully dirty old woman bought a diamond and emerald ring. She paid with a money order. Mr. Rodriguez the piano tuner, installing his bulk on the love seat, complained at length about his son, who wanted to become a mechanic instead of going to Harvard. Mr. Rodriguez, taking first one point of view and then another, finally talked himself into letting the boy apprentice himself to a machine shop for a year, to see how things worked out. "Thanks for the advice," Mr. Rodriguez said to Rennie, who hadn't said a word. Cathy Lovell came in to return the Lalique pin.

*   *   *

"My business in this town is concluded," the man with the mustache said on Friday. "I'm an engineering consultant," he offered. "I'll take the Puck."

Rennie never showed surprise. "Shall I arrange to have him delivered?" she inquired.

"No, I'll escort him myself to Devlin's Hotel," he said. "He can be my carry-on tomorrow—probably just fits in the overhead rack. Or else I'll buy him a seat," he added idly. "How much?" he thought to inquire.

She named a price higher than she expected to get—people usually liked to haggle over objets d'art. But he silently took out his checkbook. Rennie looked at the check, drawn on a Denver bank, and then climbed onto a little stool kept near the safe and fetched Puck down. He stood on the glass case between them.

"Yes," the man said at last, and stowed the statue under his long left arm, and tipped an imaginary hat with his right hand, and was gone.

An hour later Ophelia found Rennie sitting on her stool, elbows on the counter, staring into space. A check lay on the glass. "Rennie, are you all right?"

"Yes."

"Heavens, where's Puck?"

"The man who admired him bought him."

Ophelia sighed. "What a loss."

"Actually, a profit."

"I mean to me. I'll miss him. I hope his new home is—"

Rennie took a ferocious breath and broke cardinal rule one. "The man is from Colorado. He's staying at Devlin's Hotel. He's tall. He's in his seventies. He has the soul of a gentleman."

"Oh. Oh? Oh!" Ophelia now put *her* elbows on the glass case. They stood face to face, the check lying between them.

"Eyes like sapphires?" Ophelia inquired.

"Well, blue."

"Hair like wheat?"

"Snow."

"Politics is perhaps no longer so important," Ophelia speculated.

Rennie said nothing.

"Lew has been gone for less than a year," she whispered.

Rennie said nothing.

"But I am not in my first youth."

Nothing.

Ophelia touched the check with two gentle fingers, rotated it until the signature faced her. " 'John Ipp...' I can't read this, Rennie."

"Ippolito. He showed me his driver's license."

"My heart's delight—his name was Horace Cannon." She gave the check a quarter rotation so they could both look at the name. "Can we transform John Ippolito into Horace Cannon?"

"...I don't think so."

Ophelia retreated from the check, and from Rennie, who had broken cardinal rule one to no purpose. She sat down on the love seat. "Horace," she mused. "How my heart leaps at the thought of him, him and Puck. I was ready to run to Devlin's Hotel...burst into his room...fling myself onto his chest. 'It is I, Ophelia!' "

"Mr. Ippolito would have been charmed," Rennie said.

Ophelia, in a voice almost accusing, said: "You have kindled a desire in me—"

"I'm a terrible chatterbox."

"—that will not be easily quieted."

Rennie's second cardinal rule leaped to the floor and smashed itself to bits. "Hunt him down," she snapped. "Try the Internet. Call his college alumni office." Advice spurted out of her mouth.

Some of Ophelia's hair had come loose from its confining pins. Her earrings swung. Her blouse had worked its way out of her waistband. To Rennie's acute eye Ophelia became in succession everything she was and had ever been, in reverse order: a colorful grandmother, a woman who had known a long and happy marriage, a girl in love for the first time.

"Hire a detective," Rennie wound up. And she turned her back on Ophelia and climbed the little stool and put in Puck's place a blue glass epergne she had bought yesterday—an ugly and misbegotten item; but it would probably be snapped up before closing time.

Assisted Living

This Yefgin—what a rogue! Leather battle jacket, cascading Rs, and a circlet of gray hair lying loose on his head just as if it were a wig, though whenever he bent his two-timing face to examine a piece of jewelry, Rennie saw that it was real hair springing from his pink scalp. Double deception! And then, that peculiar profession—in a brown third-floor office Yefgin cured people of addictions like tobacco and scratch tickets, using a combination of hypnosis and harangue. "Special concoction," he said, with a wink. Many of his clients did quit their habits, though they often switched to new ones. When Yefgin addressed a woman he kissed her hand first, then twisted his face into a grin that suggested he'd just conceived a helpless passion for her even though they'd met only minutes ago, such things happened all the time in Turgenev. His discolored teeth inspired sympathy rather than revulsion. He was forever in debt. Rennie let his IOUs accumulate to a thousand dollars—then, until he paid up, she refused to sell him any of the dramatic prewar brooches and bracelets he bought for his mistress, and she wouldn't sell him any delicate Victorian rings either, the ones he gave to his wife, Vera. Oh, the scamp.

From time to time Yefgin brought Vera into Forget Me Not to try on one of those rings. She was a large woman with dyed hair whose garnet eyes were settled comfortably in her fleshy face. Rings meant for the fourth finger had trouble wriggling past the knuckle of her pinkie. They had to be resized. Yefgin doted on his fat spouse. He doted on his mistress too, buying her an enamel cockatoo and a bracelet of gold panels connected by diamonds—and, today, right now, a bouquet of amethysts for her lapel.

"Don't tell Vera," Yefgin said, scribbling his IOU.

He needn't have troubled to say anything: Rennie made it a point of honor to keep her customers' business to herself. Yefgin kissed her hand and scooted away.

She liked the rascal. But then, she liked most people who came to her shop here in Godolphin, Massachusetts. She liked the people who fancied tiny Edwardian desks. Breathlessly they bounded up the three stairs at the rear of the store, and through the wide arch, and into the sunlit back room where the furniture stood waiting—they might have been meeting a lover. Rennie liked office girls who called themselves administrative assistants. They spent lunch hours trying on necklaces they couldn't afford. Then, desperate to treat themselves to something, they bought stickpins they'd never wear. And the gossips who didn't buy anything at all—they sat on the striped love seat opposite the waist-high jewelry case, chattering at Rennie, who stood behind it. And the braggart dealers who tried to unload mistakes. She even liked the helpless acquisitors, people who lived only to buy, who filled their lives with one expensive thing after another. But their addiction made her uneasy. Maybe she should run a side business in cures, like Yefgin, browbeating people out of their lust. *Really, you don't need these pewter candlesticks,* she'd say with urgent sympathy. *You've got those brass ones I sold you last month.* But why defeat her own purposes. Enabling was her vocation.

Muffy and Stu Willis slid into the store at least twice a week. Like many long-married people they looked like siblings—both short, both with fine thin hair the color of Vaseline, both with a wardrobe of ancient tweeds and sand-colored cashmere sweaters. An inch of pale shirt showed at the neck of Stu's sweater. Pearls adorned Muffy's. The rims of their glasses were so thin that the spectacles seemed penciled onto their old and yet unwrinkled faces. Together they weighed less than two hundred pounds.

A quarter of a century ago, Stu's public relations firm had done well enough. But it was an inheritance from Muffy's father that allowed them to indulge her attachment to furnishings, rugs, jewelry, and dreary but costly clothing. Stu was quiet, Muffy quieter. Stu occasionally put in a word about the weather, but mostly he stood with his hands in his pockets, his eyeglasses watching while Rennie spread jewelry on the counter at Muffy's soft request. And Muffy's voice—there was nothing to it. It was as if she had once been almost smothered and then allowed to live only if she limited her vocabulary and breathed hardly at all.

When Rennie had spotted the diamond bracelet at an estate sale, she thought right away of Muffy. The bracelet was a four-strand cuff, each square-cut jewel exactly like the one beside it and behind it and in front of it, like a team of expensive mules. Rennie called Muffy the next morning, and within half an hour the couple was standing before her. How meager they were growing. The diamond cuff hung heavily on Muffy's mournful wrist. "Oh," she sighed.

Stu's palm held the bracelet Muffy had taken off—similar to the new offering, but emerald. He tossed it up and down. "Stu," Muffy murmured. *Stu* was one of her words. "Look, Stu."

He gave the diamonds something between an inspection and a glance. "Nice."

"Can I wear it for a while, Rennie?"

"Of course."

"What's a while?" Stu inquired of his wife.

"Go have a nice lunch."

And so, pocketing the emeralds, he strolled out—emaciated and out-of-fashion. Yet there was something of the dandy's spring to his step.

Muffy settled herself on the striped love seat and Rennie prepared for skimpy strings of conversation. From time to time Muffy would wonder aloud if the thing really suited her. And of course it didn't suit her any more than it would have suited a vegetable brush. The Lord alone knew what would suit her. What might improve her would be a transfusion, a perm, a toddler (her one child, an unmarried daughter, lived in California and paid two brief visits a year); an interest in something, anything— gardens, bridge, crime novels, crime itself… "Perhaps this design is monotonous," she said in her nearly inaudible voice.

"Perhaps it is," Rennie said.

Customers—regulars, occasionals, strangers—came in and went out. Some left with purchases. Rennie sold a good ring, a poor Limoges box, a set of demitasse spoons. Muffy's eyes wandered from one person to another, her braceleted wrist unmoving on her thigh. Between customers, she produced a few murmurs. She'd heard about a movie that wasn't worth seeing. Someone had mentioned a program that wasn't worth watching. They'd dined at a restaurant out in Worcester that wasn't worth the drive. The Willises tried a new place every Saturday, alone, together. On the other six nights, alone, together, they dined at the Tavern on Jefferson Avenue, walking from the town house Muffy had grown up in. They ordered the special, whatever it was, and Stu drank a glass or two of wine, and Muffy drank water. The Tavern had once been a church and boasted a stained-glass window. Its patrons included academics and young doctors from nearby Boston hospitals, still wearing their scrubs, and pairs of single women—young, no longer young, frankly old. Rennie often dined here with her friend Dr. Elissa Albright, collector of art deco jewelry. Yefgin and Vera liked it. And here, Saturdays excepted, in this thickly colored noisy place, sat the wordless couple.

"The bracelet may be too wide," Muffy said now.

"It may be," Rennie said.

"I will use the last of Papa's legacy if I buy it."

Rennie said nothing.

After a while: "Diamonds are like currency," Muffy said.

More silence.

"Perhaps it's too heavy."

"Perhaps it is."

Stu came back from lunch at last. He lifted Muffy's wrist from her lap. "Mmm," he said.

They bought the bracelet.

But not only the bracelet. It was as if this end-of-the-legacy purchase included a stake in the business too. Many mornings, on his way to his office—recently reduced from two rooms to one—Stu dropped off his wife like a day-care child. Rennie feigned enthusiasm. Muffy spent the morning inspecting the jewelry, and the Staffordshire, and the Tiffany lamps. She searched for secret compartments in the Pennsylvania desks. Often she stayed the entire day. "No, Rennie, I never eat lunch," she said to Rennie's offer. After hours of musing, she turned to the silver as if it were a sweet saved for last. Vases and platters and tea sets stood on shelves behind glass; shallow drawers were full of tableware. "Nice you've finally got an assistant," said Mr. Gadsby one afternoon. He'd stopped in to look at a barometer. When Rennie lifted her eyebrows he turned to the little figure on its knees, in front of a low drawer, holding a spoon, apparently memorizing its arabesques.

In a way Mr. Gadsby was right. Many days Muffy brought in soft cloths and silver polish. She rubbed trivets and serving forks, and then bathed them in a dappled enamel basin she'd set up on newspapers in a corner, and then carried the basin up the three stairs to the skylit back room and rinsed the silver in the lavatory whose door was hidden by a Chinese screen. When she brought it back down the stuff glowed nicely.

One night at the Tavern, Dr. Elissa treated Rennie to a description of decline. "You see, old girl, elderly people can often tolerate what their cells do to them. They can even tolerate what their physicians do. But that first slip, that first turn of the ankle—ah, that's the beginning of the end. What seems like convalescence is really weakening. Bed rest is preparation for the coffin. There'll be another incident, and another. The aging body cannot repair its skeleton. It begins to yearn toward ruin, and then it accomplishes it. Even—"

"Elissa, for God's sake..."

Elissa took a swig of beer. Seven bar pins gleamed on her broad chest. "None of this applies to you, Rennie. You'll live forever. We all need you."

*　　*　　*

Muffy fell at Forget Me Not. The skylit back room was rather bare that day. Mrs. Fortescue, who rarely bought anything, had, in the space of twenty-four hours, purchased and removed a dining table and six chairs. It was a present to her son on the occasion of his third marriage. "Fine furniture can anchor a relationship," the hopeful lady confided to Rennie. And so there was space for Mr. Gadsby's grandsons to stage a make-believe sword fight with cardboard tubes. They stood aside politely when Muffy padded by carrying a rinsed silver coffeepot. But they may have addled her. At any rate she missed the top stair, and, leaning backward, she slid down the other two. She entered the main room of the store lizard shoes first. She held on to the pot. She made so little noise that the Gadsby boys didn't notice her unusual descent, nor did their grandfather and Rennie, heads bent over a signet ring. Stu, coming into the store, saw Muffy flat in front of the stairs, legs spread as if awaiting him. Behind and above her the duel had resumed, the boys appearing and reappearing under the arch, parrying, thrusting. "Muffy," said Stu, in a tone of reproach.

Mr. Gadsby raised his glance from the ring and bounded to the silent form. Rennie too. Stu was third.

"Don't move her," Rennie said.

"Is there pain, dear?" Mr. Gadsby said.

"My wife," Stu mentioned, and took the coffeepot and put it on the floor beside her feet.

The boys had paused. "I didn't do it," one said.

Nobody had done it, thought Rennie as she telephoned 911; that had been Elissa's point, hadn't it. Muffy fluttered her fingers until Stu took her hand in his.

*   *   *

She stayed a week in the hospital—she was found to have broken a small bone in her foot, and to be emaciated and anemic as well. She was brought home in an ambulance. Two deft strongmen carried the stretcher up the narrow stairs, watched by Stu in the front hall, and by Rennie too—he had begged her to be there. "You are Muffy's best friend," he'd explained; and she turned away to spare him her surprise and horror.

She had visited their house exactly twice before: once to advise on the placement of a French landscape, all cows and mud; once to deliver a repaired clock. Both times she had been struck with the gloom of the downstairs, deprived of light by spruce trees in front and by the houses stitched to theirs on either side. All the fine appointments stood in shadows. But today, following Stu following the stretcher upstairs, she found a light and airy master bedroom. Its high windows, above the spruce, were open to the May softness. The marital four-poster faced a Chippendale chest, so important, so highly polished, that Rennie was reminded of the mirrors young couples hang on their ceilings.

The big men left, passing Stu in a deliberately slow manner. Rennie ran after them with a pair of tens. Back in the room, Muffy, whiter than her pillows, asked for a pain tablet. Stu crushed it between two exquisite teaspoons brought by the Jamaican housekeeper. Muffy took a sip of water from a faceted glass. "Stu. Have a nice lunch somewhere."

"But you...but Rennie..."

"Agnes will make a sandwich when I ring," she said. A porcelain bell sat on the night table. And so housekeeper and husband left the room.

"Rennie, I must...make an inventory of my things. It's been

on my mind. In the hospital...all I thought of." This was a prolonged utterance, and she lengthened it further, asking Rennie
to open the walk-in closet and announce its occupants. Rennie obeyed. Two pairs of black alligator pumps. Two pairs of
brown alligator pumps. Two pairs of brown oxfords. Mr. and
Mrs. Penny Loafer—that couple, or its ancestors, must have
been all the rage fifty years ago. And dozens of skirts, each of
a slightly different tweed; and dozens of sweaters, ranging in
shade from vanilla to rancid mocha. And stalwart broad-shoul-
dered fur coats in plastic capes of their own. "Now the chest,
the Stephen Badlam chest of drawers, start from the bottom,"
said Muffy's weak voice. There were two drawers of silken underpants, piled squarely like memo pads. Tidy slips, camisoles,
beige silk scarves. The three next drawers held gloves, and
stockings, and little white blouses. Rennie intoned descriptions.
The drawer second from the top held only pearls, strand after
strand, each separated from the next by pearly candles, how
clever. And finally the single top drawer, high and narrow. Rennie stood on a mahogany stool inlaid with mother-of-pearl. She
pulled the drawer out. What could be here? The good stuff must
be in a safe somewhere.

What was here was a shoe box. What was in the shoe box
was the good stuff. The diamonds, the emeralds, the rubies.
Necklaces, bracelets, rings. Worthy jewels of impeccable dull
design—some purchased in the finest of stores, some bought at
Forget Me Not—all repeating each other like crocuses. Rennie
felt rather than heard Muffy's sigh. She put the shoe box on the
bed. One by one Muffy picked up the pieces of jewelry, then put
them down, seeming to check them against a mental list—this
urgent inventory did not require paper and pencil. Finally she
put the lid on the box. "Tomorrow you and Agnes can help me

get downstairs, and we'll look at the furniture and the silver..."
She was almost asleep, but with a motion of her hand she indicated that Rennie should return the shoe box to its resting place.

Rennie could leave now. She could go downstairs and say
good-bye to Agnes and walk into the spring afternoon. She
could return to her store filled with lovely items, some of them
oddities: recently she'd had a bronze Puck, and now a graceful
brass device with a long spout and a receptacle and a miniature
pestle in a hollow cylinder. She had bought this mysterious thing
from a man who said he was a Turk...Or she could go home.

Instead, Muffy's best friend remained at the edge of the bed
listening to the shallow breaths, feeling a wet warmth within
her own body, as if she were bleeding. Was it envy oozing
there? This spoiled Muffy had known what she wanted and
had acquired it. What a rare accomplishment. And the objects
of Muffy's affection repaid that affection just by being there,
trustworthy, trusting. Something long contained burst from the
competent woman sitting on the bed, who did not love things
though she traded in them, who did not love people though she
pleased them. "We all need you," Elissa had said. "You'll live
forever." It would only seem like forever, Rennie thought, and
leaned against the bedpost, her mouth loose.

Stu coughed himself into the room. He looked down at his
wife. "Still lovely, isn't she."

Muffy fell out of bed that night. She broke her arm. She went
from hospital to rehabilitation center to nursing home. Even
there she managed to sink to the floor when an aide's attention
momentarily wandered; this time she broke a hip. Back to the
hospital...

Stu fluttered from the house to wherever Muffy lay. Muffy

whispered to Rennie—who visited, who kept visiting—that there were long stretches when he didn't come. He closed his office, and sold some silver to one of Rennie's colleagues to pay its back rent. "The stuff wasn't going to fetch much," the colleague told Rennie. "We melted it down." A breezy young couple bought the town house. They would no doubt gut the place from front to back before they divorced.

"I'll auction everything inside," Stu said to Rennie one day outside Muffy's room. "But first you take whatever you want. Buy, I mean."

Rennie selected a few things: a needlepoint chair, an eighteenth-century sewing box, and the entire dining-room set. "We never used that stuff," Stu told her. "We liked the Tavern. My new apartment is right near the Tavern." The table and chairs looked handsome under Forget Me Not's skylight.

Yefgin took an immediate interest in the sewing box. "Vera would love it," he said, waving away a starburst pin with pink jewels. But the sewing box was too expensive, even on credit. In the end he asked for the Turkish instrument.

"You mean that lamp?" Rennie wondered. It was a strange gift for either of his loves.

"It's not a lamp, it's an opium pipe," he told her. "I'll grow poppies in my window box." He paid cash, and bent his head to kiss her fingers, and he pressed his lips to the roll of twenties too.

The day before the auctioneers were to remove the furniture and paintings, Rennie and Agnes packed up shoes, sweaters, skirts, underwear; all would soon adorn the more petite guests at the local shelter. Agnes carried the boxes downstairs, and left. Rennie put the pearls into a silk sack and moved the inlaid stool to the dresser and took down the shoe box.

She didn't open it, though. She could tell from its heft that it had lost half its contents. She heard a creak at the threshold of the bedroom, and turned; and there was Stu, one tweed shoulder against the jamb, his thin lips twisted in a grin—shamed maybe; proud maybe; repulsive in any case. Could somebody find this half-man attractive? Ah, somebody probably could, somebody probably did, why, just yesterday, a couple had bought the ugliest lamp Rennie had ever handled and carried it lovingly away. She stepped cautiously down from the stool—the cracking of bones could begin at any age—and handed the sack of pearls and the diminished shoe box to the husband of her best friend.

What the Ax Forgets
the Tree Remembers

I.

The first hint of trouble came early in the morning. The telephone rang on Gabrielle's desk in the lobby—her glass-topped, strategically placed desk: she could see everyone, anyone could see her.

"It's Selene," lisping through buckteeth. "I have flu."

"Oh, my dear...you've called the clinic?"

"The doctor forbids me to leave my home." Home indeed: a heap of brown shingles in an alley in a town forty miles north of Godolphin. Three children and a once-in-a-while man... "My friend Minata will give testimony in my place. From Somalia too, and now she lives on the next avenue. She knows the fee, and that she will stay overnight in the inn. She agrees to come, and tell."

"And she has...things to tell?" Gabrielle softened her voice. "Was her experience like yours?"

"Ah, worse. Thorns were applied. And only palm oil for the mending. She will take the same bus..."

Thorns and palm oil and two fullback matriarchs, each with the heels of her hands on the young girl's shoulders as if kneading recalcitrant dough. Someone forces the knees apart. Horrifying tales; Gabrielle knew plenty of them. But would this Minata touch the heart like Selene? *I am happy to be in this town Godolphin, in this state Massachusetts, in this country USA,* Selene always concluded with humble sibilance. *I am happy to be here this night.*

Would the unknown Minata also be happy to be here this night, testifying to the Society Against Female Mutilation, local chapter? Would she walk from podium to chair in a gingerly fashion, remembered thorns pricking her vulva like cloves in a ham?

Gabrielle had first heard Selene three years earlier, at the invitation of a Dutch physician whose significant protruding bosom looked like an outsize wedge of cheese. Gabrielle privately called her Dr. Gouda. Dr. Gouda was staying at Devlin's Hotel, where Gabrielle was concierge extraordinary—Mr. Devlin's own words. Gabrielle said yes to guests whenever she could. She'd said yes to Dr. Gouda. She'd accompanied the solid woman to an empty basement room in a nearby church. After a while twelve people straggled in. Then photographs were shown—there was an old-fashioned projector, and a screen, and slides that stuttered forward on a carousel. A voice issued from the darkness beside the projector—the doctor's accented narration. The slide show—the Follies, Dr. Henry Ellison would later name it—featured terrified twelve-year-olds in a hut. Behind the girls was a shelf of handmade dolls.

The brutality practiced in the photographs—shamefully, it made Gabrielle feel desirable. She was glad that she and her stylist had at last found a rich oxblood shade for her hair; and glad that her hair's silky straightness conformed to her head in such a Parisian way, complementing the Parisian name that her Pittsburgh parents had snatched from the newspaper the day she was born. She knew that at fifty-two she was still pretty, even if her nose was a millimeter too long and there was a gap between a bicuspid and a molar due to extraction; how foolish not to have repaired that, and now it was too late, the teeth on either side had already made halfhearted journeys toward each other. Still, the gap was not disfiguring. And her body was as narrow and supple as a pubescent boy's. She was five feet tall without her high-heeled shoes, but she was without her high-heeled shoes only in the bath—even her satin bed slippers provided an extra three inches.

In the basement room of the church there was no podium, just a makeshift platform. After the slide show a white-haired gentleman unfolded a card table on the platform and fanned laminated newspaper articles across it. Dr. Gouda then stationed herself in front of the screen now cleansed of enormities. She wore a navy skirt and a pale blouse and she had removed her jacket, idly revealing her commanding bosom. The width of her hips was apparent to all. In ancient China child-buyers sometimes constricted an infant's body so that the lower half far outgrew the upper. Gabrielle had read about it: they used a sort of straitjacket. The children thus warped into human pawns often became pets at court.

But the Dutch doctor's shape was nature's doing, not man's. "This is Selene," she said, and surrendered her place to a mahogany woman.

My mother was kind to me, Selene began that night, begins every time, would begin tonight if it weren't for her flu. *My mother was kind to me. Yes, she brought me to the hut, as her mother had brought her, as her mother her, on and on backward through time, you understand.*

When she bears witness Selene wraps herself in native costume—a colorful ankle-length dress and turban. Her face is long and plain. The thick glasses, the large teeth with their goofy malocclusion, the raw knuckles—all somehow suggest the initial maiming.

My mother loved me.

The thing was done for my good and for my future husband. This was believed. I believed it too. I was held down, yes, the body fights back, that is its nature, no one scolded me for struggling. But they had to restrain me. My...area was swabbed with something cold and wet. The cutting was swift. Painful. A small curved knife cuts away a portion of your flesh, it could happen by accident in the garden or while preparing food, that tiny slice I mean, though not in that...area. The wound was salved. There was no shame. All the women in the hut had gone through the cutting.

My mother was kind to me. She was kind to me throughout her life. She procured for me a fine husband, one who would not have taken me whole, as someone might say that piano lessons had broadened her marriage opportunities. *I was sorry to leave my husband when I took our children and ran away.*

"Your experience of intimacy?" Dr. Gouda usually asks from some dark place.

The lids behind the glasses close, open. "My husband was not at fault."

"And childbirth?"

"I wished myself dead."

The listeners are still.

But I love my children, she continues. *I have a new husband,* not an entirely accurate statement, Gabrielle would learn; but the fellow was as good as a husband, or as bad. *It is the same excruciation with him. He understands.* No one asks if he spares her. *I think of my mother and I do not scream. But the cutting should stop. I hope you can make it stop. I am happy to be in this country. I am happy to be here tonight.*

That first time, the Dutch doctor stood at the table and waited until the silence turned into murmuring. Then she said that regrets were unproductive. The challenge was to save today's victims, tomorrow's. To that end...She went on to speak of the work of the World Health Organization, of associations in Europe, of the Society Against Female Mutilation she represented, which hoped to form a chapter tonight here in Godolphin, Massachusetts. The noted gynecologist Dr. Henry Ellison would serve on the advisory committee. "And we are looking for more help," said the Dutch doctor tonelessly.

Many attendees signed up, and several took out checkbooks. Two were elderly women who looked alike, as old friends often do. A pale, emaciated college girl clasped and reclasped her hands; perhaps she felt personally threatened by mutilation. There was a thuggish dark fellow. He probably had a taste for porn. The man who had unfolded the card table now folded it up again. That handsome ruddy face, that crest of white hair—he must be the noted gynecologist Dr. Henry Ellison.

At last Gabrielle approached the Dutch doctor. "I'd like to sign up," Gabrielle said.

"Of course!"

II.

There was no "Of course" about it. For half a century Gabrielle had avoided Good Causes as if they might defile her. Efficiency and orderliness were what she cared about, and her own lively good looks. She cared about Devlin's Hotel too, a double brownstone on the border of Godolphin and Boston. Mr. Devlin had transformed it into a European-style inn, Gabrielle its concierge extraordinary, Gabrielle with her clever wardrobe and her ability to say two or three sentences in half a dozen languages... Gabrielle was made for the job, Mr. Devlin had sighed, more than once.

Really the job was made for her. It left her time to read, to tend her window boxes, to give an occasional dinner party, to go to an afternoon concert. She lived alone. She wasn't burdened with an automobile—she biked to and from the hotel in all but the worst weather, her confident high heels gripping the pedals, two *guiches* of hair pointing forward beyond the helmet. She wasn't burdened with family either, unless you counted the half-crippled aunt back in Pittsburgh. The old woman loped along on a single crutch, the filthy adhesive that wrapped its hand bar replaced only on her niece's annual visit.

Until that night in the church basement this game relative had been Gabrielle's only responsibility. And yet now Gabrielle was writing her name on a clipboard and undertaking work on behalf of females unrelated to her, unknown to her, half a planet away.

Something had stirred within her. She supposed that a psychologist would have a name for this feeling. But Gabrielle would as soon discuss emotions with a psychologist as with a veterinarian—in fact, she'd prefer a veterinarian, she thought, biking home with a packet of information in her saddlebag. It was as if the kinship she felt to those pathetic girls was that of mammal to mammal, house pet to feral cat. The jungle creatures had been cruelly treated by other beasts, attacked with needles and knives as sharp as flame; whereas she, a domestic feline, had in her two brief marriages only been left cold. Free of sex at last, she was disburdened of her monthly nuisance too. The loss had been hastened by a gynecologist—not the distinguished Henry Ellison, rather a Jewish woman with unpleasant breath who advised Gabrielle to rid herself of the bag of fibroids beginning to distend her abdomen. The hysterectomy was without complications. And now, flat as a book below her waist, dry as linen between her legs, she felt pity for the Africans' dripping wounds...well, curiosity, at any rate.

III.

Gabrielle's chief responsibility within the new chapter was arranging its semiannual meeting—the visit of Dr. Gouda, the visit of victim Selene. The first thing she did was thank the church for the use of its chilly basement; then, in its stead, she commandeered the function room of the hotel, a small cocoa-colored space with three elongated windows looking out onto the boulevard. She wheedled a promise of wine and coffee and cheese from Mr. Devlin and convinced him to charge the chapter his lowest rates for the overnight stay of doctor and witness. She did other work too. She and the two elderly women—who were in fact sisters, and hated each other—designed a fund-raising brochure. She helped the emaciated girl, who had volunteered to be a liaison with the local university, withdraw without shame.

"Suffering affects me too strongly," the goose said, her hand on her meager chest.

"Of course, dear," said Gabrielle, flashing her compassionate smile with its friendly missing tooth.

And she listened to the boring conversation of the man with white hair. He turned out to be not Dr. Henry Ellison, as his dignity suggested, but a retired salesman with time on his hands. He was good for running the Follies, though he sometimes got the slides upside down. And she answered e-mails for Dr. Gouda, who hated the computer, and she wrote letters on behalf of Dr. Henry Ellison.

Henry Ellison was the man who looked like a thug. On closer inspection he was merely unwholesome. He had pockmarked skin, teeth like cubes of cheddar. His children were grown and his wife suffered from some malady. He wasn't on the prowl, though. He seemed to welcome Gabrielle's indifference to romance just as she welcomed his pleasure in quiet evenings and good wine and the sound of his own voice. He liked to answer questions. "Is the Dutch doctor gay?" she asked him one night when they were sorting new slides in her living room.

"Doubt it. She's got a muscular husband and five children." A well-trained surgeon, she could have had a splendid practice in The Hague. Instead she was now running a fistula-repair hospital. She drove a van around the African countryside, performed procedures under primitive conditions, sterilized her own instruments.

Henry held a slide up to the light. "Oh Lord, too graphic. Our folks want terrified damsels. They want stories of eternal dysphoria. This..." He kept looking.

"What is it, Henry?" And she did an eager jig on her high heels.

He didn't relinquish the little square. "It's an excellent photograph of the separation of the labia with a speculum, a wooden one for heaven's sake—the thing ought to be in a museum." At last he handed the slide to Gabrielle.

What a strange mystery lay between a woman's legs. The skin of thigh and pubis was the same grainy brown as the old instrument, but within the opening all was garnet and ruby. "Yes, too...graphic."

Henry adjusted the carousel on her coffee table. He held another slide to the light.

"What's that, Henry?"

"A trachelectomy...a sort of D and C. I hope they used some analgesic, something more than the leaves from the stinging nettle."

"Why is she sending slides we can't show?"

"She wants to remind us that despite our efforts, despite our money, the practice continues." He switched off the lights. They sat in the dark, and Henry clicked, and the wall above Gabrielle's couch—she had removed her Dufy print—became a screen. Gabrielle and Henry watched unseen hands manipulating visible instruments.

"Surgery is thrilling," he mused. "Do you mind if I smoke? These village witches probably get a kick out of it. You divorce yourself from everything except the task at hand. Your gestures are swift, like a bird's beak plucking a worm. The flesh responds as you expect. Someone else takes care of the mess."

Gabrielle imagined herself collecting blood in a cloche.

Click. "An excellent example of splitting the clitoral hood. Sometimes they excise the external genitalia, too, and then stitch the vaginal opening closed. This is known as..."

"Infibulation," supplied Gabrielle, who was growing knowledgeable. She too was enjoying a rare cigarette.

Click. "Here's a procedure not yet legal here." An instrument was attacking something within a vagina; there was a glimpse of a pregnant abdomen. "They are destroying the infant's cranium," said Henry.

IV.

With her usual thoroughness Gabrielle went beyond her official chapter assignments. Often on one of her days off, Wednesday or Thursday, she visited Selene in her town, once thriving with factories, now supported, Henry said, by the welfare industry.

There were houses in Pittsburgh too that had been home to factory hands—little brick two-stories, near the river. But there they had been rehabilitated and now belonged to young academic gentry. Here they belonged to the wretched. Here immigrants and their children and a stream of relatives packed themselves into the structures and onto their uneasy porches. The railroad station was a mile away. Gabrielle walked from the train along a broad and miserable street, never wobbling in her high heels though she was always carrying two bulging paper bags. She took a right and a left and fetched up at Selene's shanty. She distributed toys and clothing to the children, and delicacies to Selene—it would have been insulting, she knew, to bring grocery items, and anyway there were food stamps for those. She played with the kids, she talked to Selene, she learned songs, she admired the proverbs that Selene had embroidered on cloth and nailed to the walls. *A cow must graze where she is tied. Men fall in order to rise.* Some were less explicit, riddles, really. *A bird does not fly into the arrow.* "A woman does not seek a man," interpreted Selene.

At nine o'clock on those occasions Selene's consort drove Gabrielle to the last train in his pickup truck. He had a spade-shaped face, as if his jaw had been elongated by force. One Wednesday he didn't return to the house in time to drive her—as it turned out, he didn't return at all.

"Stay with me," Selene said with a shrug.

The children were asleep. It had been a mild wet spring, and Gabrielle's raincoat and scarf were hanging on a hook in Selene's bedroom. She took off her little dress and hung it on another hook, and took off her strapped high-heeled shoes that exactly matched the pewter of that dress, and in her silk underwear climbed into Selene's bed. A light blanket was all they needed. They fell asleep back to back. But during the night the weather turned cool. They awoke in each other's arms...or, rather, Gabrielle awoke in Selene's arms, her head between warm breasts, Selene's fingers caressing her area.

V.

"Minata will take the same bus I take," Selene had said.

Gabrielle met the bus. She had no way to recognize the new witness—so many dark-skinned people were disembarking. Perhaps Selene had told her friend Minata to look for a *petite femme*, stylish, nice face. Walking toward Gabrielle was a rare beauty. She wore a chartreuse raincoat made of tiny scales. Long brown hair combed back from a broad brow. Wide eyes above a simple nose. "Ms. Gabrielle?"

"Ms. Minata?"

They shook hands. *Short skinny white woman with dyed hair*

and ridiculous shoes, maybe that's what Selene had said to Minata. *Brilliant blackie in a coat of fake lizard,* she might have said to Gabrielle. Minata wore golden sandals. Her toenails were golden too. She carried a leather hatbox with brass fittings. "We take the subway from here, yes?"

"Tonight, a taxi," said Gabrielle. *Goddesses don't hang from subway straps.* She explained that the Dutch doctor and an American doctor and an American lady in pink would join them for dinner in the hotel. In the cab Minata turned her head toward the city lights. "Have you been to Boston before?" Gabrielle wondered.

"Oh, yes, it's not the moon. It's the Cradle of Liberty. My children learn that in school."

"You have borne children?" *Did you wish yourself dead?*

"Five."

Gabrielle was quiet during dinner. She was thinking of Selene, her spectacles, her teeth, her martyred air. She was remembering Wednesdays. She was feeling the probe of Selene's strong hand, the fingers then spreading like wings. Her own fingers always fluttered in a hesitant way, fearful of causing pain. Sometimes Selene guided them further inward . . . Minata too said little, was no doubt conserving her energy for the testimony. Dr. Gouda, just arrived from New York—she was on her stateside fund-raising tour—spoke in low tones to Henry. Doctor talk: the gabble of baboons.

After coffee the little group moved to the function room. There they were greeted by a group smaller than the previous one. "Female-circumcision fatigue," Henry whispered. She shook her earrings at him. To her relief, a few more chapter members wandered in. Perhaps they wanted to hear about the progress of the fistula hospital and the opening of a new clinic.

Perhaps they wanted to see the Follies. Perhaps they wanted to listen to the witness. Perhaps they had nothing else to do.

The evening followed the usual pattern.

Dr. Gouda made some introductory remarks.

The white-haired man showed the slides. Some were new, some were old, none were from the batch that Henry and Gabrielle had judged too gory.

Minata's presentation resembled Selene's, though her voice had no sad lisp but instead a kind of lilt. She talked of the cutting, of the women's belief in its necessity, of the children's bewildered compliance. She provided a few extra details. "My cousin—they left her genitals on a rock. Animals ate them." Gabrielle attended, her high heels hooked around the rung of the folding chair as if around the pedals of her bicycle. Her black crepe knees were raised slightly by this pose; her white satin elbows rested on those knees, her fingers laced under her little French chin.

"It causes immediate pain," sang Minata. "Recovery also is painful." She bowed her head.

"And the sequelae—the aftereffects," urged the accented voice of Dr. Gouda.

Minata raised her head. "Ma'am?"

"You must have suffered further...when touched by your husband," said the doctor in a kinder tone.

The head rose farther. "I have never had a husband."

"When touched by a man..." The voice softer yet.

"I do not usually talk about these things—"

"Of course."

"—to strangers. But you are perhaps like friends. To me, being touched by a man is a happiness. Perhaps the cutting made it more so. I also enjoy amusement parks."

"Me too!" from the projector, heartily.

"But childbirth," moaned the barren Gabrielle.

"Oh, one of my sons was a breech: awful. The other four children...pushing and straining, yes, you know what it's like. Pain? No." The listeners were silent. "It is a matter of... choice," said Minata. "You can choose to like, to not like. 'Wisdom does not live in only one home.'"

Gabrielle's aunt too had been childless. She had lived as a scorned spinster with Gabrielle and her parents, part of the dry severity of the family. In Gabrielle's room there had been a few books, a few records, curtains with embroidered butterflies, their wings trapped within the gauzy folds. She thought of this squeezed girlhood, her careless husbands, the restrained Henry. She remembered the slides, the jeweled vagina.

What had *she* chosen? Divorce, self-sufficiency, *an enameled piquancy*—the phrase remembered from some novel. She had achieved it all, hadn't she. But she felt weak. (Later Henry would tell her that her blood pressure had dropped.) She grew dizzy. (He would tell her that she began helplessly to swoon.) The heels of her shoes clawed the bar of the folding chair. She toppled sideways, her shoes still clinging to life. The chair toppled too, but in a delayed manner, as if only reluctantly following its occupant.

"Usually an ankle breaks from a fall because of the sudden weight that is exerted on it. But in your case it was the twist itself that did the work. You managed to wrench your left fibula right out of its hinge. And break a few other things, like the ankle joint, very important, a gliding joint, supports the tibia, which—"

"My left fistula?" she said, turning toward him from her hospital bed.

"Fibula. A bone. Poor Gabrielle."

"What pain I was in."

"You had every right to be in pain, the nerves in the foot..."

"A different kind of pain," she muttered.

"...you'd be in pain now if it weren't for that lovely drip. You won't be able to walk without assistance for a while, old girl."

"Minata," she said. Now she turned her head away from him.

"Minata had several drinks afterward with the doctor and the projectionist."

"Minata betrayed the chapter."

"Dear Gabrielle, we surgeons can never confidently predict the outcome of our work. The midwives of Somalia...likewise."

She leaned forward, and some dismayed tubes shook. He slipped a pillow behind her back. She hissed at him. "You *can't* say mutilation may enhance sex."

"Minata said it for me."

"'Choice,' she said," Gabrielle bitterly remembered.

"'Luck,' she meant," Henry soothed. "Probably rare."

Gabrielle's recovery was awful. One of the little bones failed to heal properly. "We have to go in again," her surgeon admitted. Back to the hospital, back to rehab, back to her apartment at last. Her hairdresser couldn't make a home visit. Her coiffure acquired a wartime negligence. Wherever she parted it a white stripe appeared.

Still: "I have a darling device to get around the house," she told her friends. It was like a child's four-wheeled scooter. Rising from its running board was a post, and atop that post, at knee level, was a soft curved resting place. Gabrielle could bend her affected leg at the knee and lay her plastered shin on that resting place and then grasp the scooter's handles and propel herself by means of her good leg. In this circus manner she went from room to room, from chair to chair, from bed to bathroom. With it as support she could water her flowers, even make an omelet.

She received many get-well cards—from friends and coworkers, from Minata, from her aunt. *I wish you a speedy recovery,* wrote Selene in penmanship that resembled her samplers. Men and mannish women sent flowers—the white-haired projectionist, Dr. Gouda, Mr. Devlin of course. Henry brought books. "I could go back to work now, my surgeon says," she told Mr. Devlin on the telephone. "With the scooter. Perhaps the guests will be amused..."

"Come back whenever you're equal to it," he said, sounding harried. "Not a minute earlier. But not a minute later."

Another week went by and the surgeon took off her immobilizing plaster and replaced it with a fat walking cast and a crutch. The cast was white fiberglass with wide blue straps. The monstrosity reached almost to her knee. Within its unyielding embrace her bones and tendons would continue to heal. But of course she couldn't bike. And she was to throw her high heels into the trash, the doctor said, and never buy another pair.

Mr. Devlin sent the hotel handyman to pick her up every morning. At the end of the working day sometimes the handyman drove her home, sometimes Mr. Devlin himself, sometimes she took a cab, sometimes even Henry showed up. At least she hadn't gained weight. But her hairdresser had rented a house in Antigua for a month.

"Why don't you just go gray," said thoughtless Henry.

She waited a minute or two, then asked, "What's happening with the chapter?"

"Oh, still high on the list of do-good causes," he told her. "Contributions are up, in fact."

"Minata..."

"Didn't hurt us. May have helped us. People adjust to contradictions, you know. And she's prettier than that horse face."

"She gave the lie to what we believe," said Gabrielle, furious again.

"Anything we believe may be disproven. Think about it, Gabby. The Salem women were possessed by the devil. Homosexuality was a sickness. Cancer was God's punishment. False beliefs, every one."

"The earth still circles the sun!"

"Today," he admitted. "Don't count on tomorrow."

VI.

Gabrielle was working late one evening, sitting at her glass-topped desk, reviewing tomorrow's tasks. She looked up, as was her habit: to see what was going on in the little lobby, to smile at guests in a welcoming but not forward manner. She could not avoid the glimpse of herself in the mirror beside the clerk's desk—head striped like a skunk's fur, leg awkwardly outstretched within the disfiguring cast, crutch waiting against a pillar like a hired escort.

A woman stood at the elevator, her back to Gabrielle. Though she was wearing an orange jacket, not a green raincoat, and though her hair was flicked sideways into a toothed barrette, not hanging loose, Gabrielle knew who it was. The hatbox was a sort of hint. But beauty like Minata's once seen is recognizable even from the rear—beauty originating in a place

where skin is brown and teeth white and nymphectomies the local sport. Gabrielle identified also the white-pompadoured man
pushing the elevator's button.

This is not a love hotel... She kept staring until Minata
turned. Minata flashed a happy grin, and Gabrielle gave her the
professional grimace with the gap where a tooth once resided.

Minata walked across the lobby toward Gabrielle. Her eyes
traveled downward and stopped at the boot. Her smile collapsed. "You must wear that thing? For healing? They tell you
that?"

"Yes. I can hobble now. When they remove it I'll be able to
walk."

"Do not wait. Go to Selene."

Gabrielle felt her face redden. Shame? No, desire: desire that
had eluded her for fifty-two years until Selene, maimed Selene...

"Hobble to her from the train station," Minata suggested.
"Or take a cab," she added, revealing a practical streak, perhaps
the very quality that enabled her to make the best of things.

Gabrielle frowned at her own enlarged and stiffened leg.

"Ugly but only a nuisance," Minata said. "'The tortoise
knows how to embrace its mate.'"

The Golden Swan

"The *Golden Swan* is the grandchild of the *Normandie*," said Dr. Hartmann in his frail but grating voice.

What on earth was he talking about now. His slight accent was German, she guessed.

"I mean, Bella, that cruise ships descend from the great transatlantic liners. There was a time, before airplanes, when if you wanted to cross the ocean you boarded a steamship."

His student—for Bella felt like his student, though she and Dr. Hartmann were in fact fellow passengers—fingered her limp hair. Dr. Hartmann was what you called professorial—yesterday he had delivered himself of a brief impromptu lecture on semiotics. She wished she'd understood it.

"And there was a time before steamships when, if you wanted to cross the ocean, or even if you didn't, you sailed on a three-masted schooner."

" 'Even if you didn't'?" Bella echoed.

"If you happened to be a slave."

Their small library—not theirs alone, but they were the sole occupants—was in the innermost portion of the lowest deck available to passengers. It was entirely devoid of natural light. It had a patterned rug, leather chairs, lamps with parchment shades, and four walls of shelves entirely filled with books...some stern hardbacks, some lively paperbacks.

"And now," Dr. Hartmann wound up, "these ships are constructed solely for the joys of the cruise." How joyless his voice was. "For swimming, dancing, sunbathing, eating, gambling. The ports of call, you will see for yourself, are incidental. And I have heard of ships which make no stops, giving up all pretense of purpose." And he produced an inadvertent shudder, and then affected to twinkle.

This cruise was a gift to Bella and Robin from Grandpa, a gift to his dear girls, sweet as candy, pretty as pictures. He liked a little flesh on a female, yes sir! And so, last June, when they were both about to graduate college, he offered them a trip. Anywhere within reason, he said. He didn't mean Paris.

They didn't want Paris. They didn't want Europe at all; they didn't want to exhaust themselves tramping from site to impor tant site. They wanted bright places and good food, and they knew that a Caribbean cruise promised both. An off-season one would strain Grandpa less—and so, though they could have claimed their gift along with their diplomas, they decided to wait almost a year, until the low rates of March. Meanwhile they got themselves jobs, found apartments.

"And now they'd better lose weight," Bella's mother had told Robin's mother over the telephone.

"They'll do that in their own good time," replied comfortable Aunt Dee.

Bella, listening in on the extension, stared bleakly into the receiver. Appetite had plagued her since childhood. In her teens she'd developed an awning of a bosom, though her waist remained relatively slender. Her abdomen bulged. Her large legs were shapely, though, and her ankles were narrow—again, relatively.

Bella was sallow. Robin was pale but blushed easily. She had the ready smile of a child and eyes as green as a cake of scented soap. Her body sloped downward from narrow shoulders past jutting little breasts; it didn't thicken until the tree-trunk waist; then came very wide hips.

The cousins had been close in high school and had gone to similar large universities. Robin studied child development and became a child-life specialist. Her manner with the hospitalized children she worked with was casual and reassuring. Bella majored in business. She was already the valued office manager of a busy real estate firm whose customers craved vistas, and whirlpool baths, and kitchens with granite counters.

Robin had never had a serious boyfriend and Bella had never had a boyfriend at all. Both liked to read—Robin favored whatever was popular; Bella read newspapers and a business weekly and biographies and, somewhat surreptitiously, novels written for middle-schoolers.

On the *Golden Swan* were two big dining rooms for evening meals. There were two small restaurants as well, one French and one Italian; but how spendthrift to patronize them when the rest of the food on the ship was free. All you could eat! There were four ports of call, one every other day in the middle of the twelve-day voyage. And swimming pools and a gym and a beauty parlor and a gift shop, and the library like a den in an old mansion. You could play shuffleboard and badminton. From a platform on the pelican deck you could drive golf balls into the sea. A party swirled every night; some had themes like Costume Ball and Talent Show. At the first party, Meet the Captain, a gray-haired Scandinavian with limited English tirelessly shook everybody's hand and posed for small group photographs displayed for sale later in the central reception room. Robin bought one, and Bella, after some hesitation, also bought one, though she told Robin that the uniformed man must be an impersonator. Shouldn't a captain be standing on the bridge, his eye out for whales and warships?

But to Robin and Bella the most extraordinary feature of the *Golden Swan* was the twenty-four-hour buffet. This occupied the entire aft section of the promenade deck. While eating you could watch the golf balls from the deck below soar into the sky and fall into a sea that was Wedgwood here and navy there and, late in the day, the purple of clematis. If you chose to face the buffet tables you saw colors more various. Pancakes were golden disks. Buckets of chowder sent up silvery steam. There were jeweled salads; hams as rosy as happy cheeks; mountains of tropical fruits. Mauve veal tongues lay on beds of lettuce. And ocher breads—there were glazed breads; grained breads; breads made with berries; breads made with olives; and the most delicious bread of all, a dense hard oblong cut into thin slices, tasting as if its flour had been ground from magic nuts and baked by gnomes in a forest hut. Two hollow-cheeked men spent all day carving roast beef. Another man continually dished out foamy scrambled eggs augmented with mushrooms, or tomatoes, or asparagus. There were cheeses of all varieties...runny, slippery, chewy, blue. Soufflés, one kiwi-colored, the other pale orange.

Their interior stateroom was just big enough for two narrow beds and two night tables. Cupboards and closets were built into the wall. The bathroom was a clever little wedge. Their beds got made and their bathroom cleaned the minute they left for breakfast, or so it seemed; at any rate, whenever they returned, the beds were taut and the bathroom polished. A small person took care of their rooms and other rooms on the corridor. At first they had only fleeting glimpses of this genderless figure—a flash of mustard-colored trouser; a dark elbow reflected in the mirror of someone's open room.

But on the third morning Bella was gripped in the bowels as they were on their way to tap dancing. All those pancakes! She puffed back to their room, and saw that the tiny bathroom was occupied, so to speak. The yellow uniform, its back to her, knelt before the toilet. Dense hair was wound into a thick bun—a woman, then. Her feet protruded into the room.

"I'm sorry," Bella said, but the devoted scrubber didn't pause. "I'm sorry," Bella repeated in a louder voice, and touched the yellow back. The woman sprang up. "I'm sorry," Bella said for the third time. "I have to..."

The maid, standing now, bowed without smiling. She was square-faced and plain, of an indeterminate age—sixty? She slid out of the compact john, and Bella squeezed into it and relieved herself of a pungent stool. She washed her hands, and left without looking again at the small woman. A half hour later, studying her feet in the mirror as she practiced the shuffle, she suddenly recalled that she had failed to flush the toilet. Well, that could happen to anyone, couldn't it, she said to the abdomen above the legs, the bosom... but her shame persisted, as if she had treated the servant like a robot.

This first port was the capital of a newly independent island nation. Its city hall had once been a governor's palace, and public gardens exploded with hibiscus and jasmine. Citizens hissed in Spanish. Robin had more or less kept up her college Spanish because so many of her patients spoke it. She exchanged some sentences with the proprietor of a hammock store, who praised her mastery of the polite form. Guides and souvenir sellers were fluent in English.

But there was a third language, Bella noticed, probably some indigenous Indian dialect. The darker the person and the more menial his task, the more likely he was to use this tongue with coworkers. Some form of the same vernacular was common in other ports too—all of which, by their fourth debarkation, had merged in their minds. The ports were not only incidental, as Dr. Hartmann had warned; they were interchangeable. Oh, there were some differences—the first was reminiscent of the conquistadores; the second had one cathedral and one thousand shops; the third, reputedly narco-friendly, featured trips into the jungle to listen to monkeys; the fourth was a South American coastal city famous for its university, its school for the deaf, its pre-Columbian fort. But they were all colorful, noisy, polyglot, and—Bella said, and Robin agreed—falsely welcoming. They were places you would never want to live in and were rather glad to leave, to walk up a road leading to a brief gangplank leading to a man who checked you in. Home! The *Golden Swan* had become their town—a town with few laws and a loose cordiality. In the dining rooms people sat with other people at tables for ten; urged by the headwaiter, you joined a table with empty seats remaining, or began a new table which was quickly filled. Nobody dressed up. Children—there weren't many, March not being school-vacation month—couldn't roam free; one of the blond officers who did roam free would take an unattended child by the hand and find its parents. Passengers were not allowed in the area where the staff and crew slept. But nothing else was prohibited.

Some people began to seem like neighbors. There was a family from Maine with a retarded ten-year-old son and a clever daughter of twelve who could convert knots to miles per hour and had read up on all the ports. Melinda was staying out of school in order to make this trip, to do her share of diverting her brother. There was a short, freckled pharmacology graduate student who had brought along the research paper he was working on. He explained it at boring length to Bella's silence and Robin's occasional "Fascinating, Luke!" There were three women in their fifties, happy to be together, as if celebrating a reunion. They weren't from the same city, they weren't cousins, they weren't classmates—"Not exactly," the one who was a lawyer laughed. "Something like," said the one who was a social worker. The one who seemed to be a pampered housewife merely smiled.

Some of the staff became recognizable—the thin-faced men serving at the buffet, the dance instructor, the lifeguards, and their corridor's silent maid. They met another maid too—or at least saw her closely. They had taken a wrong turn after a fitness workout; wandering down a corridor, they came to a door labeled INFIRMARY. A long-haired girl with Indian cheekbones was sweeping the floor nearby.

"Hello," Bella said. "How do we get to the swimming pool?"

No answer but a smile.

Robin repeated the question in Spanish.

The young woman leaned her broom against the wall and disappeared into the infirmary. A starched redhead came out. "Yes?" she inquired, and then gave brisk directions while the maid resumed sweeping. How beautiful she was.

Elderly Dr. Hartmann with his scrupulous goatee liked his own company. Bella had once spied him entering one of the restaurants; there, for the price of a dinner, he could sit at a table by himself. But he didn't seem to mind her joining him in the library. In his cultivated presence she was ashamed to read her usual undemanding fare, so she was laboring through the stories of Thomas Mann, twenty pages or so every afternoon.

Every afternoon... For, unlike Robin, Bella needed to withdraw from the stimulation of the ship. So much noise—splashing, laughter, piped music, the clang of coins in the little casino. Luke's talk, full of Latinate polysyllables. And worse: the outdoor buffet, the only place to have breakfast and lunch, had begun to sicken her soon after her first sight of its art-gallery brilliance. If only it were merely a picture it would have continued to please. But it was actual, tangible; it did not signify, it *was*. Real people with real stomachs jostled one another, and piled food onto their plates, and consumed the stuff, and returned for more—Robin did it; young Melinda too; the three ill-assorted women. The underweight Luke listened to Robin's assessment of various pastries and followed her advice and then had seconds of his own choosing. Dr. Hartmann inserted forkfuls of omelet into his old mouth. Perhaps he needed the moisture. Perhaps he was determined to get his money's worth. Meanwhile Bella grew helplessly abstemious. Dry toast for breakfast became all she could manage, a piece of fruit for lunch. A bit of main-dish chicken at night.

"Bella!" said Robin one dinnertime. "Are you okay? This veal is scrumptious! Try some."

"I'm fine." Obediently she speared a cube of repellent meat from Robin's plate. "Yummy," she lied.

One night a figure crept into her dream—familiar, but un-characteristically placating. "Eat, darling!" her mother cried. "You're supposed to diet, not starve."

The next morning Bella created an edifice of waffles on her breakfast plate, and topped it with strawberries and whipped cream. But she couldn't swallow more than a bite. "I have to..." she said, and left Robin and Melinda and Luke and managed to get to her room.

And there was the tiny woman, tightening the linen, smoothing the pillows. In another ten hours, during dinner, she or one of her mates would drop foiled candies onto these same pillows. Now she extended a hand toward the bathroom as if to say it was clean and ready.

"No," Bella said. "I just want to lie down." She did lie down. The woman stood still, perhaps puzzled. They looked at each other, one horizontal, the other vertical. One oversize, the other diminutive. One running a real estate office in preparation for operating a complicated enterprise, maybe a cruise line...the other skilled at cleaning people's bathrooms. The maid was younger than she had seemed that first day. Her dulled face gave an initial impression of age, but she was no more than twenty. At last she resumed her work. She polished the knobs on the built-in drawers while Bella watched. She hung the cloth on a wheeled device that carried all her utensils and pushed the thing out of the room. At the door she again looked impassively at Bella. She did not say anything: not good-bye, or *adios,* or the Swedish *ahyur,* as some of the ship's higher staff liked to do, imitating the yellow-haired officers and the rarely seen crew. Her language, whenever she did use it, would be one of those Indian ones, Chibchan, maybe, or Kuna. Yesterday afternoon in the library Dr. Hartmann had spoken of the languages. He said that certain ones were making a comeback and others were extinct, like the dodo.

"Dodo," Bella giddily called; but the maid was gone.

After the library Bella usually went to the sparsely attended casino and played roulette and surrendered, as slowly as possible, the ten dollars she had allotted to this daily indulgence. But on the final afternoon of the cruise she skipped the library in favor of the beauty shop, where she endured an overenthusiastic shearing that exposed her long neck. Her earlobes looked huge; she covered them with turquoise clips she'd bought for her mother in the colonial port. Then she went to the casino. There she won four hundred dollars. It was a gradual process, this change of luck—win a little, lose a little less, win a little more—and she realized after a while that she was being helped, now and again, by nearly invisible signs from the croupier: a frown, a nod, a tiny shake of the head.

She found Robin and Melinda and Melinda's family at poolside. "Look!" And she showed the roll of bills.

Robin raised a merry face. "Did you rob somebody?"

"She made a killing," Melinda corrected. Then, because her brother was fretful, she joined him on his chaise.

"Oh, Bella!" Robin said. "Get yourself something wonderful. In the gift shop Luke bought a darling mahogany box..."

"No...I'll pay myself back the amounts I lost. But the rest of this is the house's money—the ship's. Let the *Golden Swan* buy us a farewell dinner. At the French restaurant, or the Italian. Which do you prefer?"

"French!"

They wore their best clothing, which had until now hung in their tiny closet. Robin's outfit was a bright blue shift ending at midthigh. Its shoulder straps had little bows. She looked silly and very sweet, Bella thought. Bella's outfit was a gauzy black skirt, long but not so long as to conceal her ankles, and a black jacket. She wore high heels, and again the turquoise earrings— they seemed to be hers now. She looked fantastic, Robin told her.

Certainly Dr. Hartmann seemed to think something similar—he stood up when they entered Les Deux Fleurs, and gave Bella an intent look. "This afternoon the library was bereft," he informed her.

Bella noted his tuxedo and wondered if he had expected something different from this cruise—something other than his usual solitude. She wondered too if her malnourished state was making her fanciful, or maybe even acute. She had already guessed that the ship had taken on cocaine in the narco port. There had been some quick feverish activity on the dock, and the person wearing the captain's uniform was not the same man who had shaken her hand at the party.

There were familiar faces in the French restaurant. And while the cousins were sipping cocktails, the three women friends came in, the lawyer glamorously got up in red, the social worker in a silk pantsuit. The housewife, in sequins, looked game, looked brave...looked done for. Bella saw that the poor woman was ill—ill *again*—and she knew all at once that what the three women shared was disease, the same disease probably, a rare and desperate one. They had met in a hospital for some bold treatment, in a special hospital, maybe in a city strange to all of them. "Classmates? Not exactly," the lawyer had said. Bella confided this intuition to Robin, who said, admiringly, "Of course!"

Bella finished her onion soup. She left most of her *lapin*.

She gave all of her crème brûlée to Robin. Afterward—after Bella had paid and tipped with the lovely chance money—they walked out of the restaurant only slightly tipsy, passing the three women taking the last dinner of their last annual reunion, passing Dr. Hartmann's empty chair.

"What a wonderful trip," Robin sighed. She wanted to go to the final party. Bella would read in their room for a while—she'd finish that story about the magician—and then join her cousin.

Tagged suitcases stood in the corridor. All of the luggage would be collected at 2:00 a.m. Bella and Robin would put out their own suitcases at bedtime. Now she entered the stateroom, took off her shoes, removed the candy from her pillow and tossed it onto Robin's, and lay down. She didn't read, though. She thought instead about the three afflicted friends, about Dr. Hartmann, about the double life of the *Golden Swan*. She awarded a moment of compassion to the graceless Luke. She considered Melinda, experienced in solicitude at an early age, destined to enter one of the helping professions.

She had neglected to close the door. The maid passed, carrying an empty basket—it must have contained the candies. Bella leaped up, and from the doorway watched the narrow form slip along the corridor, avoiding the suitcases. At the end of the corridor were service stairs. The maid opened the door leading to those stairs. It swung closed behind her.

Curiosity...it was a new form of hunger. Bella, shoeless, closed her own door and ran to the service one, and paused—*uno, dos, tres*—and opened it.

The stairs were spiral, winding around a central post, enclosed within a rough yellow cylinder that matched the color of the maid's uniform. There was a groove at shoulder level for the hand to grasp. The dark head was one revolution below. Bella paused on the top stair as if it were a plank. Then, fingers within the groove, she plunged after the maid. The funnel of stairs drew them silently downward. The maid ignored doors indicating new levels. All at once, she disappeared. Bella saw that the stairs had ended. Then she herself was at the bottom, looking into a ... place.

It was a large room with no portholes. Its light was the same reddish brown of the library, the casino, her stateroom—light that had been stored, rinsed in rusty water, and then released. Shades of blue were unknown here. Sky and ocean seemed miles away. There was a trestle table in the middle of the room, bolted to the floor, and two benches on either side of it. There was the smell of baking—that heavenly bread she'd grown to detest. From tiers of bunks attached to the walls came snores. Beneath the room, the ship's engines—diesel these days, Dr. Hartmann had mentioned, not steam—throbbed. Otherwise, no sound at all.

A bowl of peaches stood at one end of the trestle table, and a pitcher of foaming liquid. Several people were playing a card game near the peaches. They did not speak, Bella realized, but rather made occasional motions with their free hands. At the other end of the table sat a woman and a man, rapidly signing. In one corner of the room, where bunks met bunks, there was a shipboard oddity—a rocking chair. In it sat a young long-haired Indian woman with a child in her arms, an infant of six months, maybe eight. Robin would have known its age.

Bella remained in the recess at the bottom of the stairs. She was grateful that she was wearing black. The maid paused to hang the basket on a hook. Then she rushed to the chair. With fluttering fingers she addressed the rocking young woman, who slid an arm from beneath the baby and answered in the same way. Then she stood and handed the child to the maid, and the maid sank into the rocker, unbuttoning the top of her uniform and unhooking an undergarment as well. She put the baby to her breast. She bent her head to meet the baby's eyes, but not before Bella saw that her face had finally attained expression—a kind of meager exaltation.

The girl who had been rocking the child was the same one who'd been sweeping in front of the infirmary the day the cousins got lost. Now she crossed the room, skirting the trestle table and the card players and the animated couple. She entered Bella's hiding place. This time she had no trouble giving directions. *Go away,* commanded the beauty wordlessly, her index finger pointing upward.

Bella allowed herself a long final look at the deaf-mute servants, whose employment here was either a kindly move on the part of a paternalistic ship company or a sensible one on the part of a smuggling racket. She took an even longer look at the hungry child, the stowaway whose presence everyone in the room and now Bella too was bound to protect. After these informative looks, she climbed the helical stairs—a journey less difficult than it would have been five pounds ago.

Somewhat later she had finished her own packing and had placed Robin's empty suitcase on Robin's bed. Certainly she could pack Robin's gifts, bathing suits...The key turned in the lock and her cousin entered, pale skin splotched, hair awry, one shoulder strap broken.

"Bella! You don't have to," she giggled. She rapidly laid clothing in the case, along with the hammock she'd bought, and a little mahogany box. Meanwhile she hummed, apparently not wanting to ask Bella what she'd been up to. And so Bella kept to herself the *Golden Swan*'s secrets, and its secret within those secrets. And her sudden distress—envy, wasn't it—she kept that to herself too.

The cousins stowed their suitcases in the hall and got undressed and went to bed, all without further speech, without gesture, though from time to time Bella glanced at Robin, and, she supposed, Robin glanced every so often at her.

Cul-de-sac

I.

Daphna invaded and then detonated whenever it suited her. Never on Fridays, though. Friday evening was Sabbath, and her husband expected a proper meal; Daphna's preparations, however slipshod, kept her busy. On Tuesday and Thursday afternoons she taught Hebrew at a local synagogue. As for Mondays, when the weekend had lost its affirmative pull—Mondays were days of sapped energy even for Daphna.

So Wednesdays, by default, were likeliest for her unannounced visits. On Wednesdays her husband taught two classes at the university—an afternoon seminar for graduate students, an evening survey for adults. He took his dinner at the university cafeteria, so Daphna could forget about cooking altogether, could toss tuna fish and a plate of sliced tomatoes onto a kitchen table already burdened with homework and half-eaten apples and Israeli newspapers. That table was so littered that sometimes the children dined on the floor. The newspapers were days old. "Stale news," Daphna said, "news that has been superseded or even proven false, lifts me to dizzy heights, like the works of magic realism. Have you read García Márquez, Ann? Saramago?" She didn't pause for a reply; I could have slipped away.

The kids often ate the tuna right out of the can. Three smart and pretty girls—eleven, thirteen, and fifteen at the time the family moved in. They had adapted to their mother's habits, had learned to take over from her. It was they who set up and then reminded her of parent-teacher conferences, they who organized shopping expeditions for school clothing, they who commanded the housecleaning on Sunday mornings. Sometimes they made additions to the Wednesday-night cuisine—raw carrots, buckwheat kernels. While the buckwheat boiled on the back burner of the ancient stove, the oldest girl sautéed the onions. I saw her doing it one night when Daphna pulled me in for a consultation about the kitchen fan—it was on strike, she said. The girl's dark hair was bound loosely at the nape. Her lovely, long-nosed profile bent toward her task. When the telephone rang in the hall the youngest picked it up and then called the oldest's name, and the middle girl took over the onions without a word.

"This malefactory fan?" said Daphna, never without a word.

"Call an electrician," I advised, and fled.

And so, on late Wednesday afternoons, Daphna, not needing even to chop those onions herself, was free to call on her four resistant neighbors.

We each had a way to avoid her.

Lucienne—seventy-five or so, widowed, overweight—could duck under her kitchen counter as fast as a girl. Fat legs bent, fat arms encircling knees, the whole round self keeping company with a trash can and a bin of root vegetables, Lucienne rested in her makeshift cave until the doorbell stopped ringing. Then she crawled out and struggled to her feet, retying whichever romantic chiffon scarf she was wearing that day.

Connie, who worked mornings at a clinic, had a more deliberate Wednesday defense. At four o'clock she popped a chicken into the oven for her family's dinner, then ran upstairs to her little alcove of an office, where she could remain unseen. She unlocked her briefcase and did paperwork for two hours; sometimes the bird shriveled, but so what?

I had an easier time than either Lucienne or Connie. I am divorced and my children are out of the house. Perhaps once a week I poach a sole for my friend Rand, but otherwise the kitchen rarely claims me. (Saturday nights he takes me to the dining room at his club: long windows, long portraits, a lengthy evening.) At the real estate agency that bears my name I can always arrange to show a property, and so on those dangerous Wednesday afternoons I was usually convincing a customer to buy some house, mostly by not talking. My height and slenderness alone can make a sale, my staff claims; my golden hair, they add, if they really crave a bonus.

But Sylvia, our street's spinster, was easy prey. Sylvia started nipping after lunch, and a few hours later she often opened the back door in a fuddled error. Her blouse had by then crept out of her skirt. Her gray hair, which had started the day in a bun, was now a limp corkscrew hanging below its elastic band.

"Ah, Sylvia, I'm so glad to find you at home. Have you time for a cup of tea?" But Daphna didn't say that. She didn't say that to any of us when she succeeded in making a capture—of Lucienne, standing in plain view at the window over her sink, having forgotten it was Wednesday, fixed by Daphna's stare; or of Connie, daring to run downstairs and baste her chicken at just the wrong time, stopped by a knock on the glass door from the deck; or of me, home early, the sale accomplished, intercepted on a dash from garage to back door.

What Daphna did say was some version of this: "Shalom, dear friend. Scandals here, scandals back in Jerusalem, and the French minister of tin cans was found in bed with his biographer. All politics is local, the gentleman said. Local? Smaller yet: household, if you ask me, though who asks me. My gutters are clogged with leaves. I can't stay long—cranberries are simmering on my stove." Cranberries were frequently simmering on her stove, and were often forgotten there. Sometimes on trash-collection day, Daphna's pile of newspapers was topped with an aluminum pot whose interior was glazed an unscrubbable purple. "More than two million bushels of cranberries are produced each year," she might go on. "The plant is cultivated on acid soils of peat or vegetable mold. Such scrupulous recycling of natural elements—it is as if the Talmud decreed it. The Hebrew word for cranberry is *hamutsit*. The French is *canneberge*. The Linnaean term is…" The briefest pause here perhaps—during which opportunity, still in my backyard, I claimed to hear the telephone ringing; or, leaning against her jamb, Sylvia softly belched; or, at her window, Lucienne, adjusting her scarf, mentioned that it was time for a nap; or, sliding open the glass door to the deck, Connie indicated in her flat Wisconsin accent that the monologue might continue inside.

It continued inside anyway, whatever any of us did, as Daphna followed me into the house, cocking her head at the silent telephone; or advanced on Sylvia; or ignored Lucienne's invented fatigue until the poor woman plodded to her back door and opened it. " … *Vaccinium macrocarpon*, the Linnaean cranberry." By this time Daphna was seated at Sylvia's breakfast table, Lucienne's, Connie's, or mine; and Sylvia, Lucienne, Connie, or I was seated opposite her, our fingers splayed on wood or cloth. We gazed at the backs of our hands. We avoided eye contact with her as we would with a rabid dog.

"Politics, you were saying?" Daphna remarked. "The things husband says to wife at breakfast, wife to husband, determine the course of the day, the year, the nation; they influence everything from some grocery clerk's nervous mistake to the idiocy which commands our destinies." She leaned forward. "They influence the policeman on the beat." She leaned farther forward. "My youngest child has the highest mathematical aptitude of all eleven-year-olds in the town of Godolphin." Another of her boastful hyperboles. "What shall I do about the leaves in my gutters?"

She had quantities of brown frizzy hair and a perfect lozenge of a face—brow narrow, chin narrow, cheekbones curved like almonds. Her large gray eyes were calm as water, her full lips about to froth. She favored ankle-length skirts and long overblouses, wore sandals in winter and no shoes at all the rest of the time. She might have stepped out of the pages of a child's illustrated Old Testament, just as her husband might have stepped out of a photograph taken in 1890 on Hester Street: an immigrant tailor, wearing black pants, black vest, white shirt, and a little beard. No skullcap, though. They were not pious, Daphna assured me—their Friday-night meal was simply a reenactment of Jerusalem life. "Every family, the godless, the *frum,* they all sit down together Erev Shabbat. To interrogate each other. It's our tradition."

They were thorough Jerusalemites, she said, all born there—Avner during the Mandate, Daphna during the Suez Crisis, the older girls during the First Intifada, the third during the Madrid Conference. They had lived in a beautiful part of the city: "Stones so golden they are almost pink, like very expensive face powder." Then Avner accepted the offer of a professorship of political science at the university here, and they arrived pell-mell in August, and somebody gave them my name, and I sold them the crumbling stucco house on my own swab-shaped street. Its feeble owners, after boldly installing a new furnace, had entered a nursing home. For house and furniture they'd take a low price. A low price was what they got.

Avner was sixty years old. Daphna was forty-five. How, once upon a time, had the little scholar won the tall beauty? We didn't have to speculate. "Ah, my Avner, his mind makes me think of a high-rise hotel, on every floor something is going on. I was twenty-six. He proposed on Mount Gilboa. We had climbed to look at the irises. I ran through the fields. He ran after me. He proposed again on Ben Maimon Street, under a eucalyptus. Again on Rav Kook Street. He asked for my hand from my father, in my father's house, in my father's study lined with books in seven languages, no, nine, no, eleven, he speaks ten, my beloved Abba, there's one he only reads. And that one is? you inquire," she might demand of whichever neighbor was at that moment studying her own knuckles at her own breakfast table. "Persian."

Daphna seemed to consider the four of us one woman—one ear, really—though she acknowledged certain individual attributes. Lucienne, who'd had a French mother, knew about sauces. Connie the social worker could recommend a course of action to take with a daughter's brief defiance. (In fact Connie made no recommendations; she kept her mouth locked, like her briefcase.) When Sylvia wasn't drinking she was thinking. She had grown up on the campus of Swarthmore College, where her father had taught philosophy; she was acquainted with meaning. She was probably acquainted with sorrow too.

And I? "You are American royalty," Daphna said. "You are a direct descendant of John Adams, I know that for a fact."

It is a fact. It is another fact that the Adams descendants number in the thousands. And there is a third, unrelated fact, an odd one: though I avoided Daphna, as did my three neighbors, because, as Sylvia said, give her a sip and she'll gulp you entire; because, as Lucienne said, she's *dérangée;* because, as Connie said, her intensity makes you feel charred—an insightful remark, though it slid with no emphasis from Connie's mouth, as if it were a standard lease form received on the fax...though I avoided her, I did half enjoy—well, quarter—the times I got captured. Her nonstop talk included celebrity gossip (she knew something about everyone in the universe); bits of information like the word for "cranberry"; and comments about her dry motherland. "We are parched, we worship water, our phlegmy consonants are the result of our nonlubricated pharynx." A change, this *dérangée* stuff, from my usual conversations about mortgage rates and bridge loans and house footprints and zoning bylaws. A change from Rand's solemn pronouncements about the decline of civility in the Western world.

"Every time we look around, Avner is being summoned to the councils of the great. He is great himself." Certainly the little tailor traveled often. We imagined him at unworldly academic conferences. When he was away, his females ate tuna fish out of the can every night. "He has embezzled my dreams," she said. "I am his favorite," she told me. "His favorite thorn," she told me. "His favorite demon," she told me, told me, told me.

Saturdays we were safe from her. Avner and Daphna disdained synagogue worship, but the family devoted Sabbath mornings to scriptural study at home and the afternoons to those shopping trips led by the daughters. Sunday mornings they all cleaned the house. But the rest of the day we were at risk. On Sunday afternoons—at other times too—Daphna occupied herself by vigorously sweeping her seven front stairs. Sometimes she mopped them as well, and then swept them again. Depending on the season she engaged in conversation with the widower on one corner clipping his hedge or the elderly bachelor on the other corner shoveling his snow. The conversation would be conducted in a yell, woman to old man, old man to woman. Soon, though, Daphna would walk diagonally across the street to the hedge trimmer or down the street to the shoveler, dragging her broom like a nightmare tail. Eventually the chosen man would go indoors, probably to pour himself a stiff drink. Then Daphna would select one of us. Maybe Lucienne in the house next to hers ("handsome Tudor," I'd say, if I ever had to sell it). Maybe Sylvia in the neglected house directly across the street ("Victorian fixer-upper"). Maybe Connie, next to Sylvia ("Colonial with deck, mint condition"). Maybe me, located at the end of our cul-de-sac like a hostess ("split-level charmer").

But Daphna knew that Sunday was my busy day and that she was unlikely to find me at home. If I did happen to be in the house I might watch from between the slats of my upper-level bathroom as she made her rounds—loopy rounds, for she never rang the front doorbell, always the back. Barefoot, now holding her broom upright but upside down, she would disappear and reappear, cross and recross the street. The broom's horizontal bar of whiskers was level with the top of her head. She looked like a peasant girl who had acquired a military suitor, or maybe a constabulary one.

*   *   *

Every Thursday afternoon I meet Rand in a coffee shop in Godolphin Center. I go home first to freshen up. One Thursday in October—it was Daphna's second year in town, so I knew her schedule—I gave the street a once-over, then left my house on foot. Of course, to be safe, I walked on the side opposite Daphna's house, and of course I walked fast.

"Shalom!" she screamed. She was standing on her top step, broom in hand. She must have been watching from a window, waiting to pop out. "Where are you going?"

"Coffee...with a good friend." I didn't break stride. "I'm late," I said over my shoulder.

"The Marigold Café?" she yelled.

I nodded. My head was facing forward now, my right arm behind me like a wing. I wished it really were a wing.

"I'll walk with you!" In a moment she was by my side. Her hand clutched the upended broom around its waist. Her unshod feet kept pace with mine.

"Daphna, don't you teach on Thursdays?"

"It's Sukkoth; no class." Of course: in various Jewish backyards leafy structures had sprung up overnight. "You are enjoying that book under your arm? My oldest reads everything she can get her hands on. She reads upon rising, she reads when she goes to bed, she reads while she's chopping onions, she reads in the shower..."

"A remarkable feat."

"She accomplishes it. The teacher of my middle one tells me that she is the best science student he has ever encountered. She will become a physician, of that I am utterly sure. She will work on a Native American reservation with victims of fetal alcohol syndrome."

"My husband was a drunk."

"Ojibwa?"

"Episcopalian."

We were passing a string of double-deckers. "These houses are advised to devote two-thirds of their land to grass, or something green," she said. "But some are utterly blacktopped. Why? For the sake of the automobile." Her family did not own a car; they used trolleys and an occasional taxi. They didn't have a television either. "Did you see the sky at sunset yesterday? Royal purple, like the irises on Mount Gilboa. I stood in the attic of my home. There is a window facing west. The telephone rang several times, but I refused to abandon my post. Anyway, the calls are always for Avner or the girls. My oldest is sixteen. There are boys already in love with her. That is her destiny."

We had reached Godolphin Center. The Marigold Café is a shallow place, mirrored to provide an illusion of depth. Rand was seated at a table in the back, against the mirror, his silver hair and distinguished shoulders doubled behind him. "Goodbye, Daphna."

"They all want to pierce their ears. What do you think? Yes, mine also are pierced, but in my youth we stopped there. I am afraid that after the lobes the lips, after the lips the belly—"

"Good-bye, Daphna."

She stood glaring at me, her feet bare on the pavement, the broom bristling beside her head. "When will you come to us for dinner?" She issued this question often.

"Soon," I falsely promised, just as often. I turned in an abrupt manner, as if she had insulted me. It was the best method of breaking away. I entered the Marigold and leaned across Rand's table to kiss his finely honed cheek. I sank onto the chair opposite him.

"Heavens," he said, apparently noting my exhaustion. Then: "Heavens" again, looking past my ear. "Isn't that your neighbor outside, getting in people's way?"

I looked past his ear into the mirror. I saw, through the window of the café, that Daphna was still standing on the sidewalk and that passersby had to swerve to get around her. Some looked annoyed. Some stopped to talk. The human knot around her grew thicker, further irritating those wanting to keep going. *Dear, aren't you going to hurt your feet?* that old lady must be saying. *A good-looking broom,* from a wag. *Would you like me to take you to the shelter?* Daphna turned her head from one to another. At last a policeman joined the little crowd and offered her his arm.

I later heard from Connie's husband that he'd seen the two of them and the broom proceeding down our street, Daphna talking and the policeman listening; and that he, Connie's husband, couldn't tell whether his neighbor was under arrest or whether, at last, she was getting somebody's full attention.

II.

The policeman's name was Sam Flanagan.

He was tall and auburn-curled, snub-nosed and broad-grinned; and if I had ever brought him home my father would have thrown him out. Jews, Daddy could just tolerate; Irish, he despised. Sam had been born twenty-five years earlier on Magazine Street in the section of town we real estate people still call Whiskey Point. He was as thorough a Godolphinite as Daphna was a Jerusalemite, and he lived in his parents' shabby house with eight of his nine brothers and sisters. The oldest, married to a man from Bhutan, had moved out.

"Can you imagine the chaos there?" Daphna said to me. "Siblings and their friends, assorted uncles and aunts, everyone drinking and watching television and utterly making a racket. They might as well be Arabs. What an atmosphere for a scholar."

Well, Sam was a scholar, of sorts. He had graduated from the police academy and achieved a bachelor of science as well, and now he was studying law part-time. Our town pays for that sort of thing for its public employees, but of course it doesn't provide a study house or even a carrel. "Within our family a person is able to reflect, to contemplate; and the girls have hundreds of those yellow highlighters."

And so Sam on his red Vespa came to that dreadful house ("prewar spaciousness; new furnace") almost every weekday, sometimes in the afternoon, sometimes in the evening. "Sometimes in the morning," Lucienne reported, her cheeks as pink as that day's scarf.

"Policemen have shifting shifts," I told her.

"He takes one of the girls for a ride before school."

I knew that. When Sam rounded the widower's corner with a daughter riding pillion, I was reminded of my splendid horse, Patrick. He was a Hanoverian, seventeen hands. I had stabled him at Prides Crossing. During my teens I rode him three afternoons a week, taking the trolley from South Godolphin to North Station, then the train to Patrick. And so I was reminded too of my parents, bravely maintaining that South Godolphin mansion ("Italianate villa on two acres; swimming pool and carriage house")—reminded of Daddy's bankruptcy and the taking over of his company by two well-dressed Italians. "Goddamn foreigners." And reminded of my misguided marriage, entered into in the wake of Daddy's ill fortune. All those memories, occasioned by a young man and a girl on a motor scooter. Lucienne in her soft chiffon and tippling Sylvia and Connie the determined empath probably had youthful things to be reminded of too. I don't know what those things were because around here we don't discuss regrets or triumphs. And I certainly don't know what Avner thought on a particular morning when he descended his front steps just as Sam rode up, Daphna behind him, her arms around his leather jacket, hair streaming. I know only that he waved at them.

Daphna was now often seen at the supermarket, accompanied by the youngest daughter, who examined each item and calculated its price per ounce and chose the cheapest, and at the same time kept a running total in her head—I knew she did that; Connie's remarkable intuition saw tumblers spinning behind the girl's forehead. Daphna began to cook almost every night—I knew that too; Lucienne provided her with many of the recipes. Sam and the family could probably fit themselves around the kitchen table, especially if the debris were removed. But Sabbath dinner had always been served in the dining room, heavy with the dark furniture that came with the dark house. On Fridays, driving by, slowing up, I could see six people around the table, could see Sam's curls brazen in the candlelight.

Wednesdays became safe. Every day was safe. Daphna had retreated into her expanded family. I wished them all good listening.

III.

It was on a Wednesday that the package came—Wednesday morning, a few days after New Year's Eve. The postman held it out to me at arm's length. The package was oblong and bore Israeli stamps and was addressed to Daphna in English. "Nobody's home there, not even Flanagan." (Postmen know everything.) "Would you sign for it?" As a proper Godolphin citizen, I complied.

I forgot about it for a day. But on Thursday when I got home from the Marigold Café I noticed it on my Stephen Badlam chest, the one item of furniture I'd salvaged from Daddy's house. I picked it up and hurried down the street, still wearing my otter coat, twelve years old now but once stunning, still wearing my high-heeled boots. The evening was misty, and warm enough for me to unbutton the coat as I walked. Rand had proposed that afternoon. I was thinking it over. I liked sailing with him off Wings Neck. I'd like being moneyed again. I could sell the business. And though I would never forget Patrick, I could buy another horse...

I walked up the seven moist steps. No one answered my ring. I walked down and made my way along the driveway, past the red Vespa. I rang the back doorbell.

Who opened it? The youngest girl, I think, scrambling up from the floor where she and the middle one were sitting, each with a bowl of stew—one of Lucienne's recipes, probably. One girl was eating with a spoon, the other was not. The stew proper was in a large enameled pan on the stove, and its fragrance almost banished the odor of cranberries burning in another pot. Other things cooked on other burners. Something sweet baked unseen in the oven. The fan, never fixed, did not dissipate these aromas. The room was steamy and it was illuminated only here and there, like a Rembrandt tavern. Some light came from a tipsy lamp on the table; some from a butterscotch disk, circa 1930, embedded in the ceiling; some from a bulb on a pole with a shredding shade; some from a weak fluorescent bar imperfectly attached to the stove. Daphna was standing at the stove, stirring and tasting, then raising her wooden spoon like a scepter. She and the girls wore golden hoops in their ears—the daughters had apparently prevailed in the matter of lobes. Their long hair was loose and lustrous. The oldest was sitting on a high stool, reading. Avner and Sam, at the table, argued in a peaceable way, each gesturing with a wineglass. The table was littered as usual, but a few plates had been laid.

I approached Daphna. "This is yours." Garlic and rosemary threatened to overwhelm me. The two men belatedly stood up. Sam overturned his wineglass. I handed the package to Daphna.

"From Abba!" she cried. She tore away the stiff mailing paper and unwrapped corrugated cardboard from three books. I saw that one was French and another German. The cover of the third was embossed with beautiful, curly letters. She pressed all three to her breast. I motioned to Avner to sit, and he did, and so did Sam, and they resumed their amiable dispute, which had something to do with the Bill of Rights. They spoke English, of course. The two younger daughters were speaking Hebrew. The oldest daughter, her paperback in her left hand held open by her thumb, slid off the stool and retrieved the wrapping paper and the cardboard from the floor (Daphna was already reading one of the new books) and stuffed it into an overflowing trash basket and picked up Sam's fallen wineglass and refilled it and handed it to him, raising her eyes briefly from the page. I imagined her in the shower, one arm extending beyond the plastic curtains to keep the book dry.

In the center of this mess of a mealtime, I felt my thoughts whirl. How would I sell the place when they left? How would I ever find people as oblivious as these? The furnace might be new but the oven was as old as the house. The electricity was so faulty that no lamp could sustain more than a sixty-watt bulb. I knew that in other rooms, as in this kitchen, crown molding was separating from walls and plaster was cracking. There was a particularly deep fissure in the ceiling of the master bedroom. Avner and Daphna had probably learned to ignore it. Sam was too besotted to notice. Someday this house would defeat me.

But the family was defeating me already...these people occupying a chiaroscuro kitchen, these people of many languages, these people indifferent to the ordinary conventions of table manners, these people of no restraint. These people steamed in happiness.

Daphna put down her book. "Join us, Ann," she commanded. And then: "We would like you to share our meal."

Join them? Share their meal? Nudge the oldest off her stool and snatch her book for myself? Sit at the table with Avner and Sam and twirl a wineglass? Sink to the ruined linoleum and eat stew with a spoon, with my fingers? If I dined there just once I might move in, never leave, marry myself to the lot of them. Just what Daphna wanted.

"I have an engagement."

"Oh," tragically.

I edged backward.

"Please, the front door," Daphna said. She escorted me out of the kitchen and through the dining room used only on Fridays—there was an awful zigzag crack from ceiling to floor, as if lightning had once struck—and into the hall, all without flicking any switches, so we proceeded in semidarkness to the front vestibule. The broom leaned against the wall like a shotgun. Daphna opened the door. We stood at the top of the glistening seven steps. "This brief seasonal warmth is called the

January thaw. The Gulf Stream sends balloons of hot air, and the arctic winds retreat. Even the global warming meshuggeners don't use the thaw as evidence, it was occurring in Eden already..." She flung sentence after sentence at my escaping self. But standing in her kitchen, looked up to and looked after by daughters, husband, and at last a courtier, she had said no more than a dozen words, probably fewer. I turned toward her from the bottom of the steps.

"You must come sometime!" she urged.

"Go back," I said, and hurried down the street.

IV.

I haven't married Rand. I couldn't say yes to his offer. Daphna's kitchen ruined any charm it had. I couldn't say yes to Daphna's offer either. It's too bad I didn't marry my beloved Patrick thirty years ago. I would now be the widow of a horse, contentedly remembering that laugh of his whenever we took a fence.

So, having not disposed of my business, I must now dispose of Daphna's house. Soon after that night, Avner accepted a position in the latest Israeli government—apparently he does move among the powerful—and within a week of his appointment the entire family decamped for Jerusalem. Never mind the contract with the university—in fact, the university trumpeted this faculty-government connection. Never mind the house they owned—luckily I found two Pakistani doctors to rent the place furnished for a few years; they work long hours at the hospital and we never see them. And never mind the girls' interrupted schooling. The family did stay in town long enough to watch the middle daughter receive a first prize at the science fair.

Daphna said farewell by leaving a brief note in each of our mail slots: *Off to the Cabinet. Shalom.* Probably she sensed that she had outworn our tolerance of her garrulity. And anyway she was returning to Jerusalem, where, I'm told, everybody talks at once, brags all the time.

But Sylvia was home when the note popped through her slot. It was morning; her hair was still in its bun. She opened the door. She told us later what she learned. Avner had indeed taken a ministerial post, but he could have done so several times in the past; his wisdom is valued by many parties. This time he accepted, not because of the usual parliamentary crisis but because of a domestic one.

No, he had not come home to find Sam and Daphna warm under the cracked bedroom ceiling. "We Godolphinites do our share of sinning," Sylvia pointed out, "but we do not abuse hospitality."

"Oh," said the disappointed Lucienne.

Sam had fallen in love, yes—with the oldest daughter. And she with him.

"They are utterly too young," Daphna told Sylvia. But Sylvia with her fine, marinated intelligence saw through that small truth to the larger one beyond. As enlightened as Avner and Daphna wished to seem, they could not wholeheartedly welcome an Irish cop into their bloodline.

"See how you feel when we return," Avner advised the lovers.

"Write every day," Daphna added. "Promise to remember each other!" What cleverness; they started forgetting each other before she finished the sentence.

Sam Flanagan never visits our dead-end street. On the corners, in their seasons, hedge clipping and snow shoveling go on undisturbed. And once every few months, Connie and her husband invite Lucienne, Sylvia, and me to dinner, served in a cool green dining room with a view of the deck. I'll have no trouble selling *that* house.

"Do we miss Daphna?" Sylvia wondered on one of those occasions. She was well into the wine; a helix of gray hair fell over one shoulder.

"Yes, no," Lucienne said. "She was too hungry."

Connie said slowly, "She wanted to . . . mean so much to us. It was . . . inappropriate."

"Also doomed," I added.

"Indeed," Sylvia said. "We mean so little to each other."

Deliverance

The hiring committee—the three members of the staff and Rabbi Stahl from the board, who begged to be called Steve—were briefly taken aback by the candidate's looks. Donna could feel a ripple of confusion. The woman's name was Mimi. Her blunt hair was dyed the crystalline color that old-movie buffs called platinum. She had a wide lipsticked smile. As she advanced toward them across the large basement dining room, it became apparent that she was very pretty. She'd stated outright in her cover letter that she was a divorcée with three grown daughters. She must have borne them young. She wore a long suede coat and high-heeled boots. A fur pillbox rested on the platinum bob.

You are not what you wear, as the staff knew well. Some of the most crackbrained guests at Donna's Ladle could rummage through a pile of donated rags, select a few, and with those few convert themselves into a dead ringer for a CEO or, if you want to talk really elegant, a high-priced call girl. This Mimi, so bewitchingly chic, might have a heart of gold.

The hiring committee, sitting side by side at the long table, took turns telling Mimi about the facility ("a soup kitchen for women and their children") and the general nature of the work ("cooking, plunging toilets, bossing volunteers, hanging out") and the sometimes strained relations with the Unitarian church whose basement they occupied.

It fell to Donna to define the particular duties of a new staff member. "When my baby comes, three months from now, I'll go on indefinite maternity leave, though I'll volunteer in the kitchen one day a week. Pam here"—an affectionate look—"will take over my administrative and fund-raising chores, and so her old job as resource coordinator is up for grabs."

"Scrounging for supplies," Pam explained. "Wheedling donations, buying food cheap. Batting eyelashes at pro bono plumbers."

Mimi's eyes were blue under black lashes. "Pleading with restaurants?" she asked.

"Yep."

"Have you thought of those unopened airline meals that go begging at the end of each flight?"

No one had thought of them.

Mimi had worked as a volunteer in a children's hospital; she could do light carpentry; she was, by her own grinning admission, a better than fair cook. Her hat was now in her lap. She asked a few questions about guests fighting with each other and workers burning out. "I'm afraid I have no cellular telephone," she said at the end of the interview; she'd already confessed to having no car.

"You communicate through your familiars," the rabbi said with a smile.

Mimi beamed back at him. "And travel on an old broomstick, you've got it." Then she left, carrying her hat, walking away with an unhurried ease, her radiant hair dimming as her figure receded.

"I'll bet she owns jeans," Donna said.

"I liked her," said the other two staff members, almost in unison.

The rabbi shrugged. "What's not to like? Her hat reminded me of one of my grandmother's. She was a Brooklyn hysteric, claimed that animal skins were essential to tranquility."

"Wasn't that thing fake mink?" asked Pam anxiously.

"It was real sable," Donna said. "This Mimi doesn't know about animal rights. She has no experience with people who are down and out. She has no experience with mental disorder or substance abuse."

No. But Donna aimed to give her guests a haven from do-gooders and mental-health busybodies—people who pushed change. When a woman lunched at the Ladle she couldn't indulge her habit but she wasn't badgered about renouncing it. She couldn't slug anybody but she didn't have to listen to antiviolence yak. She couldn't flush socks down the toilet, but she could warn her friends about the socks' radioactivity as long as she kept her voice reasonably low. She could be herself.

Mimi's closest rivals during the hiring process were a light-skinned black woman who sang in a church choir and whose grandchildren had made her wise in the ways of the street, and a social worker serving as adviser to a radical state senator. Either candidate would have been a breeze to justify to the board. But the staff sensed a streak of punitiveness in the first and a wearying righteousness in the second. Mimi wanted to make things better for people, but she seemed to have no wish to make people better. "Or she keeps that wish under her hat," the rabbi sighed. "I do warm to that singing grandmother." Then he agreed to hire Mimi.

"You are very gracious," Donna said. "Steve," she managed to add.

Mimi at first gave Donna no cause for regret. She was indeed a much better than fair cook. She could take a meager amount of cod donated by a fish market half an hour before it turned and make it the basis for an abundant chowder. "Toss that out," she said to a volunteer who was refrigerating the leftover soup. "If we eat it tomorrow we'll be dead by nightfall." Mimi could transform a few scraps of lamb into a bountiful shepherd's pie. "Potatoes, all you ever need is potatoes," she explained to Donna with her gleaming smile. "I can make potatoes into a dessert. Into a shake, too, with a little whiskey. I'm part Irish, you know."

"The other part must have studied at the Cordon Bleu," Donna said.

"The other part—part of the other part—is Romany. I come from a long line of horse thieves."

Maybe—she was wily enough. When the board of health decreed that kitchen workers cover their hands, Mimi teased a gross of surgical gloves from a dental-supply house. When a restaurant failed in New Hampshire, she borrowed Rabbi Steve's car and drove north and returned with hundreds of stainless place settings, purchased very cheap. She flew to every yard sale in town and bought defective board games for a quarter each. After several weeks of collecting, she persuaded a few guests to spend a rainy Friday making whole games out of parts. By the end of the day they had three sets of Monopoly, two sets of Clue, two Connect Fours, and lots of full sets of checkers. While the women were working, Mimi knocked together a Lego holdall, a knee-high case with subdivided shelves. She fenced the compartments halfway up with nylon and labeled them: TWO-BY-EIGHT; EIGHT-BY-EIGHT; FLAT PIECES, WINDOWS...

Donna, on her way out, paused to admire this construction: what a boon to kids whose only play space was the Ladle's small children's room. "That barrel we kept the Legos in was driving me crazy," Mimi said. She was kneeling on the floor, still hammering. There was sawdust on her jeans, her tee, even a few yellow grains on her translucent hair. She spat out the last nail. "The kids had to turn the barrel upside down anytime they wanted to build a tower."

As a reward for the afternoon's labor Mimi took the women out for pizza and a bottle of Chianti. On Monday Donna offered reimbursement from petty cash.

"Oh, Donna, the wine, I shouldn't have, you don't want the Ladle to enable anyone..."

"It was grape juice; I have it on the best authority. Thirty-five enough?"

"A little too much. But I know where I can get some Lego wheels."

Donna's baby was due in December. By the beginning of November a sense of imminent maternity seemed to hang over the Ladle. Or was it imminent madness? More people than usual were touchy, defiant, in trouble with caseworkers, in trouble with parole officers. Several got picked up by the police because of threatening behavior. Donna knew she was partly responsible for the unraveling—she was providing one more desertion for souls who had been deserted too often.

Miss Valentine and O-Kay were cruelly bedeviled. Unwelcome visitors inhabited Miss Valentine's large black body. Voices told her what to do and say, even when what she did and said caused her landlady to call the police and the police to suggest that she keep a nonactionable tongue in her mouth. Miss Valentine's children had all been taken from her except for the ones she herself had abandoned on the island where she was born. When the voices were silent Miss Valentine muttered to herself, as if keeping the conversation up.

Pale O-Kay talked out loud to anyone who would listen. She bragged that she was in charge of innumerable children, some hers and some awarded by the state. She was the little young woman who lived in a shoe. The shoe was her old car. In fact, O-Kay's children were illusory. She slept alone in her car. She had an unnerving tic; often her whole body shook.

Mimi talked often with Miss Valentine and O-Kay. Donna saw their three heads bent toward one another over bowls of cooling soup. She couldn't catch the conversation, but she could see O-Kay's shoulder quiver and Miss Valentine's mouth move, and she could hear Mimi's tone of priestly softness. Had the Ladle been infiltrated by a religious in drag? That legislative aide they'd thought about hiring, for all her high-flown ideas, was at least an atheist like the rest of the staff.

"Miss Valentine is possessed," Mimi reported to Donna in her ordinary voice. "O-Kay is possessed too."

"I suppose *I* am possessed," Donna said lightly. Her baby stirred.

"Literally you are. And you'll be delivered of a lovely infant. But Miss Valentine and O-Kay can't rid themselves of their demons, not without help."

"Miss Valentine and O-Kay have gone off their medications."

"Not without help," Mimi repeated with a husky intensity. "Those demons, they cling to the innards with red claws."

"It's our mission to meet the women where they are—"

Mimi's blue gaze caught her like the beam of a lighthouse.

"—and not to interpose our own values," Donna finished, blinking helplessly.

In early November, on the Friday afternoon before a long weekend, a guest's child—the middle boy of three—staggered in with his arms around a wood and mesh cage. He had won a lottery: he got to take home the class gerbils. "Home!" his mother snorted. "We ain't got room even for the TV—had to sell it. Your aunt is having another baby—did you forget that?" She turned to Donna. "We leave these critters here, right? And you'll visit them on Monday," she said to her son, who was silent. He was accustomed to disappointment, and he didn't dare appeal to Donna, since he knew that she knew that he often left the Ladle with Legos in his pockets.

The mother stormed off with her progeny. "All right," Donna said to her retreating back. Donna herself could drop in on the weekend to feed the animals. The boy's mother would probably decide to suffer them on Monday night.

But she didn't. She didn't come in on Monday or Tuesday. Then one of the volunteers got word that the whole family, pregnant sister included, had left for Mississippi. Who knew where in Mississippi? And who knew where in the Boston area they had lived? It was the Ladle's policy not to ask questions. Who knew what third grade in which school was grieving for its lost gerbils?

At the staff meeting Mimi suggested that the gerbils be declared official mascots. Donna proposed finding them a berth elsewhere. She pointed out that deprived women first go weepy over animals and then identify with them; the Ladle would soon drown in self-pity.

This reasoning met silence. That singing grandmother would have agreed with Donna—she'd no doubt sent many a stray cat packing. Donna mentioned the wretched guest who, by carefully leaving wrapped food for the alley rats, had brought the wrath of the church upon their heads.

Mimi leaned forward. "The gerbils are entertaining," she said calmly, "and maybe we'll find some off-label use for them," she added, looking first at Donna and then at Pam, who said, "Let's give it a try," and the management of the Ladle passed from Donna to Pam at that moment, as it was supposed to do, as Donna had meant it to do, as she had dreaded its doing since the day she noticed that her period was late.

Donna, swallowing, reminded herself of Pam's fidelity to the Ladle's values of nonintervention, uninquisitiveness, and tolerance.

At first the two gerbils seemed indifferent to their good fortune. They just sniffed their toys, rode their wheel, gobbled their pellets of food, chewed on cardboard toilet-paper rolls. Then one weekend Mimi built a platform for the cage, and on Monday she placed it in the middle of the dining room. "Now they are integrated into our community," O-Kay said. To Donna they looked above the community, little high priests. Sometimes they stood up with their claws on the bars and silently orated, bits of cardboard clinging to their mouths like cigars.

"They speak in tongues," Miss Valentine claimed. *"Français,"* she clarified.

The gerbils' new position in the center of the room tempted guests to feed them. Pam warned that the gerbils would soon refuse their usual food. "They'll become tyrants." But some women couldn't resist spoiling the animals, and on certain days the gerbils' confused friskiness followed by torpor indicated that they had been treated to booze as well as salad. After a few overfed weeks they grew bored with their wheel. Instead of chewing the cardboard rolls they crawled inside them. "They're shooting up," O-Kay said.

By December, a very wet month, almost everybody was sharing lunch with the gerbils. Pam stopped urging restraint, since the animals now turned up their snouts at anything except fresh vegetables. Also, constant rain was making the whole crowd more irritable than ever; best not to notice minor infractions. In front of the church the street ran like a river. The newspapers used the word *deluge* every day. "The Almighty wants to get rid of talk radio," Rabbi Steve explained.

The church's subcommittee on social action, dripping, made a surprise inspection of the facility. The chairwoman, speaking for the committee, suggested that the presence of rodents so near food was unhygienic. Mimi treated the speaker to her level gaze; the chairwoman looked alarmed, as if she sensed that her own coven could be dispatched by a wink of that sapphire eye. Then Mimi lowered her lids and stood like a penitent with the rest of the staff, their hands in hastily donned surgical gloves crossed on their breasts or clasped at their waists, except for Donna's, whose were splayed on her belly.

One of the volunteers interrupted the tense silence by suggesting coffee. Miss Valentine, talking to herself, appeared with a tray of unopened dinner packets that had just been delivered by a Sabena airline steward on his way home. The site visit turned into a party.

The rains continued. Mushrooms appeared overnight on

lawns. O-Kay fed some of them to the gerbils. "Enjoy your sweet life while you can," she told them. "Because someday soon..."

"Shut your hole," Miss Valentine said, and she hit O-Kay on the side of the head with her pocketbook. Miss Valentine was immediately barred for twenty-four hours by the staff. A volunteer put her arm around O-Kay. O-Kay ducked under the arm, embraced Pam, and began to shake uncontrollably. Pam suggested that O-Kay lie down. The volunteer burst into tears. Donna suggested that *she* lie down. The gerbils passed out, but they woke up half an hour later with no apparent ill effects.

Still the rains came. Storefronts gleamed coldly in the brief intervals of pale sunlight. The alley behind the church bubbled with mud, and a black lake formed in front of the stairs leading to the Ladle's door.

Donna too would soon be awash. Her sac of amniotic fluid was just holding. On the Wednesday of the second week in December she felt a mild wrench. She had a doctor's appointment that afternoon. Leaving, she recklessly told a little clutch of women that the baby, male, would be theirs to name.

"Oh, Jesus, Donna," groaned Pam, but her voice was drowned out by suggestions: Achille, Nelson, Steve...

The obstetrician looked pleased during the examination. "Any day," she said.

Donna returned to the Ladle. The Cuisinart had broken again; maybe she could fix it before the baby came. And O-Kay's car had sprung some new leaks. She'd speak to O-Kay about spending a night or two in a shelter.

In the alley Donna paused dreamily before the big puddle. The rain had stopped, probably only briefly, just to tease them. The sky was a deepening mauve. The puddle was the color of garnets. Beyond this jeweled lake the three stone steps descended damply to the Ladle's door, which was slightly ajar, as if by inadvertence. But that heavy door couldn't have been left ajar accidentally. Donna squinted. A brick made of Legos had been inserted between the door and its jamb. She walked around the puddle to the nearest ground-level window and lowered herself into its well, her sneakered feet sinking into decaying leaves. She peered into the dining room.

O-Kay and Miss Valentine and Mimi sat side by side at one of the long tables. On the back of each chair was draped a coat—O-Kay's schoolgirl parka; Miss Valentine's black sateen trench coat, plucked from donations one lucky day; Mimi's suede garment, the fur hat resting on its shoulder. The cage of gerbils had been removed from the platform and now occupied most of the center of the table.

For a while all three gazed at the cage. Then Mimi lifted its gate. The gerbils ran out. Mimi lowered the gate.

From the window well Donna moaned aloud. The creatures would head right for the pantry. They'd get into the rice or the cornmeal. She'd have to call the exterminator again, and throw out half the dry produce.

But the animals surprised her. They raced not for the kitchen but for the hall leading to the back door. She lost sight of them. She stood up in the well in time to see them leaping over the Lego brick. Pell-mell, with all the willfulness of the crazed, they ran up the cement stairs and into the lake. There they drowned.

Donna sat down again. Mimi was replacing the cage on its platform. O-Kay and Miss Valentine were putting on their outerwear. O-Kay wasn't shuddering and Miss Valentine's mouth was closed. Even on medication they had never looked so placid. Then the two disappeared from Donna's view, like the gerbils. She transferred her gaze to the door and saw Miss Valentine pushing it open. Miss Valentine and O-Kay climbed the stairs. They skirted the puddle and companionably got into O-Kay's car and drove away.

Mimi, wearing coat and hat, stooped to pick up the Lego brick. She put it into her pocket and pushed the door open and climbed the steps while the door closed behind her, locking itself. She bent over the puddle where the drowned animals eddied. She retrieved them with her right hand, which was protected by a surgical glove. She lifted the lid of the nearby dumpster with her ungloved hand. She tossed in the corpses and lowered the lid.

"What about that empty cage?" Donna called from the well.

"Steve will deliver a new pair of gerbils tomorrow," Mimi said. She peeled off her glove and raised the dumpster lid again. The glove arced palely into the trash. She walked to the window well. "If you stay there any longer, your baby will be born with the sniffles," she predicted.

Donna extended her hand and Mimi took it and helped Donna climb out of the well. They stood for a moment, hand grasping hand, like friends who have known each other long but never intimately and who now must say good-bye.

"I look forward to volunteering under your supervision," Donna made herself say. She discovered that once said it sounded true and perhaps even was true. "That business with the beasties—an inventive cure for madness, transferring the demons. Though of course you need animals always at the ready..." She trailed off.

"We'll have them," Mimi said.

Fishwater

Truth lies within a little and certain compass.
—*Viscount Bolingbroke*

It took my aunt Toby twenty years to profit enough from ficto-historiographia to give up teaching, to release the two of us from New York, to realize her dream of buying a house on Lake Piscataqua in New England. But at last, the year the century turned, we could afford the very house she had in mind. We packed up the little Eighth Street apartment—furniture and a few treasures: the Turkish rug, the Dutch menorah. Toby held what you might call an exit interview. The interviewer was a young reporter from a literary rag. I sat in.

"Fast and loose? I?" Toby repeated to him. "With men or women?"

"With data. It's been suggested. I heard," said the flustered fellow.

"No. Not. Not on your backside," Aunt Toby said. "Never have I claimed something to be true that I knew was not true—or claimed something to be true that was discovered to be false."

"Fabrications, they say..."

"Oh, fabrications. Literally, yes. I make things up out of whole cloth—that's *to fabricate* definitions one and two. One:

'to make; create.' Two: 'to construct by combining or assembling diverse parts, as in to fabricate small boats.' However, three: 'to concoct in order to deceive, as in to fabricate an excuse'—I don't do that, darling." He blushed. "I concoct," she continued, "but only to illuminate! How could I possibly write a history of, say, the Slavic cleverness employed in the Battle of Thessalonica without adding some tricks of my own divining?"

The Battle of Thessalonica left traces of itself in old histories. All the rest—the winged mercenaries, their pinions fabricated from cloth, the boy spy Dimitry and his pal the giant Vladimir, one on the other's shoulders—is Toby's doing, imagined by her dedicated intellect, unprovable, also undisprovable. The art of fictohistoriographia has been perfected by her, and without it the world would be a poorer place. So always said Mr. Franz Szatmar, her steady admirer. Franz Szatmar of the deep eyes, the major nose, the transparent hair fluttering on either side of his narrow forehead.

I always called him Uncle Franz, though his poor frail wife I addressed as Madame Szatmar.

"Lance, your aunt is generosity itself," Madame Szatmar once declared, addressing me while Toby strode from our Village living room into the kitchen to brew a deep blue tea that might just prolong the old lady's sad, barren life. "Discretion too. She keeps secrets as if her tongue has been torn out."

I am Lancelot. Toby inherited me from her brother and sister-in-law, my parents—dead tragically early. I have no memory of them. I have been Toby's adoptee and later her assistant during the two decades in which her books, never claiming to be factual history, claiming only to be possibly true, found favor among young people, though they never threatened to outchart the witchy-wizard series.

Toby's version of history depends on the principle of parsimony. That is: her accounts are the most economical way of explaining what cannot be explained in a briefer way. The rout at Thessalonica required subterfuge and optical illusion. As for the Alchemist of Rotterdam, his existence is postulated by the metaphoric pricking of the infamous tulip bubble. We know now that the prized tulips were made multicolored by a virus. The virus inducer is Toby's, a scientist who understood that invading organisms could work their will within a plant. He infected bulb after bulb, using a rudimentary syringe. Gorgeous, those tulips were. The second generation died.

"Produce evidence of the existence of that protobiochemist," said some rigid historian.

But, wrote Toby's most admiring reviewer, *she does not fill up her books with data and a bogus sense of the past. It is her genius to be able to imagine time and place and person so fully that they are as good as real—or better. History as diversion.*

We bought the cottage on Lake Piscataqua with the continuing royalties from *The Spy of Thessalonica* and *The Alchemist of Rotterdam,* and with the honoraria from Toby's appearances on panels and platforms. A devoted suitor brilliantly invested the money.

Toby was by now sixty—I was twenty. She was tall as a young tree, thin as a spear. Her hair that had once been blond, my hair that had once been blond, both had darkened to the brass of an ancient Greek drachma. She wore pants and shirts of a similar shade. Her chin was cleft, like mine. Her eyes were pewter. (Mine, certain young women told me, were dark chocolate.) Her tales unfurled behind a brow broad as a garden spade. (My own brow is narrow, like a dibble.)

At Piscataqua we repaired the little stone house and white-washed its inside, and in the middle of the one room (the bedrooms were lofts, a minimal kitchen occupied a corner) we spread the Turkish rug that had inspired *Who Set Fire to Smyrna?* In that tale the incendiarism was caused by Turks dressed as Armenians and Armenians dressed as Turks. No one could tell friend from foe, according to the twelve-year-old Jewish narrator who observed the entire conflagration, running and hiding, running and hiding, scribbling all the time...

Behind the stone house we staked out a plot for a vegetable garden and began digging the foundation for a gazebo—Toby would write her next work there, whatever it was. We became regulars at the post office—Toby's letters to the Szatmars, along with photographs of me, went out twice weekly. We made friends with fishermen. Every morning at four they came with their glistening catches to the docks at the sea, ten miles away from us.

Our smooth lake in sunlight resembled Toby's tea of immortality. Under the moon, ruffled, the lake looked like the carbon paper that lay crumpled in our wastebaskets. Toby disdained computers and word processors, typed her work on an old Hermes. Carbons for copies she had always purchased in the secondhand typewriter store on the third floor of an East Side building, a store right next to Uncle Franz's shop. Uncle Franz was a numismatician, dealing in history himself. But he *was* history himself, Toby mentioned more than once; he embodied a grim horror—a schoolboy who, alone among everyone he knew, was not murdered. Toby's eyes grew dark, her jaw stiffened when she referred to this.

"Will you put Uncle Franz into a book someday, his miraculous escape? It's time you told *me* about it, anyway."

*   *   *

A day passed before she responded. Then: "Here is how Franz escaped. A large group of Jews including his family had been marched from their small city to a village near a forest some miles from Budapest. They were crammed into a three-story wooden structure. They knew they would be moved any day to a cruel and permanent place. Franz and his family were on the third floor. Snow covered the hard earth. The building was unguarded.

"'Jump from the window,' his mother hissed that first night.

"'Mama...'

"'Jump.'

"'Mama.'

"She opened the window and picked him up—he was a slight twelve-year-old—and held him to her massive chest. Then her iron hands grasped him under the armpits. She thrust him through the window toward the icy night, and held him in the air like a blanket to be shaken. He had stopped saying 'Mama.' She held him and held him and held him. Then all at once she bent double over the sill and released her child. He landed un-harmed on snow, and stumbled into the woods, and kept going. He met others. They survived the war there, some of them: the ragged, the starving, the ill. If you put your ear to Franz's chest you can still hear the rattle of an old lung disease.

"Could I offer that story to the world, Lance? What could I add to it that would not degrade it? Winged soldiers, Dutch-men poking needles into flowers, scamps on the docks of Smyrna—they are my material, history as diversion, the fellow said. They are my antidote to the unbearable past." She added in a labored voice, "Franz was the only member of his entire family to survive, the only student from his school."

"Franz and Madame . . . they met as refugees?"

"Yes."

"They couldn't have children together, Franz and Madame?"

"No."

"Uncle Franz is the last of the Szatmar line."

Silence. Then: "You could say so."

We attended the annual business meeting of the lower valley historical society. "Piscataqua?" Toby inquired during the social hour that followed.

"An old name dating from the centuries when the area was populated and governed by its aboriginal inhabitants," said Mr. Jennings, the chairman, bending his head toward the beautiful woman with the metallic hair. "It has been determined that the names of the lake and the river came from the Abenaki language, the word being a probable combination of a syllable meaning 'branch' and another meaning 'a river with a strong current.'"

"How ancient is Abenaki?"

"Oh, it was spoken before Columbus."

"Latin was spoken before the Babylonian captivity."

"Nevertheless."

"Nevertheless," she repeated in her golden voice, "linguistic economy indicates that the river and the lake were named not by the Abenaki but by the Roman-Briton arrivistes."

"My dear Ms. Bluestein," he said, falling in love before my eyes—well, he wasn't the first to do so—"Romans didn't arrive on these shores until the nineteenth century, when they came in droves. Mostly shoemakers and fruit farmers."

"My dear Mr. Jennings, you are talking about Italians, as you well know. The Roman-Britons came in 500 A.D."

"How on earth—on sea, ha-ha—did they travel?"

"In Roman longships, descendants of Roman galleys, themselves descendants of Roman quinqueremes. The longships made it to shore and then crumbled."

"Then there is no proof of their existence."

"There is no proof of their nonexistence."

Mr. Jennings produced a smitten smile. "What do you think they were like, these ships that sailed the sea before the era of sails?"

"Oh, they had sails. And oars, of course."

"The last of the Romans left Britain in 410," Mr. Jennings said. "They did not sail the Atlantic, then called Thalassa. They sailed only to the Continent and then made their way home on foot. According to popular belief, the first European to reach North America was Leif Eriksson. He landed on the coast of what is now Newfoundland in 980."

"I respect popular belief," Toby said. "It's mostly guesswork, like my own endeavors. Mr. Jennings, there are things we know without knowing that we know them."

"Yes, but…" He didn't finish the sentence. Both he and I could tell there was no stopping her.

So she started her next book before the gazebo was begun. She wrote in her bedroom loft. The book's hero was young Titus of the port of London.

For Titus in the shipyard, working with the oaken, the sea always beckoned. It beckoned with the crooked finger of death, for he had lost father, brothers, uncles, and a cousin to the foam. Some with his history might have fled inland and become a laborer on a farm, or made his home in a town, or joined an abbey. But water was Titus's passion.

"How are you getting on?" asked Mr. Jennings, whose feet

were planted on the Turkish rug. He had dropped in with a basket of zucchini; I was slicing the squash on the tiny counter.

"Getting on fine," Toby called down.

Titus was in charge of the construction of the longboat. The Roman/British longboat, unremembered by historians, was graceful, narrow, light, with a shallow draft hull designed for speed and which allowed navigations in waters only one meter deep. The longboat was fitted with oars along the length of the vessel. It bore a rectangular sail on a single mast which was used to replace or aid the effort of the rowers, particularly during long journeys like the one planned now.

The next time he brought wine. "Full sails ahead," Toby informed him.

They left London, Titus on the seventh oar—for though he was master and captain, there was no provision made for rank; everyone rowed. He was a short, muscular young man with a Saxon profile grafted onto a Roman head, and his hair was dark... Months later, his battered ship sighted the coast of what would one day be called these United States.

"Would you like to give a talk at the library?" Mr. Jennings asked on his now daily visit.

"Love to."

A coastline of cliffs and gorges and rocks presents an unwelcoming aspect. The newcomers rowed on. Romans were aware of premonition: the feeling that imminent disaster is hiding behind every cloud, every wave. They lived in a permanent state of anxiety. Titus feigned boldness, but he constantly fingered the good-luck coin his sweetheart had given him, which hung on his chest. Where on this earth would they land?

*They landed in the estuary formed by the then unnamed river
and the sea. Now called Piscataqua, of course.*

"Would you read me some of your work?" said Mr. Jennings,
looking loftward from the chair I'd provided.

" … Okay.

" 'After the brave beginning came the deaths by disease, by
unknown poisons in plants, by animals; came wars with natives,
peace with natives, children. Came hurricanes, surely sent by
the God. Came the final disease, a mercilessly lengthy fever;
and then came the collapse into itself and then into dust of
everything remembered, everything that could be remembered,
obliteration as complete as that of … ' "

"Atlantis?" wondered Mr. Jennings. "Troy?"

"I am thinking of a Hungarian community in 1943."

He was respectfully silent.

She continued …

" 'Titus had taken a wife, had become chief, as was his destiny. He burned his dead children one by one on rafts sent out
to sea (the Vikings did not invent the Viking funeral, just added
the dog at the feet of the deceased). He himself was slain by
fever, and the few remaining Piscataquans, dying themselves,
managed to bury him, not burn him. He became part of the dust
of the encampment beside Lake Piscataqua.' "

Well, everybody knows about the publishing business today, per-
ishing like the longboats. Toby's usual editor had escaped into
another line of work; the imprint which had sponsored the editor
immersed itself in a larger company and that company into one
larger. That conglomerate assigned to its greenest editor the new
offering by an author from, as they saw it, the generation previous, though *Who Set Fire to Smyrna?* was still on the backlist.

We met in the young editor's office. "The thing's just too fucking unlikely," he said. (He didn't say *fucking*, but the word was essentially printed on his curled lip.) "Your other stories... you could make a case for them. Not this one."

Toby tapped her manuscript with two fingers. "Much here might have happened."

"Viking artifacts are thick on the ground in the Piscataqua area." He had done his homework. "There's not so much as a Roman fishhook. Your other heroes, your children as it were, have a habit of seeking their fortunes and finding them. That still sells books. But poor Titus finds only oblivion. Please change tack. Write something different... And, Ms. Bluestein," he added as she was walking with that cleft chin raised, "no more carbon copies, I beg you."

We met Uncle Franz in our favorite Hungarian place. He wore a black ribbon on his lapel; he had been a widower for several months. "There are other publishers," he said.

"Not for me. Fictohistoriographia is out of style. Everything is out of style except sex"—Uncle Franz reddened—"and money."

"About that..."

"There's plenty to live on."

Silence. "When," he said.

"Now."

"I must alarm the store." While Toby went to Penn Station to buy him a ticket I accompanied Uncle Franz. He busied himself for a few moments among his display cases. A small satchel was beside the door, already packed. We met Aunt Toby at the train. We passed woods, farms, glimpses of the sea.

We'd left our car near the station. Uncle Franz and his satchel took the backseat. We drove the two-lane highway, then a smaller road, then a dirt road. And finally the water beckoned us, purple-blue in the afternoon, its surrounding pines blue-green.

"As you described it," Uncle Franz said. "An economy of palette." His sigh quivered. "Beautiful. Beautiful no matter who discovered it first."

When we got to the stone house, Toby threw the manuscript on the couch and Uncle Franz settled his satchel beside it. We went swimming. Despite his age, Uncle Franz was fit, and a good swimmer, though he avoided jumping off our little raft, merely slid into the embrace of the water. His swimming shorts flared like a skirt. He must have bought them just after the war, when the Joint Distribution Committee brought him to New York.

At dinner he said, "The vegetable plot needs immediate work."

The next day the three of us harrowed, raked, created furrows, planted tomatoes and lettuce and cucumbers. We dug up artifacts—barrettes, number 6d nails.

One day Uncle Franz brought inside an object covered with mud and laid it on a newspaper on our trestle table. He washed it with water and a cloth and detergent from his satchel. A magnifying glass emerged from the satchel too.

He passed the thing around and then held it in his palm and inspected it. "It's copper," he guessed. Once perhaps green, it was now as pale as the wings of his hair. "A woman on one side, a ruminant on the verso. The coin dates from about 400 A.D. It originated in Rome, traveled through the empire, perhaps spent time in Britain, who can say..."

Uncle Franz had once given me a lecture on fakes. "Sometimes the fakes are tooled... authentic, but improved by the tooling. Sometimes they are fantasy coins, or modern coins made to look ancient." But this wasn't a fake. Lifted by his loving fingers from the New England soil, it was metal money from Rome. "It has been deformed by age but the only deliberate defacement is that hole near the animal's horns. It was probably worn as a lucky charm."

"You could show it to that ass of an editor," I said to Toby.

"I will show it to Mr. Jennings."

She did. And Mr. Jennings, not questioning provenance or authenticity or age, accepted the coin on behalf of the historical society with the grace of a vanquished lover. He provided a display case on legs, and a card which read ROMAN COIN C. 400 A.D. Somebody snapped a color photograph for the Piscataqua weekly—Mr. Jennings, Toby, me, Uncle Franz, all but one of us looking down at the coin. And then I saw what I had already known without knowing I knew it: I might have Aunt Toby's hair and chin, but I had Uncle Franz's cylindrical brow and chocolate eyes, those eyes that preferred to look at me rather than the coin, though I don't think he was ashamed of either of us.

I had long considered the train-wreck death that Toby had supplied for my vague father and mother unworthy of her imagination.

Uncle Franz (I will always call him that) sold his shop and said good-bye to New York. He moved in with us. Toby gave up fictohistoriographia and turned to writing adventure books, frankly invented. So she never told of the heroism of a mother who let go of her child to save him. And she never revealed the story of a woman of forty and a man considerably older who briefly combined in order to perpetuate a Hungarian family, their secret connivance encouraged by another heroine, one who would have performed the task herself but could not.

And I, my provenance acknowledged at last, my parents together at last, went off to seek my own fortune, as Toby's children are destined to do.

Wait and See

I.

L yle stares at a lemon.

How does the lemon appear to Lyle? The rough skin is what he has been taught to call yellow, and he knows many modifiers of that word—pale, bright, dull; he knows also metaphoric substitutes—gold, butter, dandelion, even lemon. What he sees in the humble fruit, though, and what he knows by now other kids don't see, is a tangle of hundreds of shades, ribbons of sunlight crushed into an egg.

And baby oil? His mother, Pansy, works baby oil into her pale satin face and neck before going to bed, and a drop inevitably spills from her fingertip: transparent, translucent, colorless, or so anybody else would say. To Lyle, however, the drop is a rosy viscous sphere. The shade of *his* skin—caramel or butterscotch or café au lait according to foodies, mulatto to those interested in mixed races—incorporates movement too: on his forearm writhe all the hues in Pansy's drawer of muddled lingerie.

And the neon sign projecting from the exercise center on the second floor of a building in Godolphin Square? Neon plasma has the most intense light discharge of all the noble gases. To a normal human eye it is red-orange; it also contains a strong green line hidden unless you've got a spectroscope. Lyle sees the green line unaided, the flowing molecules of it. It is as if the sign, GET FIT, has given him a gift.

But then, Lyle has been given many gifts, including Pansy's love. Bathed in that love, Lyle in turn is gentle with other kids, especially with kids uneasy under their bragging, kids really as frightened as rabbits when a hawk darkens their world. Lyle's underweight presence steadies them, and he is sought after—but not exactly as a friend. He is more like Anansi, the helpful spider of his favorite tales—a quiet ally and trickster who prefers his own company but skitters over to join you when you need him.

Yet another gift is money. These days, money resides in electronic bits; Pansy has plenty of bits inherited from her Alabama grandfather. And there is, or was once, the gift of a small amount of yellowish fluid containing enzymes, acids, and lipids. Semen, not to put too fine a point on it.

The unknown bestower of the semen had been living on the edge. He'd come from Africa in a troop of lost boys—not the famous ones from Sudan but less famous, less numerous ones from elsewhere. But the situation was similar: civil war, carnage, a few boys running from their ruined villages all the way to the United States.

One particular lost boy ended up in Massachusetts, lived in a house with other lost boys, got through high school, and at the time of his gift was employed in a lab in the area. But he was poor. And so he did what many people in his situation did: sold his blood. He thought about selling his sperm too, but he considered it too valuable to be made a commodity—he was proud and he was free and he wanted freely to sire a thousand American sons. So he did not sell but gave his sperm to a bank—really a hospital roomlet provided with facilitating magazines.

II.

And then there's a submicroscopic gift, the consequence of a genetic mutation that has passed mostly unexpressed through the millennia. It was bestowed by evolution not directly on Lyle but on a primate who was his remote ancestor. The gift was a mischievous gene, which, if it meets its twin, can affect vision.

"Primate vision unadulterated is trichromatic," said Dr. Marcus Paul. "*Tri* means 'three,' and *chroma* means 'color.'"

"Yes?" Pansy encouraged from the other side of the desk.

"Well, Mrs. Spaulding—"

"Miss."

"Miss..."

"Or Ms., if you want to be correct." She grinned.

"Ms., then," the flustered man said, and took refuge in a disquisition. "You know the retina, at the back of the eye, the thing that captures light and color and ships them to the brain. The retina uses only three types of light-absorbing pigments for color vision. Trichromacy, see?"

"See," she agreed, still grinning.

"Well, almost all nonprimate mammals are dichromatic, with just two kinds of visual pigments. A few nocturnal mammals have only one pigment. But some birds, fish, and reptiles, they have four."

"They see more colors than we do? Damn it all."

"They probably do. And some butterflies are even pentachromatic. Pigeons also. And there is one twig on the *Homo sapiens* tree whose members—a small fraction of them—are believed to be pentachromatic too: the Himba tribe. Himbas endure their usually short lives in Namibia...Lyle seems to be of mixed race."

"Yes. I asked the sperm bank for a black donor. I believe miscegenation is an answer to the world's ills. All people one color: tan."

"Oh," said the doctor, whose skin was the shade of eggplant. "Your donor was African?"

She shrugged her slender shoulders. "I didn't ask, and they didn't tell."

"Well, I think Lyle's a pentachromat. Those colors he reports."

She nodded. She was all at once serious. "Yes. No wonder he has headaches, my poor boy." Then she paused, partly to let this young Jamaican take a frank look at her, as he was clearly eager to do—at her inky curls, at her small straight nose that angled upward a degree more than is usual, robbing her of beauty and instead making her irresistible; physiognomy's gift to Pansy, you might say. The doctor could see also her wide mouth, her dimples, her long neck and long hands. Her long legs were hidden from him by his desk, but he must have noticed them earlier. She hoped so. Oh, yes, and when she parted her lips, out flashed the bright white of her perfect incisors. Men often remarked on that...She continued now: "What's it like to be a pentachromat?" Though she knew, or had an idea; Lyle had told her of

the numerous dots of color he could detect on a plain manila envelope. She had taught him a new word: *pointillism.* "Doctor?"

What's it like to have a face like yours? He said: "Neither
we nor they have the words to describe this sort of thing. How
would you describe color to someone who was color-blind?
What we do know is that tetrachromats and pentachromats
make distinctions between shades that seem identical to the rest
of us. For example, I read about a woman in California, she's
dead now—"

"From hyperchromaticity?"

"From old age. She was a seamstress, the article said. She
could look at three samples of taupe fabric cut from the same
bolt and detect a gold undertone in one, a hint of green in another, a smidgen of gray in the third. She could look at a river
and distinguish relative depth and amounts of silt in different
areas of the water based on differences in shading that no one
else was aware of . . . So it's probably safe to say that tetrachromats and pentachromats have a richer visual experience of the
world than the rest of us." *But my own experience has become
richer in the past fifteen minutes because of this woman sitting
in front of my normal, trichromatic eyes. I hope she likes my
dreadlocks.*

III.

Lyle had been an unfretful baby, though for a while he confused
day and night. Pansy slept through the days along with him.
Gave him breakfast at twilight and took him for a walk, sometimes across the river to Boston but usually around Godolphin.
Lyle lay angled on a pillow in his old-fashioned perambulator,

facing her or staring upward at the dark green of trees, the charcoal sky. He turned his head to notice glossy books in the window of the bookstore, always open late. There was a full-length mirror embedded in the door of the pedicure place. Sometimes, again turning his head, he stared at mother and child, and she did the same. There she was, in black leather pants and a glistening white poncho; there he was, a baby whose skin had not yet begun to darken. Her own skin had never darkened, though her southern ancestors had no doubt mingled with their slaves and then admitted the lighter progeny into the mansion. A gene for a dusky epidermis might lie embedded in each of her cells. In his early childhood Lyle went from phase to expected phase—resisted the occasional babysitter, considered the toilet fine for other people, couldn't bear carrots. He played with blocks in a bored way. Idly he mentioned headaches. The pediatrician found no cause for them.

He continued his habit of staring at everything. He himself was odd to look at—the skinny arms, the thin beige face, the unsmiling gaze. When he took a walk with his mother, he put one hand in hers, like collateral, while his mind wandered somewhere she couldn't follow, and she had to relinquish the treasured notion that mother and child were one.

He didn't like picture books—all those primary colors, he wouldn't look at them. It made her wonder.

The psychologist she took him to said no, he wasn't on any spectrum. "He's not interested in those little board books—so what. He's intrigued by the wider world. Wants to wait and see what catches his fancy."

She thanked him and stood up, a vision in her striped black-and-white sundress and her black cartwheel. She walked toward the door.

"You too," the psychologist called. "Wait and see."

She'd waited several years. One day irregular blurred lines appeared on the wall of her bedroom. Their interiors filled in; now they were splotches. Then they turned into continents. The plumber found the leaks that were their source, and fixed them. Pansy hired a painter and brought home a color wheel. It was a collection of about three hundred long slender cards of thick laminated paper, each with a hole at one end, allowing them all to depend from a metal ring, to be held in the hand at once, or fanned out into a circle. Each card bore seven contiguous squares of similar hues, with names, about two thousand colors in all. She dropped the device with idle grace beside Lyle, prone on the floor. He abandoned his book—he was reading adventure stories now, aping his classmates, though he frequently returned to those old trickster tales.

He inspected this new toy. He knew what he had before him—paint samples. He guessed that these two thousand colors were about as many as human beings could create—in their labs, their paint factories, their electronics workshops. He had endured years of feeling different, of possessing something that was a secret to others and also to him. Now the color wheel enlightened him... People gave hues such hopeful names. There was a square called Orange Froth and next to it Orange Blossom and next to that Florida Orange. Lyle could see the Froth globules deepen to a color that almost matched Orange Blossom but didn't, and the Orange Blossom itself acquire a gloss as it approached but did not attain Florida Orange. "Mom," he called.

"Yes, darling?" from the other room.

"I have..." he said, and paused. In the Anansi tales, secrets were meant to be stuffed into the heart and never pulled out; there could be unforeseen results if they were.

She walked in. " ... Something to tell me?"

"Well..."

And then came the visit to Dr. Marcus Paul; and then came the tentative diagnosis of a condition, though not an ailment, unknown to most scientists probably because of its weak grant potential. And then came romance. Love at first sight? It can happen. There's often a lot of palaver.

"I love you not only because you're beautiful," Marcus told Pansy a few weeks after they met. "I love you because of your admirable politics, your wish that the world's population become one color. Because you mop floors in a soup kitchen. Because you cook like a four-star chef."

She kissed him then, and she caressed his hip with her knee, a gesture that cannot be achieved unless both parties are lying on their sides facing each other. They happened to be lying on their sides facing each other—Lyle was at school—and so the caress impossible under other circumstances was now possible, probable, necessary, unavoidable, though who would want to avoid the deep shudder each felt as joint saluted joint. Then Marcus entered his lovely woman.

Afterward she took over the colloquy. "I love you because of your single-mindedness," she said. "Your voice. Your dreadlocks. I love you because our coupling feels like destiny."

"Arranged by Anansi."

"Anansi? Lyle reads stories about him ..."

"He's a powerful spider who used to make his home in Africa and now lives in Jamaica. But he gets around."

"Please thank him if you see him ... And I love you because together we belong to Lyle."

"And Lyle belongs to us," Marcus said. In a state of postcoital clarity he realized that he had found his life's love and his life's work in a single ophthalmologic interview. "We are Lyle's caretakers, guardians, keepers of his secret."

"It's like the housemaid marrying the butler," Pansy said.

"If you say so." He felt like the stable boy marrying the princess.

There was a brief three-person honeymoon. They visited Italy, where plump lemons offered even more yellows than the ones Lyle knew. They went to Iberia, where the tiles of Lisbon and the airport in Madrid presented a chromatic joy, many colors new and glorious to Marcus and Pansy and about twelve times that many to Lyle.

Marcus's clinical practice was easy to transfer to a colleague. He'd been mostly engaged in research anyway. After returning from the colorful honeymoon, he built a lab behind Pansy's spacious house and invited his cousin David to join him. The reclusive David, an optician, was interested in the changes to vision that curved or beveled glass, glass within glass, prismatic lenses, all those things, could make when placed in front of the eye. The two cousins had already designed a number of spectacles that helped people with eye diseases see better.

Their little optical laboratory—incorporated, after a while— produced many improved devices. Telescopic eyeglasses for everyday use. Microscope lenses, and surgical snakes with tiny cameras in their heads, and smoky instruments for astronomers. These tools became much in demand.

The company flourished, and Pansy's return on her investment was substantial. She was proud of the men's success. Still, when Marcus and David entered their laboratory day after day, she liked to imagine that, in addition to their other products, they were working on a superinvention that would grant Lyle's vision to everyone. Performance-enhancing, you might say. When perfected, it would encounter regulations; when produced, it would inspire inferior imitations. Even so, it would be a vehicle for public good.

But after four years it had not yet appeared. So one day the patient Pansy inquired.

"I don't think we can do it," Marcus admitted. "We've tried; it was one of our original purposes. But we cannot duplicate work that nature took millions of years to accomplish. We cannot invent an external instrument which will produce an internal variant. The butterfly has a genome, the pigeon too. But where does the pentachromatic gene lurk? We cannot tell. And if we could tell, and could extract it, and could transfer it to a human cell, would the cell survive? And if yes, yes, yes, yes . . . for what purpose? To give people headaches?"

"It would be only a carnival attraction," Pansy slowly acknowledged. "A rich man's plaything. But oh, Marcus. No one else can ever become like Lyle. He's stuck being unique."

IV.

And what of the unique Lyle during these years? Well, he had things to occupy him: school, cello, baseball, walks at night with Marcus or David or Pansy. Music was blessedly colorless. When he stood in center field, the sky showed him its myriad blues and the field its hundreds of greens, but none of that distracted him from the flight of the sphere, a headless wingless bird, a ball white and off-white and off-off-white. Nothing distracted him from the task of predicting the bird's destination and putting himself beneath it, mitt at the ready.

He played in the school orchestra. Once in a while he went

to a party and talked to whoever seemed left out—talked awkwardly but soothingly, or maybe soothingly because awkwardly.

He thought about someday becoming a doctor. He liked looking at anatomy plates, vivid to begin with, garish under his inspection. He wondered whether his vision, trained, might develop an X-ray component. Marcus doubted it. They discussed diseases of organs other than the eye—diagnosis, treatment, treatment failure.

But despite the error-free fielding record and despite the mild friendships with his peers and despite the comfort of nocturnal darkness in the company of one of the three people he loved, Lyle, heavy with his secret, often felt sorrowfully alone.

When he was sixteen, he began to spend Sunday mornings with last year's biology teacher. They drove to a nature preserve and then hiked its trails. And then one Sunday, during a forbidding rainstorm, she invited him to forget nature for a day. She was forty, the ideal age to relieve a sensitive boy of his virginity and satisfy his curiosity too. He noted that her areolae were not sepia, as novels said, but pulsing pink rose mauve...This dear woman would be fired without a hearing if her generosity became known—he knew that, and he realized how uncalibrated were the rules that claim to protect us from one another. But Lyle was used to keeping things to himself, and anyway he would never betray Ms. Lapidus. Their Sunday-morning explorations continued—in the nature preserve if the day was bright, in bed if otherwise.

He shared his secret with her—she would not betray him either.

"But, wow!" she said, turning to look at him, her head on her palm, her elbow on the mattress.

"Wow? It's an affliction."

"Really? By me it's an opportunity. Think of the things you could do with those special eyes. Detect art forgeries."

He blinked at her.

"You could tell the difference between Rembrandt's paint and pseudo-Rembrandt's paint," she explained. And on another occasion she said, "You could identify altered substances. Traces of banned pesticides."

"Or find the fault lines in a rock," he unenthusiastically contributed.

"Or see a smear of makeup on a man's tweed shoulder."

"Huh?"

She told him that adulterers usually tried to keep their activities hidden, and that their wronged spouses often hired detectives for a substantial fee. And on yet another rainy Sunday she suggested that he could identify fish misnamed by dishonest restaurants. "And sometimes they serve brains masquerading as sweetbreads, or maybe it's the other way around. You could bring miscreants to court."

He didn't answer. He was again looking at her breasts. The areolae were mauve, yes, but mostly by contrast to what he now noticed as yellowish skin; and when he raised his eyes he saw that her sclera were curdling. To foresee the coming of disaster—that was not how he wanted to use his gift.

"Would you do something for me?" he managed.

"Just about anything," she confessed.

"Would you have your doctor do an MRI of your abdomen?"

"What? I feel fine."

"And a pancreas biopsy," he said, and began to cry.

V.

Another year. And then, one August afternoon, Marcus emerged from the lab and found Lyle practicing hoop shots by himself.

"I have a story to tell you," Marcus said.

"Okay." When Lyle read, the black letters sometimes shuddered on the page. But when he listened, his closed eyes found a sort of repose behind the patchwork cerise of his lids.

"It's a Jamaican tale," Marcus said.

"Oh, then about Anansi."

"Anansi plays a part. But it's about a young man."

They sat on the ground, their arms around their knees and their backs against the trunk of a beech, as if they were in a Caribbean village leaning against a guango.

Marcus began:

"Once upon a time there lived a youth who was never happy unless he was prying into things other people knew nothing about. Especially things that happened at night. He wanted secrets to be laid bare to him. He wandered from wizard to wizard, begging each of them in vain to open his eyes, but he found none to help him. Finally he reached Anansi. After listening to the youth, the spider warned:

" 'My son, most discoveries bring not happiness but misery. Much is properly hidden from the eyes of men. Too much knowledge kills joy. Therefore think well what you are doing, or someday you will repent. But if you will not take my advice, I can show you the secrets you crave.'

" 'Please!'

" 'Tomorrow night you must go to the place where, once in seven years, the serpent-king summons his court. I will tell you where it is. But remember what I say: blindness is man's highest good.'

"That night the young man set out for the wide, lonely moor belonging to the serpent-king. He saw a multitude of small hillocks motionless under the moonlight. He crouched behind a bush. Suddenly a luminous glow arose in the middle of the moor. At the same moment all the hillocks began to squirm and to crawl, and from each one came thousands of serpents making straight for the glow. The youth saw a multitude of snakes, big and little and of every color, gathering together in one great cluster around a huge serpent. Light and colors sprang from its head. The young man saw brilliance usually denied to mortal eyes. He saw iridescence, bioluminescence, adularescence, opalescence. Then the scene vanished. He went home.

"The next day he counted the minutes till night, when he might return to the forest. But when he reached the special place, he found an empty moor: gray, gray, and gray. He went back many nights but did not see the colors. He would have to wait another seven years.

"He thought about the colors night and day. He ceased to care about anything else in the world. He sickened for what he could not have. And he died before the seven years was out, knowing at the end that Anansi had spoken truly when he said, 'Blindness is man's highest good.' "

After a while Lyle said, "But, Dad, not complete blindness..."

"No. Fables are not literal. Freedom from supervision... supravision...overvision...hypervision..."

"Freedom from second sight," Lyle added. "I can have that freedom?" He turned toward Marcus. His remarkable eyes, an unremarkable brown, seemed to swell a little—tears had entered from the ducts.

Marcus put his arm around the boy's shoulders, scraping his elbow grievously on the back of the tree. "I think so."

The next week, Marcus appeared at dinner with a pair of spectacles—rimless, with wire earpieces. The lenses were constructed of hundreds of miniature polyhedrons.

"Prisms," said Pansy, and went on dishing out *lapin aux pruneaux.*

"Involuted prisms," refined David, who now lived with the family. He had become comfortable at last with his celibacy and inwardness; he was sometimes even talkative.

Marcus turned to Lyle. "These are for you," he said, and he handed the eyeglasses to the boy. "Put them on whenever you like."

"They will give you a different kind of vision," David said. "And, Lyle—it's all right if you don't like the spectacles."

Lyle did not put them on inside. He went out onto the lawn with its commanding beech tree and its flowering bushes. He looked around at the normal thousand-color summer scene—normal to him, at any rate, though he understood it to be his alone. Now maybe he'd know a competing normal. He put on the glasses.

It was as if someone had turned out the lights or a thick cloud had passed in front of the sun. Most creatures see things less brilliantly in the dark, he knew that. He was seeing things less brilliantly. The house, made of flat stones, was gray. Perhaps the gray contained some gold. On the laboratory's green siding, each slat cast a slightly darker green on the one beneath it. The beech tree was a combination of brown and red. The geraniums were a shade of magenta—one shade of magenta. He looked at his skin. Plain tan. He looked at the sky. Blue, slowly deepening—it was dusk now. Dark blue.

He went inside. "I like the glasses."

"And the colors?" Marcus asked.

"Duller. Many fewer. Motionless. Perspective is less noticeable. Things seem to have only a touch of a third dimension. I'm glad for the...diminishment. Now I have two ways to see. Thank you, Dad. Thank you, David. You've given me a wonderful present."

"We have given you a choice," Marcus said. "Always an ambiguous gift."

Lyle said suddenly, "Spiders—what's *their* vision like?"

David said, "Spiders usually have eight eyes placed in two rows on the front of the carapace. The eyes have a silvery appearance. The retinas have relatively coarse-grained mosaics of receptor cells, and their resolution of images is..."

"Poor," said Marcus, finishing David's lecture and answering Lyle's question at the same time.

Lyle wore his gift every day, all day, until he went to bed—and even then he took the new glasses off only after he'd turned out the light. His classmates were incurious about the glasses—they were teenagers, after all, not interested in much outside themselves. But Lyle's new and commonplace vision gave him new and commonplace manners. He no longer stared into space, his conversation became less effortful. Girls phoned him. He got included in more activities. Marcus and David made sunglasses for him, and swimming goggles, biking goggles, wraparounds for chemistry lab. They made him a pair of pince-nez, which he wore to a Halloween party, along with a stiff collar and a frock coat and a false beard. "Chekhov," he explained. He joined the chess club. The club met Sunday mornings. His Sunday mornings were free. Ms. Lapidus had recently died.

In the lab Marcus and David were now constructing wide-angle micro-optical lenses. The lenses could be implanted—and were, after the proper trials—in a sufferer's eye. They made new tools for photography and tomography. They made corneal inlays. Pansy was running the business aspect of the enterprise, and managing the staff of five. Having learned so much about the tricks of the eye-brain double play, she became expert at standard optical illusions, and then invented some of her own, with which she beguiled the twin sons who had been born to her and Marcus. ("Their complexion is Unglazed Bisque," Lyle said of his brothers, remembering the old paint wheel.) Pansy began a side venture selling games of her own design. Some elaborate inventions she used at the twins' birthday parties, held in a newly built room off the lab. The kids' friends entered an illusory universe for half an hour, then gobbled up Pansy's sweet-potato ice cream, which was real.

VI.

At eighteen Lyle was accepted at St. John's. He was looking forward to reading the Greats. The day before he was to leave for Annapolis, a thick autumn mist enveloped Godolphin and Godolphin alone—the sun was out in Boston. A graduation gift from Anansi, Lyle thought. He walked down to the river. There the mist rested, soft and colorless. Slowly, deliberately, he took off his glasses.

Mist. Still mist. Then, gradually, colors returned, filled the scattered bits of moisture. According to the laws of physics, each drop should have contained a rainbow—but no, on this eve of departure, the drops, directed by the spider, were breaking the laws, each producing a singular shade for his pleasure, all together producing a universe of colors. Purple deeper than iris, laced with yolky lines. Bronze striped with brass. He saw the indigo of infected flesh, he saw the glistening fuchsia of attacking bacteria, he saw the orange of old-age crinkles that wait invisibly on every smooth young arm. Yes, all colors, in all their headachy variations, colors as they had once been.

His man-made glasses, his trickster specs, had made life less sorrowful, but at a cost. They had deprived him of this sheen of blue blue blue violet seeping into blue blue violet violet pressing itself into blue violet violet violet that yearns to become shadow. Vanilla hectored its neighbor papyrus. There was moss concealing like a mother its multigreened offspring. There were squirming nacreous snakes, slightly nauseating. Much is properly hidden from the eyes of men, Anansi had said... Chartreuse slashed like lightning across his vision from upper left to lower right and also from upper right to lower left, both slants remaining on his retinas that were so cursed, so blessed. Where one diagonal intersected the other in this chartreuse chiasma rested an oval, deep within the intersection, for of course the mist in which these shapes and colors shudderingly resided was three-dimensional or maybe three-and-a-half, and it was in motion too, the color drops assaulting one another in a chromatic orgy. The oval within the chartreuse X was scaled with overlapping hexagons of nearly transparent turquoise—there must have been hundreds of turquoises, each different from the other by so little, so little, yet, by that little, different. *What's your favorite color?* people used to ask, as they always ask children. *Red,* he would answer, divining even then that they had no idea how many reds there were: a cloud at sunset, a cloud at sunrise, blood from a scratch, blood from a nose, a run-over cat; the dappled skin of a tomato, with all reds swimming upon it…He wondered, not for the first time, who his original father was.

He put his glasses back on. Mist returned to mist, ordinary mist, mist in whose every drop curved what people called the spectrum, such a paltry number of colors. This sight was no truer a reality than the glory of a few minutes ago; no less true either. Truth had nothing to do with the witness of the eyes. What he saw now was simply what other people saw. He chose their limited vision; he meant to live in this world as an ordinary man. He would not remove his glasses again.

Flowers

On a bright Monday morning in February, Lois and Daniel were reading in their monochromatic living room—gray walls, gray carpet, gray furniture. It was the kind of room that could soothe a panic attack, or cause one. From the stereo Scriabin flung a cat's cradle of notes.

The doorbell interrupted the Russian madman. Daniel was still in bathrobe and slippers—this was his day without seminars to conduct or office hours to show up at. Lois answered the summons. She was already dressed: stovepipe pants, tee, jacket, all black. Iterations of this uniform in various dark colors hung in her closet like a line of patient men. She had not yet put on her shoes. But even barefoot she was six inches taller than the lanky teenage boy in the doorway, though the offering of gladioli he thrust into her hands rose above them both. "'Mrs. Daniel Bevington,'" the kid read from a yellow slip. Lois nodded. "There's a note," the boy said, and raced to a curbside van that bore the name of a local florist.

Daniel, noiseless as always, had followed Lois to the door. "Have we a vase long enough for those?"

"No." You can't really bury your nose in a gladiolus, but she tried. Meanwhile, boots pulled on because of the snow, he headed for the garage. She followed him, still barefoot, the purple shafts in her arms. He scanned the garage's tidy innards, chose a tall rubber basket the color of earth, picked it up and rinsed it under the outside tap. Then he filled the thing halfway with water. He put it down and returned to the living room, Lois still behind him, her feet turning blue. He spread the automotive section of the newspaper on the floor in front of a bookcase. He went back out for the rubber basket. Lois went into the kitchen.

She laid the flowers on the kitchen table and loosened their wrapping. She slipped the note from between the stalks. *Happy Valentine's Day*, it said. *Love, Daniel.*

She returned to the living room, the gladioli now horizontal in her arms. "Daniel! How sweet of you. So sweet." She put the flowers in the rubber basket.

"I'm glad you like them," he said, looking up, sounding briefly young, younger than their twin college-age sons, younger even than the delivery boy, who had probably thought he was fleeing a house of mourning.

"Like them? I love them," Lois said. *Especially since I'm not really dead*, she added silently. She walked to Daniel's chair and kissed him. This was the first time he'd sent her flowers since her lying-in.

He noticed that her eyes were unnaturally bright.

The doorbell rang again.

This time the truck was from a florist in a neighboring town. Another teenager said, "Lois Bevington?" He handed her twelve tall bloodred roses in their own vase.

She placed this gift on the low coffee table. Daniel was suddenly at her side. "Heavens," he said.

"Heavens," she echoed. She fingered the little pink envelope before opening it. He took the delay as an invitation to move still closer. Finally she slid out the card. *From one who loves,* it said. No signature. The words had been printed by a computer.

"Century Gothic," he identified. "I too was offered the use of the keyboard. I could have selected that font or any other. But I used my own pen."

"I prefer handwriting," Lois said in an earnest tone.

They returned to their chairs, though not to their reading.

The third truck belonged to a notable Boston florist. Its delivery person was a middle-aged woman. "Bevington?" she said.

Into the kitchen again, both of them. These flowers erupted from a shallow bowl. The elaborate ribbon and cellophane bright as tears at first prevented their identification, but when she cut the ribbon and removed the cellophane a rush of glory met their two gazes. The flowers were mostly white lilacs, with occasional sprays of heather and spikes of something very blue. She carried the bowl into the living room and placed it on the piano. An envelope fell to the floor. Daniel picked it up, as if the gift were for him. But it was meant for *Lois,* the four letters rounded, perhaps to disguise the penmanship, perhaps to make it legible.

"Open it," Daniel said in an unlikely bark. "Please," he amended. She extracted the card.

Love consists in this: that two solitudes protect and touch and greet each other.

Neither could identify the quote. Side by side on the gray couch they consulted their *Bartlett's.* The source was a letter written by Rilke.

"I don't believe those lilacs were sent to you by Rilke," said Daniel. "Not the tulips either."

"Roses," she murmured.

"Roses. They didn't come from a dead poet."

"No," Lois said, but whether she meant accord or disagreement or let's not speculate . . . that was anybody's guess.

In order to understand the sudden beflowering of an unadorned room, one must go back a month in time and half a mile in space—back to the evening McCauley Bell selected the menu for the fiftieth birthday party he was throwing for his wife, Andrea. Lois had been hired to cater the event. She waited in her outsize kitchen, dreading the interview. McCauley Bell was a cardiologist, and so of course he'd forbid meat, soft cheeses, pâté. He'd turn thumbs-down on her signature tiramisu, any mouthful of which could kill you if you were genetically inclined. He'd probably demand fruit salad and hardtack.

But he turned out to be a paunchy man of sixty with a voice as rich as Lois's seven-layer frivolity. She offered him a slice of frivolity, and then another. He indicated that he wanted to serve his guests exactly what his caterer liked best to make. He took all her lethal suggestions except Brie *en croûte;* he explained that he had a relationship with a cheesemonger who supplied him every so often with very special wheels of Camembert.

"And every so often you scrape out his arteries?" Lois asked.

He smiled at her. "That's the surgeon's work." He felt a curious sympathy for this bony woman. She seemed to find smiling difficult—was it the slight malocclusion; had no one ever told her that buckteeth were sexy? He knew she was married, but he suspected that she was insufficiently attended to.

"Yes," Andy said later, at home. She had taken an adult-education cooking course taught by Lois—Sweet Soups and Saucy

Pies—and she had formed one of her shallow friendships with the tall teacher. They'd gone to *Pirates of Penzance* together. "The husband is out to sea and she doesn't know how to haul him in—that's my guess. He teaches algebra or something." In fact Daniel Bevington was a world-class mathematician, but McCauley didn't trouble Andy with that information. "Lois does know how to monkey with ingredients, combines things you'd never think of. Chilies and melon, say."

The night before the party, the Bevingtons carried hors d'oeuvres and pastries into the Bells' permanently disordered kitchen. Lois opened the refrigerator that McCauley and Andy had emptied that afternoon. The Bevingtons stacked trays inside the fridge, taking turns, never bumping into each other. Then Lois and Andy walked through the downstairs discussing the placement of the bar, the various routes from kitchen to the other rooms, the fact that the piano player could play just about anything if he was kept drunk enough.

McCauley watched the two women confer, Andy's soft freckled beauty facing Lois's profile. The sweet awning of the caterer's upper lip did not quite cover the uncorrected teeth. Her husband was still in the kitchen, looking out the window. There were probably rabbits in the backyard; there might also be coyotes. Rabbits with their rapid hearts, 335 beats a minute in some breeds, can go into shock when a coyote comes close: convenient for the predator. But McCauley saw as he too neared the window that there were no rabbits just now. The mathematician was staring at something else, maybe the birches, white as the snow. . . . The man's pulse was seventy to eighty if his heartbeats were normal. McCauley estimated them to be on the slow side.

He positioned himself in the dining room so he could see both husband in the kitchen and wife in the living room. He already knew that the caterer was competent and reliable, and she probably was master of the renunciation you often saw in people who cooked for a living: she knew she must taste only enough of her creation to test its merit and not enough to satisfy her appetite. But she had that streak of inventiveness Andy had reported...He shook his big head. Other people! Other people's marriages! He himself could be considered imperfect as a husband: he never noticed clothes, he'd be damned if he'd make the bed. As for Andy: she buried herself in idle novels, talked forever on the telephone, played tricks on people. *All is lost. Fly*—once she had telegraphed this message to her cousin, an importer of wines; and the fellow did leave town for a while...She forgot to buy toilet paper and pick up his shirts and complain to the electric company about the bill. But he loved her tolerant nature and ready arms and generous bosom and the light laugh when he reached his peak—he was still capable of it, even if the postcoital heartbeats had become more irregular and the breathlessness more prolonged. Then she'd laugh again, again lightly, while his slow detumescence brought her to her own pleasure. All couples have their peculiarities. Suddenly he wanted to get rid of the skinny pair who had invaded their house to do their work so capably, like dancers who knew each other's moves.

"Darling," he said to Andy and Lois. "I think you've obsessed enough about the pianist; just make sure the minions keep his glass filled." And then, gliding into the kitchen, his belly shaking just a little, he said to the mathematician, still staring out the window, "You must be sure to come back in the spring and see the three hundred tulips I planted last October, like the

October before, and the October before that. Many of the old ones keep coming up. Nature has its way with us."

Daniel had not been looking at anything in the yard. Instead he'd been recalling an episode he'd witnessed earlier. It was brief, and soundless, and reversed—he'd seen it through the black mirror of the window, superimposed on the backyard geometry. He had been standing here then as he was now. All the stuff had been brought in. His dogsbody role had been played and he was at liberty. Lois was rearranging a tray of carved carrots and little pots of condiments. The Bells had been standing in the dining room behind Daniel. That is, in reality they stood behind him, but reality be damned; they were stationed right before his eyes in the very middle of the backyard. McCauley's left arm slid across Andrea's shoulders. Her right hand busied itself unseen, no doubt thrusting itself into his back pocket, curving her fingers around his pouf of a buttock. They didn't look at each other, but she moved her head a couple of millimeters so her hair would tickle his nostrils, and he bent his head to ensure that result. That was all, decorous foreplay reflected in a window, yet he'd felt as if one of Lois's wooden spoons was stirring his entrails. He roiled first with jealousy and then with painful relief: for why envy the fat cardiologist his unkempt wife when he had as his own companion a gentle-voiced person who had painted all the rooms of their house gray and had grayed the rest of his life too, just the way he'd wanted it, perfect for contemplation. She'd even developed an interest in Scriabin. But such consideration must be commutative, or should be—what had been placed on *her* side of the equation?

And so, three days before Valentine's Day, he'd ordered the gladioli.

Oh, the roses? Lois had sent them to herself—perhaps they would light a flame, and fan it...

And the lilacs? They were paid for in cash at the Boston florist's—both Daniel and Lois separately winkled that information out of the proprietor. But the lady would say no more—probably knew no more. So Lois had to be content with the discovery that the deception she had concocted had doubled itself. Apparently she did have an admirer. It would not be the first time.

Daniel's interior was again contorted with anxiety. Two other bouquets! His wife was so desirable that unknown persons— persons unknown to him, anyway—sent flowers to her. Attention must be paid. And you can say this of him: he had a good memory, a strong resolve, and an ability, once something was brought to his notice, to keep noticing. Certain attributes could not be changed—he found numbers more interesting than anything else—but an affection that had once been planted in his heart now belatedly flourished. Nature does have its way with us.

After a time Lois found herself smiling more readily.

The day after the birthday party the Bells went to the Caribbean, and on Valentine's Day they were still there. Early that morning, while Andy still slept, McCauley padded to the office of the little resort, and collected the camellias he'd ordered, and took his pill. He returned to the cabin and strewed the petals over her naked form. Brushed by this silken shower, she opened the hazel eyes that had brought many men to their knees, some literally, and smiled at the one she'd chosen, and slipped out of bed to go to the bathroom, disturbing only a few blossoms. She came back and lay on the petals and opened herself to her husband. As he was entering, she remembered the lilacs she had impulsively arranged to be sent anonymously to her caterer and wondered if they had done mischief or good or anything at all, and then—Oh, my love, my darling, McCauley panted—she stopped thinking about the flowers and devoted herself to the work at hand.

Conveniences

Amanda Jenkins was having a little trouble with her article, "Connubis."

"*Not* cannabis," she explained to Frieda, the girl from downstairs. "Do you really think anybody would read yet another dissertation on grass? Be your age."

"I'd rather be yours," said Frieda, who was fifteen to Amanda's twenty. "What's *connubis?*"

Amanda hesitated. Ben Stewart, eavesdropping from the bedroom, could hear for a few moments nothing but the sound of crockery being stacked. He and Amanda had agreed that dishes would be her task, laundry his. Now, at five thirty in the afternoon, she and her young friend were washing last night's plates, which had lain odorously in the sink all day.

"*Connubis,*" Amanda resumed, "a coined word, refers to being married. Or being as if married."

"Like you and Ben," Frieda said.

"More or less."

Ben wondered why she was so wary. They were indeed living together as if married, a conventional enough arrangement these days. Only the difference between their ages was exceptional. But that difference was a mere ten years...

"Actually," Amanda was saying, "I am not Benjamin's lover but his daughter."

"Stop it," Frieda sighed.

"His niece," Amanda smoothly corrected. "By marriage," she further invented. "His relationship with my aunt soured considerably when he fell in love with me. We eloped. Now we live in fear of detection. If a large weeping gray-haired woman should one day appear—Ben's wife, my aunt, is a great deal older than me—please tell her..." She paused. Frieda waited. Ben waited too.

"Tell her what?" Frieda said at last.

"To peddle her vapors elsewhere," Amanda said triumphantly.

"Mandy!" shouted Ben.

She appeared in the bedroom doorway, curly-haired and ardent. Her T-shirt said AUTEUR.

"Please stop feeding nonsense to poor Frieda," said Ben. "What will she think?"

Amanda joined him on the bed and lay on her side, propped on an elbow. "She'll discount the nonsense and think what she already thinks. That we're libertines."

"Ah. And are we that?"

"I don't know. What are we, Benjy?"

Ben considered the question. He himself—dark, thickset, Brooklyn-born—was a respectful sort of person. He particularly respected Amanda, whose upright Maine family he also respected. Once, years ago, he had loved her older sister, presently married. Now he loved Amanda, but in a casual way. And impudent Amanda—what was she? At the least, an excellent student of literature. He wished that the college kids he taught were as clever.

"I am a conformist," he said, illustrating his words by curving his hand around her breast. She giggled. He muzzled the Auteur, then put his chin into her curls and noticed that her double stood in the doorway. Frieda's T-shirt read GODOLPHIN HIGH, CLASS OF '82. "But, Frieda, you don't even live in Godolphin," Ben remarked across Amanda's head.

"The shirt belongs to my cousin," Frieda said with her usual blush.

Godolphin was the town—really a wedge of Boston—in which Ben, who worked in New York, and Amanda, who went to school in Pennsylvania, had elected to spend the summer. They had sublet a snug apartment at the top of a three-decker house. On the first floor lived an old couple, and on the second lived Frieda's aunt, Rennie, a young divorcée with a son at camp. This aunt exhausted herself day and night in her antiques store. Frieda herself was a child of Manhattan. Her parents, both art historians, were spending their summer in Italy, and Frieda had chosen Godolphin over Florence's I Tatti.

"Your cousin would not recognize his garment," Ben said gravely to Frieda.

Amanda was on her feet again. "Come into the kitchen with us, Ben," she said agreeably. "Have you been asleep all afternoon?"

Ben got out of bed. "I'll be with you in a minute."

He used the bathroom, then paused in the dining room. He and Amanda were in the habit of eating at the round table in the kitchen and reserving the heavy oak table in the dining room for work. Their two typewriters, one at either end, looked like combatants. Each machine was surrounded by papers and books,

Ben's piles orderly, Amanda's in disarray. Though he had no intention of working at this hour, Ben sat down in front of his typewriter in order to groan.

Frieda had an affinity for jambs. Now she stood aslant between the kitchen and dining room. "What are *you* writing about?"

"Hawthorne," he said. "The first novel," he expanded. "Name of *Fanshawe,*" he summed up.

She waited for a while. "Oh," she said. "I haven't read any Hawthorne."

"Do so soon."

"*Fanshawe*. A book of Gothic posturing," Amanda called from the kitchen. "But the setting is excellent. And there are a couple of more or less comic characters. I find Hawthorne a not-bad writer."

"Hawthorne is grateful," Ben muttered.

"What are you going to say about *Fanshawe*?" asked Frieda.

"I wish I could tell you," Ben said. In truth he wished he knew. "But reticence is essential to the scholar. Ideas have to be nurtured in the dark silence of the mind before they can live in the bright light of discourse. When they can bear your intelligent scrutiny I will reveal them." He went on in this vein for some time, unable to stop. Finally Amanda called him to dinner.

"Will you stay, Frieda?" she said with her beautiful smile. "Your aunt's at the store tonight."

Frieda did not have to be asked twice.

In the kitchen hung some plant that had been in beautiful condition a few weeks ago. The framed squares of needlepoint on the walls were the work of Mrs. Cunningham, from whom, through the proxy of Frieda's aunt, Ben and Amanda had sub-rented the apartment. Mr. and Mrs. Cunningham, both school-teachers, had gone to Iowa for the summer.

"What are the Cunninghams like?" Amanda asked as she served the tuna fish salad.

"I arrived only a week before they left," Frieda said cautiously.

"Tell us your impressions."

Frieda cleared her throat. "Clean and tidy and traditional."

"All of those china cats in the living room," Ben agreed. He helped himself to a carrot. "Couldn't you have scraped this, Amanda? When it's my turn to do dinner I always scrape the carrots."

"I forgot."

"I never forget."

"But you often forget to flush the toilet," she reminded him sweetly.

Ben addressed Frieda. "The Cunninghams, I am persuaded, never argue—"

"I don't know."

"—for she has her needlepoint, and he has his *Time*. Such mutuality. Theirs is a marriage of two minds. Did you remember to pick up some strawberries, Amanda?"

"Have a pickle," Amanda said. "Mutuality is exactly the point I was trying to clarify last night. Mutuality isn't the least bit important in marriage, Ben. It counts only in romance. Marriage has no truck with the smarmy mutual gratification that you just attempted to extol by sarcastic, by sarcastic..."

"Implication?"

"Implication. The idea in my article, 'Connubis,' is that—"

"Will the idea bear scrutiny?" Frieda asked. "Will it live in the light of day?"

"Of course I'm beginning to realize that conventional wisdom about the reasons for marriage is out-of-date. Like most conventional wisdom. People do not marry for security anymore. Security is provided by the welfare state."

"But we live under capitalism," Frieda said.

"Maybe you do at the Brearley School. The rest of the country is on welfare. In some form. Where was I? Oh yes, security. Security is out. And people don't marry for status either, because marriage no longer confers it. Nor do they marry for sexual satisfaction, because anybody can attain that at any time—"

"I hadn't noticed," said Ben, looking hard at her.

"—as easily single as wed," she blandly went on.

"So why should a person get married?" Frieda asked.

Amanda considered the question. Ben meanwhile thought of Hawthorne's wedded contentment.

Finally Amanda answered, "There are two creditable reasons to get married. Financial and dynastic."

"Financial?" Frieda said. "You told me we were already secure."

"Secure isn't prosperous."

"Dynastic?" Ben wondered.

Amanda turned on him one of her shining gazes. "Think of it! To raise a family a couple need not be passionate. They need not even be compatible."

"Need they be of different sexes?" Ben asked.

She waved an impatient hand. "They *must* be, as a pair, complete. Whatever they want for themselves and their progeny has to be provided by one or the other. If my family has influence, yours had better have cash. If I am worldly-wise, you had better be empathetic—"

"Empathic," Ben said.

"—and so on. We choose each other on the basis of the needs of the future family rather than on our personal desires. Those we satisfy elsewhere...the *mariage de convenance!* That's it, in a word."

"In a phrase," Ben corrected. "The old *mariage de convenance* had nothing to do with love."

"Neither will the new," Amanda said.

Ben gave his pretty paramour a long look. Did she believe this stuff? Or were she and her sidekick playing some deep, female game? He knew he would not marry her. He was proud of her, and he enjoyed her company, but she was not what he had in mind as a lifetime *partner*.

For her part, Amanda claimed loftily that she was employing him to guide her through earthly delights. They would emerge from the summer as warm friends, nothing more. After college she intended to embark on an adventurous career. She would live amid palaces, and also dung.

" 'Life is made up of marble and mud,' " he had quoted softly.

"Hawthorne?"

"Hawthorne."

"Hawthorne was right."

She was in some ways as green as Frieda. Now he looked across the table at the two sweet faces, Frieda's still vague under a cloud of hair, Mandy's excited. Her dancing eyes showed that she considered her new theory to be revealed truth. He knew she would not rest until she had revealed it to others. It had been base of him to suspect her of clever falseness. Oh, her Yankee honesty! And, oh, his Brooklyn suspiciousness. Such a misalliance. And what on earth were the two of them doing here, messing up the Cunninghams' place and overstimulating the worshipful Frieda? His stomach rumbled, as if in protest.

"What have we for dessert?" he formally inquired.

"For dessert," Amanda told him, "we have nothing."

The summer wore on. Amanda went every day to her typist's job at the offices of Godolphin's weekly, the *Gazette*. Then she came home to work on her article, which was going better. Ben taught his two courses at the university, and then came home to work on *his* article. Frieda continued to hang around their doorways.

"Connubis" got retitled "Mariage de Convenance." Amanda had conceived of it as an intelligent young woman's guide to marriage customs past and present. But it was now a manifesto, a call to common sense. "If marriage does not confer an advantage," she declared one night, "it would not be undertaken. The new woman must not wed for sentimental reasons."

"I think the dinner is burning," Frieda said.

Mandy took the pot off the stove and served the baked beans. When they were all eating she continued. "The Roman custom of *concubinitas* might have demeaned the institution of marriage, but it didn't demean the participants. However, *dignitas,* despite its name, was exploitative. The woman was expected to bear children, and she and the children were under the *potestas* of the male. As for the trustee marriage in the Dark Ages, it is being revived today in the much-touted 'extended family.' But the eager beavers who want to restore and strengthen the extended family don't realize that the trustee system involved blood vengeance, bride purchase, and sometimes bride theft."

Silence from her companions. Finally Ben said, "Take out *eager beavers*."

"What? I was just making conversation."

"You were quoting nonstop."

A hand fluttered to her curls. "Oh, was I?"

"These beans are awful," Frieda said.

United for once, her hosts glared at her.

"I was just making conversation," Frieda protested. "Listen, tomorrow night I'll do the cooking."

Soon she was making their breakfasts as well as their dinners, running up early in the morning to start coffee. Amanda and Ben enjoyed sleeping late. Frieda cleaned up too. Ben liked coming home to a well-kept apartment. Each afternoon he sat down at his dusted typewriter with a vigorous feeling. Worthy pages began to pile up on the table beside the machine. He felt more and more benevolent toward Hawthorne's first novel. The great author himself had repudiated *Fanshawe*—had even cast all available copies into the flames—but he, Dr. B. Stewart, would rescue the work, would reveal it as the precursor, however flawed, of the later masterpieces. It was a help on these afternoons to know that there was a bowl of strawberries in the refrigerator, and a pound cake on the counter. Frieda herself was never in the way.

"All daughters should be like you," Ben said one night.

Frieda flushed. Amanda frowned at him.

"All younger sisters, I mean," he said, getting the same response. "Silent partners? What do you consider yourself, toots?"

"A helpmeet," Frieda said.

"Like Phoebe in *Seven Gables*?"

"Yes." She had been doing her homework.

Every Friday the three of them went out for pizza and a movie. Every Tuesday Frieda went off with her aunt to visit another aunt, and Amanda and Ben were left to amuse themselves. They took the girl's absences with the same good nature as they took her presence. Sometimes they talked about her devotion to them.

"She adores you," Amanda said.

"She adores you," Ben returned politely.

"She adores us both. My exuberance. Your scholarly wit. It's wonderful, being adored. But whatever will Frieda do back on West End Avenue with those two aesthetes her parents?"

"I'll call her every so often," Ben said. "I'll come up from the Village and treat her to a concert. I'll buy her tea afterward, like an uncle."

"Where?" Amanda asked.

"At the Palm Court," said the expansive Ben.

"Will you really do that for Frieda?" Amanda asked unjealously.

It was midnight. They had just made love. Mandy in a long nightshirt sat on the porch glider looking at the moonlit streetscape of three-decker houses, each with its maple tree. Ben kissed her, then stood up with his back to the scene and leaned against the railing. "I don't know if I'll really do anything for Frieda." He yawned. "I can't look past this moment."

But that was untrue. He was looking past this moment at this moment. Gazing at the tumbled young woman before him, he could see clearly another version of that young woman, wearing a cap and blazer as befitted a college girl. The maples were yellowing. Amanda waved good-bye. He saw himself, also purposefully clad, headed back to New York and the intense, exophthalmic psychiatric social worker whom destiny no doubt had in store for him. He groaned.

"We'll always be friends," Amanda soulfully promised.

*   *   *

It became Ben's turn to do the dinner-table lectures.

"Hawthorne had a surprisingly gloomy view of life, considering how conventionally domiciled he was. That supportive wife, those devoted children. Yet his point of view remains tragic. Especially in *The Marble Faun,* with its plot of murder and paganism, its theme of sin and suffering, does he—"

"Supportive wife?" Amanda sniffed. "Sophia Hawthorne was a milksop, if you ask me. Letting him wallow in free love at Brook Farm while she waited celibately in Salem."

"There is no indication of sexual irregularity in the Brook Farm documents."

"I can read between the lines."

"Nathaniel considered himself saved by his marriage."

"Sophia knew herself ruined."

"They went off to Italy, didn't they?" Frieda said. "What a pair of nitwits. Please have some more bouillabaisse."

Ben considered arguing further but chose the bouillabaisse instead. Mandy's sassy comments did serve to illuminate the novels, in which placid arrangements within the house were threatened by the turbulence without. Only away from the hearth could the moral order be upset. This seemed particularly true of *Fanshawe,* which was now revealed to him as a morality tale: domestic continuity triumphing over unregulated passion. Afternoons, sitting in the Cunninghams' dining room, Ben felt the rightness of his position. In their comfortable place it was possible for him to gaze long and hard at Hawthorne's devils. Frieda's lemonade helped too.

The summer was drawing to a close. Late one hot August

night, Ben and Amanda sat on the porch drinking wine and watching the stars over the three-deckers. Amanda was on the glider, Ben on a canvas chair.

For a while they were silent. Then: "We've been happy here," Amanda began.

"Of late we have not been miserable," Ben allowed.

"So happy," she said again.

He refrained from further comment.

"But would you mind terribly if I left a bit earlier than we'd planned? Say, just before Labor Day weekend? Because I have an invitation."

He examined his heart. Certainly there was a twinge. "An invitation? From that self-centered jackass you see at school, I suppose. He's back from abroad?"

"His family has the loveliest house at the Vineyard. Would you mind, Ben?"

Well, would he? Her eyes glittered at him. Oh, the darling. "I'll mind a little," Ben said truthfully. "But I myself have an invitation to Fire Island," he lied. "So go, sweetheart."

"Come sit beside me," came her soft voice.

He found his way to the glider. He slipped an arm around her shoulders. "'What we did had a consecration of its own,'" he whispered.

"Poor Hester."

"We *have* been happy here," he said.

"Like an old married couple," she said.

"Or a brother and sister."

"It's the same thing. The best marriages have a strong incestuous component."

"Is that so?" he murmured into the side of her neck.

"That's so. The best marriages have complementarity rather

than similarity. The best marriages have a sense of the past as well as a sense of the future. The best marriages—"

"The best marriages," said Ben, suddenly enlightened, "have a maid."

Frieda hated to cry. Instead she was baking a Queen of Sheba cake. "I thought you'd get married," she loudly complained, "and here you are splitting. You've ruined my summer."

"Shh," Amanda said. "Ben is trying to work."

Ben, in the living room, sent up a corroborating clatter on the keys. Then he resumed his eavesdropping.

" . . . madwomen in the family, and certain inherited disorders in Ben's," Amanda was explaining. "Gingivitis, that sort of thing. No, no, it would have been impossible. Not to mention illegal, Ben being already married to my aunt."

"Shove it," Frieda said.

"The place looks wonderful," Amanda went on. "I hope the Cunninghams are grateful. We certainly are. We'll miss you."

"Won't you miss each other?"

"Oh, excessively!" said Amanda, forcing Ben the didact to shout, "Exceedingly!" after which he rushed into the kitchen and with promiscuous joy embraced both girls.

Hat Trick

"B oys are such boys," Marcie moaned. "Adolescent, locked into latency, infantile."

"Neonatal?" said Sallyann.

Marcie ignored her. "Oh for an experienced man. Minimum age twenty-five. Others need not apply."

She was lying on the floor looking at the ceiling lamp. Its glow made the porch seem an amber cube, floating alone in the night. Sallyann's mother wished that the cube would detach itself from the house; from the town of Godolphin; from the entire state of Massachusetts; from the globe. She wished that the porch and its five passengers, herself included, would sail off to Noplace, or at least Elsewhere...

"I'd like a pianist," June was saying, her fingers trilling on her bare thighs. She herself played the cello. "The Beethoven piano and cello sonatas," she explained, "the Dvořák..."

From the creaking old glider Helen spoke. "I want to be... taken care of," she said. Her voice was hesitant—dependency was already going out of fashion.

"My ideal mate," Sallyann said—she paused for effect, taking off her glasses, putting them back on—"will speak French, raise horses, solve mathematical paradoxes in his spare time, and write poems, paying strict attention to meter."

They were inebriates, thought Sallyann's mother. They were invaders. There were a hundred of them, a thousand...

But in fact there were only four, one her own daughter; and they were drinking unadulterated iced tea. She herself had made the tea. They were eating cookies she'd made too, though Marcie was only nibbling, having declared that shortbread was an invention of the devil and could permanently ruin her waistline. Marcie's waistline measured eighteen inches.

Helen, narrow-shouldered and wide-hipped, ate each cookie slowly, without complaint.

June munched and munched.

Sallyann just sipped.

Her mother sighed. Of course these nubile creatures weren't drunk—not on spirits, anyway. They'd bounced in from a summer movie that ended in a wedding, and they were intoxicated by their renewed belief in Love: ennobling love; love that hurtles toward blissful marriage; love that lasts beyond the grave. A perfect man waited somewhere for every girl, and her agreeable task was to find him.

For every girl, yes. They called themselves girls—this was the 1950s, and they were nineteen. In another few years they'd drop that sobriquet, all except Marcie. Marcie would be a sweetness. Poor Helen no doubt took refuge in nasty imaginings.

June had the face of a pixie—alert hazel eyes, a firm little chin. Her slender five-foot-nine-inch frame was mostly legs, or so her shorts would have you believe. She had performed a solo at the high school graduation two years ago, her long limbs making chaste love to the cello.

Sallyann had messy red hair, a long mouth, and a small nose. Sallyann was...promising, her mother hoped.

And Marcie of the endangered waistline? Golden skin, blue-green eyes, a banner of black hair, and a grin that suggested that you not take these features too seriously—she would age like everybody else, wouldn't she; she would grow lined and fatigued, wouldn't she. Yes, she would, the smile assured you—in a century or two. Marcie was the town beauty. But some boys were too awed to ask her for a date.

So she was planning to turn those jeweled eyes toward men of the world.

And Helen was hoping for a strong pair of shoulders.

And June required ten talented fingers.

And Sallyann, God help her—she wanted a Renaissance man. She was still chattering. "I wouldn't object to a noble profile."

"Oh!" cried Sallyann's mother. They all gasped, no doubt fearing a heart attack. "Oh," she repeated softly, to reassure them. "My darling fools. You dream about musical fellows, brainy guys, masterful ones, sophisticates...Let me tell you something: all cats are gray at night."

Respectful silence. Then: "What does that mean?" June asked.

Sallyann's mother struck her left palm with her right. "It means that, by and large, excluding criminals and the feeble-minded and the psychopathic...men are interchangeable."

"That can't be true," Helen said in a tone of dismay; and "Really," June said in a tone of curiosity; and "Mother," Sallyann said in no particular tone; and "Lord!" Marcie shouted from the floor. She sat up. "I do beg to differ. There are amusing men, there are learned men, there are tall ones and short ones

and ones who can't stop biting the sides of their nails; and there
are—"

"Listen to me," Sallyann's mother said.

In those days girls paid polite attention to women. Marcie
wrapped her arms around her calves. Helen stopped the glider
with a discreet motion of her heel. June on her chair leaned forward and rested elbows on bare knees. Sallyann took off her
glasses.

"There are four of you—"

"Four darling fools," murmured Sallyann.

"—and there are twenty nice young men buzzing around
Godolphin. Some are buzzing close to some of you, I've noticed.
Any of you can make do with any of them. Yes, you can, Marcie." Four stubborn silences. "Here's an idea," she barreled on.
"Choose, together, oh, twelve decent fellows. I'll write their
names on little pieces of paper and fold the papers and throw
them into a hat. Each of you will pick one paper. You'll read the
name on it..."

"Out loud?" inquired the explicit June.

"No, silently. And then set your cap for whoever you draw.
You've got charm, you've got determination. You'll catch your
guy."

"And then?" Marcie demanded.

"You'll marry him."

"And then?"

"You'll be very happy. Well, happy. Happy enough."

"Happy *enough?*"

"Happy enough," Sallyann's mother repeated to the princess.
"It's more than most people are granted. Look," she said, with
urgent sympathy, "these will be like arranged marriages." Four
blank looks now. Oh, maybe she ought to yawn, and rub her

eyes, and creep upstairs to her untenanted bed. "No backing-and-forthing," she continued, "no dubious enthusiasms." *Let's talk some other time*—perhaps she ought to say that. "No broken hearts!" she said. "And the marriages will be arranged by the best matchmaker in the universe..."

"Who?" Helen asked quietly.

"...Chance."

Silence for a while, finally broken by June. "What hat?"

Sallyann's silly beret? Her own pillbox? "...My late husband's fedora."

"How many names do we get?" said Marcie, extending her graceful hand.

"One. Bigamy is illegal."

Sallyann's three friends assented.

"And Dad," Sallyann drawled. "This is how you chose him?"

They had met on the fast train from Boston to New York, and for many years, on the anniversary of that encounter, they had raised a glass to the New Haven Railroad. "More or less," said mother to daughter.

Helen picked up a pad of paper from the table next to the glider. She fished a pencil from the pocket of her skirt. She handed both to Sallyann's mother in the gracious manner that so pleased her family. She practiced petty thievery, Sallyann's mother suddenly knew, and told little black lies; anything to lighten the weight of being overvalued.

Sallyann resumed her glasses and drifted out of the porch and walked through the living room and into the front hall. There she opened the coat closet. Two raincoats hung like culprits— hers and her mother's. Her father's coats had been bundled up with the rest of his clothing and given away; but, without discussion, widow and orphan had withheld the fedora. On the high shelf—there it rode. Whenever she saw the hat—with her glasses, without them—she reconstructed his head beneath it, the big brow and big nose, the smile; and his broad male body in topcoat and muffler, the trousers sturdily below the coat; and below the trousers the shoes, oh those big shoes. As a child she'd stood on the shoes, stood on his very feet, and together they danced.

She returned to the porch. June, still in her chair, was stretching her legs forward; they seemed to have lengthened an inch since Sallyann left the room. Sallyann's mother was still in her chair as well. Her right hand held the pad and pencil. The thin fingers of her left hand touched her own cheekbone, her ear. The wedding ring glowed. Her hair, once cinnamon like Sallyann's, had darkened to nutmeg. She would probably marry again, Sallyann thought with mild revulsion; some women of forty-five did manage to marry. Perhaps she'd pull a husband's name from a hat...Helen still occupied the glider, wearing her mask of serenity. Marcie under the lamp looked ready to be plucked and put into a buttonhole; or maybe devoured.

Sallyann gave her mother the upturned hat and her mother laid it on the floor between her sling-backed feet. Sallyann retreated to the doorway and lounged against its jamb.

"Helen, dear," said Sallyann's mother. "Name a potential husband."

Helen said nothing. She would have liked to name Jim Fitzwilliam, who had never graduated from high school and now worked in his father's auto-body shop. His uncle was in jail. His muscles were extraordinary.

"Biff Gray!" Marcie shouted.

What a waste, thought Sallyann. Handsome Biff Gray had recently graduated law school. He dated young women who had already finished college. The foursome on the porch were just kids to him.

"Biff Gray," repeated Sallyann's mother, her pencil working. She tore this first entry from the pad and folded it twice and dropped it into the hat. "Helen?" she said again.

And again Helen was silent. In addition to Jim Fitzwilliam she wanted to name Jorge Leibovich, an Argentinean Jew who owned a watch factory. In the summer he wore white suits and Panama hats and deep blue shirts that matched his eyes. He walked on the pads of his feet. He was at least fifty, and had four children and a wife.

"Maurice Armand," offered Sallyann, hoping that June would draw his name. Maurice Armand was the son of émigrés and played several instruments.

Sallyann's mother wrote, folded, tossed.

"Steve Folkster," said June. Shy Steve Folkster, now the third name in the hat; how pleased he'd be if only he knew.

"Larry Reimer," said Helen at last. He was her second cousin. His name went in, as did Larry Stubblefield's, and Larry Mady's, too. And a few more nice guys, non-Larrys.

"Anyone else?" asked Sallyann's mother.

"I guess not," Sallyann said. "I'll mix them up." She stepped forward and picked up the hat with its light burden of twice-folded papers. The brim felt warm. She moved the thing gently from side to side, hardly disturbing the prophecies within. Marcie leaped up and grabbed the hat from Sallyann and shook it vigorously. June shook it too. And Helen as well, still sitting.

"Ready?" Marcie said.

Sallyann's mother stood. She picked up the fedora. *Go home, darlings,* she might say even now. *Widows are notorious witches.* "Sit down, girls" was what she did say, though Helen had never left the glider. Sallyann's mother held the hat in her upturned palms and offered it to June. June's hand dived in like a baby seal. It surfaced, a folded paper between thumb and two fingers.

Helen next.

Marcie.

Sallyann.

Then the four girls retreated to separate corners of the porch. Sallyann's mother carried the hat out of the room. She followed her daughter's earlier path from porch through living room to coat closet, its door now closed. She moved on to the kitchen. She placed the hat in the empty sink and lit a match and dropped it among the unclaimed bridegrooms. They burned quickly. She ran water into the hat before the little bonfire could do more than singe the silk lining.

When she returned to the porch she found Sallyann alone.

"They all thanked you, Mom."

"Such sweethearts," she said, her voice light, or perhaps trembling. Both went to bed.

Greedy Marcie had deftly lifted two tickets to happiness. The first bore the name of one of the Larrys, a tall, awkward boy. Sitting at her frilled dressing table, she looked up into the mirror. Larry would be dazzled if she turned her attention his way. But he would respond—there was a confidence within his clumsiness. In fact, she thought, now studying his name as if she were studying him—the thin chest, the mouth frequently marred by cold sores, the dreams, the ambition to become a doctor like his father—he had an excellent future. She considered him for several minutes. Then she looked again at the other paper. Biff Gray.

Biff. He had flirted with her at some graduation parties, and once at the beach. He had overlooked her at other times. Something more than merriment was needed to captivate him—some quality she had not yet achieved. She would make it her business to achieve it.

And so, the next time she ran into Biff, at the tennis courts, she nodded briefly and returned her full attention to the game she was playing with June. She played better than usual, and won. June, accustomed to beating Marcie, threw her racket into her bike basket and pedaled off—she said she had to babysit. Marcie bought a Coke and settled herself on one of the slatted chairs. After his game Biff sat down next to her. She gave him a smile—not her usual broad one, however. She did not show her teeth, perfect though they were; she kept her chin lowered; she concentrated on a storybook sequence of thoughts. The unusual blue-green of my eyes indicates that there is a cache of emeralds hidden somewhere in my father's house. Some of them may have been distributed about my person. Only the brave deserve the fair. Concentrating, she said nothing, not even hi. He began to talk.

That was the way of their courtship—Biff talking, Marcie listening with her eyes. Her high spirits, her healthy optimism, her clever chatter—all were restrained in order to perfect the new talent. Once she had been a thoughtless tease. Now she was a seductress.

They were married two years later. At the end of the celebration Marcie turned her back to her bridesmaids and threw the bouquet over her buttermilk shoulder. It was a wide flattish nosegay, all yellow flowers, and it looked rather like a garden hat. Helen caught it.

*   *   *

Helen had drawn Steve Folkster's name. She'd known him since third grade. He was a diligent student, a good athlete, an everyday sort of fellow. But in Sallyann's mother's graceful script he became someone fresh, a young man with interests to reveal—a yearning for the mountains, say, or a passion for bees.

Helen did something unusual for those times—she telephoned Steve and, without preliminary remarks, invited him to the movies.

"I didn't know you liked me," he said that night, wonder steaming his face.

"I always liked you," she fibbed.

"I've always been crazy about you," he said. That claim probably wasn't true either, but no matter. She liked him now. He was crazy about her now. And it turned out that he was a passionate woodworker, and that he was devoted to his three young nephews, and that he was slow to anger, and that he was able to forgive her spurts of unkindness.

And so, when Helen caught Marcie's bouquet, she left the other bridesmaids and carried the flowers to Steve. He drew her into the harbor of his embrace.

She was protected by his devotion for the next forty years, through all their woes: his job lost, twice; a malformed infant who lived a week; her brother's intractable depression; the prolonged defiant adolescence of each of their surviving children. Even when she briefly left him, haring after a woman who had no long-term use for her but who liked to be tied up, liked to be taken from behind—he gravely withstood the desertion, gravely welcomed her back.

There was nothing written on Sallyann's paper.

In the corner of the porch, she folded it again and then unfolded it, looked at both sides several times, took off and put on her glasses. She held the paper up to the moon.

Was it accident? Was it the intervention of fate? Through the years that followed she sometimes remembered to be puzzled. At the time, though, she felt only blessed. A delay had been granted: a secret reprieve.

Many decades later she did mention the queer incident to her mother.

"No!" Her mother raised head and shoulders with such sudden force that the IV pole shook.

"Lie down, dear," said Sallyann, glancing at the monitor.

Her mother subsided into the pillows. "I assumed that you drew Maurice."

"I drew a blank."

"You married Maurice," her mother reminded her.

"Among others," Sallyann reminded her in turn. "Franco and Nils—who knew then that they existed? Their names weren't even in the hat."

"Franco," her mother murmured; and even though her voice had been weakened by the troublesome business of dying, it managed to convey the distaste she had felt for Sallyann's middle husband.

Sallyann smoothed the pillows. "My gorgeous Franco had a bad character but he was passion made flesh. All cats are *not* gray at night...Did you really think they were?"

Her mother's heart was unstoppably failing but she was in no pain and her mind was clear. "I thought—I still think—that people are more similar than different. I think that any reasonable couple can...invent its own romance...make its own happiness. See how right I was with Helen and Steve, with Marcie and Biff."

"Marcie and Biff both play around, I hear."

"Look who's talking," her mother said. Her affectionate hand found her daughter's.

Sallyann wore contact lenses these days. Her still fiery hair was coiled around her head. She had fulfilled all possible promises: had become stunning, had become worldly, had become an important anthropologist, had lived in various places, had married and divorced and borne interesting children. Though nearly seventy she would probably marry yet again. It had become a gratifying habit, more enjoyable each time she did it; but the man in the fedora still occupied pride of place in her heart. Now she had returned to Godolphin to nurse her ancient, twice-widowed mother.

"So it was you who drew the blank," her mother was whispering. "All along I thought it was June."

No one will ever know the name of June's intended. She pocketed the paper she had lifted from the hat. While the other three girls were reading theirs—or, in Sallyann's case, trying to read hers—June was merely musing. Once home, she went into the bathroom and, face averted, tore the paper into many pieces and flushed the pieces away.

She too felt relief, deeper than Sallyann's. She would not merely delay; she would retire. She could pretend that Celibacy was the name she had drawn; she was freed now to become that endearing thing: an old maid.

At college in Maine she had been languidly studying the history of music. Now she switched to biology; and in graduate school she made fungal morphology her specialty; and there, among the mushrooms, she found her life's sustaining interest. It was a particular organelle called individually the parenthesome, though it always came in pairs. She spent her postdoc investigating its properties, and, with a succession of cherished lab assistants, she spent the years afterward discovering its many uses. She, and they, received awards and honorary degrees. When she was fifty she bought a cottage on a hill. She grew roses and dahlias and poppies. She was the cellist in an amateur string quartet that met faithfully every week and gave occasional recitals. She kept in touch with old friends.

"You knew there was a blank?" Sallyann asked her mother.

The old woman briefly lifted her chin: Yes.

"Did you put it into the hat?"

The barest side-to-side motion: No.

"But you let it stay there."

This was not posed as a question; and she hadn't the strength to reply; and anyway there were too many answers. Because she had been acting as agency, not executive: she'd been as passive as the fedora. Because chance allows itself an occasional collaborator. Because Helen needed an opportunity to discharge her malice. Because the one blank paper made the game more interesting. It was only a game, after all. Who could have known that the girls would play it so seriously. Who could have predicted that a woman addled by bereavement could wield such influence over four sprites with their lives ahead of them, with choices thick at their feet.

Sallyann saw that her mother could no longer speak. She bent over the loved face. "You did a marvelous thing," she said. "We are all happy enough."

Sonny

Of all the books Mindy's father received during his illness and convalescence, his declared favorite was *Legends of the Jews*. Fat warty Rabbi Goldstone lugged the set into the sickroom on one of his unwelcome visits and deposited all six volumes with a godly thump onto the bed, as if the learning inside might overcome ills of the flesh. Mindy's mother, Roz, gave the rabbi one of her ambiguous smiles—this one, Mindy knew, meant "Strike me dead if I open one of those tomes." The book Roz grabbed from a stack sent by patients was *B.F.'s Daughter*—the first J. P. Marquand since the war. She admired Marquand's well-bred characters.

As for Mindy and her two sisters, they liked best the optical-illusion book, *Masters of Deception*, brought to the door by the maid of Mrs. Julius Barrengos, who lived in a grand house on the next street. *Masters of Deception*'s illustrations included paintings and engravings by Dalí and Magritte and Escher. Impossible things made possible—a hat floating between clouds like a bird, a watch dripping like syrup. Transformation was the game: just what the Margolis girls were looking for.

Retransformation, really. Their father had already been transformed from a hearty man into an invalid. So Mindy and her sisters wanted to return to what they'd all lately been—a reasonably contented family of six: two parents; one maiden aunt, Cecile—*she* chose the latest Perry Mason from the stack; and three princesses, otherwise called daughters. "Fairy tales always have three daughters," Thelma noted. "The older two are mean, the youngest is nice." At twelve, Tem was the youngest. "Though Beauty's sisters are not so bad…"

"Three sisters are endemic in drama," said Talia, the oldest. "Chekhov wrote a play of that very name, and think of Lear…"

"I never think of Lear," said Mindy.

"What's a Lear?" said Tem.

Talia at sixteen was the family intellectual. She was in the eleventh grade's first group in the three-track high school. Mindy, two years younger, was in the ninth grade's first group. Tem was still in untracked grammar school.

Talia persisted. "Lear, a king, had three daughters: Regan, Goneril, and Cordelia."

"In the gender category our family doesn't balance," Mindy said, disregarding those made-up names.

"Dad and Mom hoped you'd be a boy," Talia told her.

"After me they hoped that Tem would be a boy," Mindy said.

"I *am* a boy," Tem said. "Sometimes."

Whatever Dr. and Mrs. Margolis had hoped for, they expressed only satisfaction with the brainy, underweight Talia, the curly, pretty Mindy, the sturdy Tem. Tem had a talent for drawing—faces in particular—which she exercised with particular vehemence during her father's recovery. It was Tem who had first lit on *Masters of Deception*. She soon learned to reproduce the optical illusions at the beginning of the book. Her favorite was the standard schema of profile confronting matching profile with a space between them. Anybody staring at the drawing got freed suddenly from profiles and found herself looking instead at the silhouette of a vase created by slanting foreheads, prominent noses, rounded lips, and jutting jaws. Tem drew pairs of matching profiles with a neat vase between them, and then pairs of nonmatching profiles producing severely asymmetrical vases in danger of falling over.

As for *Legends of the Jews,* all three girls could see Dr. Margolis, through the half-open bedroom door, propped up in bed with one of the volumes splayed on his lap. Every so often he turned a page. So Talia abandoned *Deception* and chose a volume of *Legends* for herself and read it in the living room on her father's leather recliner. She copied phrases into a spiral notebook. Uninvited, she read pages from the *Legends* out loud to her mother, who, Mindy noticed, only *seemed* to listen; to Tem, who glared as if annoyance could transform Talia into a pillar of salt; and to Mindy, who liked the thought of God becoming soft, melting like a watch, saving Isaac, saving Jonah.

But Mindy liked best the paintings of Arcimboldo. He was a famous sixteenth-century Italian, the book told her. His portraits were composed of fruits, vegetables, and flowers. That is, he painted representations of fruits, vegetables, and flowers so arranged that together they formed the likeness of a grotesque person. They had helpful titles, and after a while you saw that, say, the portrait called *Autumn,* a face in profile, had a pumpkin for a hat, grapes for hair, a potato for a nose, a cherry for a wen. His cheek was an apple, his ear a lemon slice. *The Gardener,* an assembly of oversize root vegetables, bore an unhappy resemblance to Rabbi Goldstone. Each vegetable or piece of one was rendered so precisely that Mindy wanted to eat it right off the page, or, if hygiene demanded, plunge it into boiling water first.

Fruit played its part in the *Legends* too, Talia told her: Eve's apples of course, but also many other juicy foodstuffs, like pomegranates. " 'Moses was commanded to cause a robe to be made for Aaron,' " she read. " 'Upon the hem of it thou shalt make pomegranates of blue, and of purple, and of scarlet... and bells of gold between them... Aaron's sound shall be heard when he goeth unto the holy place before Jehovah, and when he cometh out, that he die not.' "

Mindy's class had done mythology last year. "In Ancient Greece the pomegranate was a symbol of death."

"Shut up," Tem said to both her sisters.

There were no pomegranates in Arcimboldo's work, but there was all that familiar produce. It reminded Mindy of Louie the vegetable man.

Louie the vegetable man was not composed of fruit or vegetables. He was composed of a cap, a face with little eyes and a big nose and a mouth missing some teeth, and a pile of assorted clothing from a junk shop. He was called the vegetable man because he owned a fruit-and-vegetable truck.

Before Louie the Margolises had had a different vegetable man—Paci, born in their middle-size New England city but of Italian descent, like almost one-third of the population. Another almost-third was Irish. The third nearly third was Yankee. There were Negroes too, slighted in so many ways—housing, city services, schools, employment—that it was a wonder they didn't revolt. To Roz, instructed in hierarchies by her beloved Marquand, the city's ethnic groups formed a ladder—Yankees on top, then

Jews, then Italians, then Irish, then a bunch of others like Armenians, then Negroes. She graded Jews within their category too. On the Jewish ladder the rungs were occupations: professors on top (there was one Jewish professor in the local college), then doctors, then lawyers, then businessmen (unless very successful, in which case they moved above lawyers). Beneath middling businessmen were high school teachers, inevitably unmarried, living with their mother or taking up residence in their younger brother's house, like plain Cecile; and then people who worked with their hands, like chiropodists, and then tailors who worked on their knees. Beneath tailors were vegetable men. Like the lone professor, there was just one of those, Louie.

These rankings were flexible; personal characteristics like beauty, musical talent, and tragedy could elevate a person's status. Murky pasts, schnorring relatives, disappointing children, and the failure to marry could lower it. This ordering of people, Talia informed her sisters, was rather like the divisions in heaven, where…

"Don't tell us!" Mindy said.

Talia's eyes watered. Mindy had noticed that Talia was less know-it-all these days, even though her new glasses made her look like a genius. That was *paradoxical,* Mindy thought (she was improving her word power).

"Okay, tell us," Mindy relented.

"*You* are not heavenly material," snapped Talia, recovering. "Here on earth Mom's rankings show how uneasy she is about us." Though by being children of a doctor they occupied the next-to-highest rank, Talia explained, there was always the danger of unfortunate friendships leading to inappropriate attachments or—God forbid—inappropriate marriages. "Mom's seen it happen in life, she's seen it in—"

"I will marry an appropriate prince," said Tem, who was apparently a girl today.

"—Marquand. So she wants to teach us where everybody stands."

Their mother's instruction was casual: murmurs over the slender shoulder as she stood at the sink, her face not quite in profile—curls obscured a portion of the smooth brow and the cheek, and all you could see was the brief nose. Or perhaps during a trip to the ice cream store: pretty Mrs. Margolis and her girls. Of Mr. Shapiro, who sold insurance, she confided: "Men in the insurance business can't make a living doing anything else." Of a nurse at the hospital, an ebony beauty: "I wonder if white boys fall for her." Sex appeal could lead directly to miscegenation. Of Mrs. Barrengos, who'd attended college out of town and didn't play canasta and wore prewar clothing: "She's like a Yankee." Embezzlement could move somebody's level from high business to criminal (below vegetable man). The discovery that a seeming aristocrat was in fact Jewish moved him above even the Yankees he had infiltrated. Roz Margolis liked Houdini, or at least the idea of him.

In fact, she liked just about everyone. Position on the ladder did not indicate human worth. She liked Louie. She had liked Paci too, even though he'd left the vegetable trade for a position in an unspecified enterprise. The city had an active Mob.

Louie arrived in the back vestibule every Thursday afternoon around four. Usually his son came with him. His son was in Mindy's grade, but he was in group two with mostly Italians. He was Louie's image, but a little shorter. It would have been hard to be much shorter. He had the same large curved nose, and he wore similar secondhand clothing. Louie called the boy

Sonny and referred to him as Sonny, though Mindy knew his name was Franklin. Sonny had inherited or adopted Louie's deferential manner.

"Hangdog," defined Talia.

"Preoccupied," Mindy said. She thought that Sonny had things on his mind, even though his mind was not superior... not yet, anyway. Talia knew of a few kids who had started in group two and got shifted to group one and ended up at Harvard. Talia herself was planning to go to Harvard.

"Sonny has green eyes," Tem said.

Mindy hadn't noticed. On the following Thursday she did notice. Yes, large eyes the color of blotting paper. They must have come from Mrs. Louie.

Despite the impoverished look of Louie and Sonny, their truck was a royal wonder. Paci's wares had been arranged hodgepodge, heaps of beets consorting with mountains of potatoes only more or less separate from apples. Bruisable items were slumped in boxes blackened by age and weather. Perhaps Paci's vehicle had sometimes been swept, but what could be seen of its floor was always covered with dirt and twigs and the squashed remains of things stepped on.

In Louie's truck, boxes filled with produce were fixed to the sides, large ones below, then middle, then small, in a hierarchy of size. Louie kept his lettuces silvered with moisture—Sonny watered them at various stops in the journey. Sometimes Sonny filled a watering can from the Margolises' outdoor spigot; Mindy, wandering outside from the breakfast nook where she did her homework, admired his deftness even at this low-value task. He didn't waste motions, though he would pause briefly to say hello.

"Hello," she'd say.

He watered the lettuce. Behind him, within the truck, potatoes were dotted with the wholesome dirt they'd been wrested from. Carrots came in mischievous shapes. Summer squash and zucchini lay side by side like gloves in a drawer. There was a makeshift aisle between the wares for the convenience of Louie and Sonny. It narrowed sharply as it approached the rear (really the front, just behind the cab), distorting perspective; the aisle seemed to go on for a mile. In the very back, a treasure within treasures, seasonal flowers stood in buckets. Every so often, after business was done, Louie would go into his truck and return with a bouquet which he presented to Mrs. Margolis, his cap still on his head.

Arcimboldo's work reminded Mindy of the vegetable man, and the vegetable man's abundant stock reminded her of Arcimboldo. Sometimes, standing at the rear of the truck, Mindy spotted a butternut squash like a bulbous nose or strawberries that side by side would have made a perfect mouth. You could put those tiny pearl onions between the berries, she said to Talia. Teeth.

"Nature imitates art," Talia explained. "That's an apothegm," she added. Again there were sudden tears behind her glasses. "I wish Daddy would get better."

On Thursdays Mindy continued to watch Louie or Sonny or both fill several slatted baskets and carry them into the kitchen and leave them there. Next week, emptied, they'd be waiting in the vestibule. Louie's system was considerate, his truck was pridefully kept in order, and though he couldn't have made a living in the insurance business, he was an excellent vegetable man.

And Sonny, second group notwithstanding, was an excellent apprentice. After awarding him her one-word greeting, after silently admiring the truck, Mindy always returned to the breakfast nook. She had a good view of the vestibule. Louie stood there having his audience with her mother. Mindy watched the two of them, Louie recommending, her mother thinking, and saying, Yes, two pounds; or Yes, a couple of good ones; or No, not today. Louie wrote the requests in a spiral notebook. Beside him, Sonny did the same, in a notebook of his own. When enough had been ordered for a one-person haul from the truck, Louie nodded at Sonny, and Sonny went outside. The rest of the Margolis order was inscribed in Louie's notebook alone. Then Louie joined his child; and soon they both entered the kitchen with baskets.

Mindy guessed she'd feel sorry when she had to stop watching this routine. But next year she hoped to play her viola in the school orchestra, which had afternoon rehearsals. Or she might go out for basketball. And sometime in the future there might be embarrassment between her and Sonny. She was destined to become desirable—all three sisters were. Their mother, like a good witch, had promised them loveliness one Saturday after an afternoon of unproductive shopping. Talia sniffed, as if she knew that tall skinny bespectacled girls rarely underwent transformation. "Can't I be a lovely boy?" Tem wondered. But Mindy trusted the prediction—she already resembled her desirable mother. She was destined to become the prettiest daughter of an acclaimed doctor—of a late acclaimed doctor, if the worst happened. Sonny was destined to remain a vegetable man's son. If he loved beyond his station, loved Mindy or some other elevated girl, that love was doomed. But this predictable disappointment seemed as far away as the receding back of the truck; now, on this year's Thursdays, Mindy still sat in the breakfast nook taking silent part in the domestic performance.

One Thursday Sonny didn't show up.

"Sick," Louie said to the inevitable question.

Also the following Thursday and the one after that, and he seemed to be absent from school. Mindy was used to seeing Sonny with the other group-two students as they trooped through the halls. She didn't see him now.

Sonny's absence coincided with Dr. Margolis's reappearance. One Saturday morning he came downstairs in his robe. Tem like a four-year-old hurled herself at his shins. Talia stood still, her mouth working. Mindy slid her arm under his and laid her head against his heart. The following day he came downstairs wearing slacks and a sweater, carrying *Legends*. A few days later he joined them for dinner; afterward he helped Aunt Cecile with a crossword puzzle. Retransformation at last... Soon he would go back to his office.

Louie was still working unassisted.

But one week, like their father, Sonny stopped being sick. He was in school on Monday, and on Thursday he came with his own father to the Margolis back vestibule. It was raining. Louis and the boy wore yellow slickers, Mindy observed from her nook—did they think they were fishermen? Her mother completed the first half of the order. Sonny went out to the truck.

"I'm glad he's gotten better," Mindy's mother said.

Silence. Louie raised his head. Then he said in a dull voice: "He hasn't. He hasn't gotten better. He's not going to get better."

That was all. Her mother did not say *What* or *I'm sorry* or *Doctors can be wrong* or even *Oh, Louie*. She remained standing in the vestibule looking down at the vegetable man and he remained looking up at her, and the space between their dissimilar profiles formed a misshapen vase. Then her mother turned away. Louie went out. The vase disappeared.

The girl went outside too. The rain had stopped. Around

their backyard hung a mist. Sonny's slicker was folded neatly on the grass. She watched as within the illusive length of the bright truck the condemned boy, soon joined by his father, silently filled baskets with squash, apples, melons—noses, cheeks, chins—the two working with their rare efficiency, as they would continue to do while they could, until they couldn't.

Her throat ached. Sonny, intent on his task, was losing a future, *his* future, maybe stunted and loveless and second groupish, but his.

Friday night, Mindy and Talia sat side by side on Talia's bed, their legs dangling as if from a raft into a lake. Side by side but not hip to hip; they were separated by an expanse of tufted bedspread. And so they managed to face each other by twisting their slender torsos. The profiles did not match: Talia's nose was long and commanding, Mindy's straight and agreeable. Mindy's non-Jewish features might serve to move her even higher on her mother's imaginary ladder, might even allow her to swing over to the Yankee ladder, onto a Yankee rung, next to a Yankee boy. Her parents would wring their hands but they would not declare her dead. "Sonny has a lethal disease," Mindy said.

"Fatal," Talia corrected. "Sonny...? Oh, yes, the vegetable boy. Which disease?"

"I don't know." Mindy repeated the conversation she'd overheard.

"That's too bad," Talia said.

"It's terrible."

"Terrible, then."

"I mean...suppose it was us."

"*Were we.* You're always thinking of yourself."

Mindy only guessed that *Suppose it was us,* though brief and ungrammatical, was a necessary first step toward putting one-self in someone else's shoes, for you had only to reverse subject and complement to say *Suppose we were Sonny*. Suppose we faced pain and then darkness; pain, what is it like for Sonny; darkness, how will it be? But she was sure that Talia, not far from her on the bed, was insulting her and that what might have been a moment of closeness between the girls had turned into a kind of spat. "I'm sorry," Talia muttered, but too late—Mindy stood up and left her hard-hearted sister.

Hard-hearted? Talia would have said *other-minded*. Though she thought of Sonny as a kind of vegetable, she knew he was a human being, and therefore worth saving, like all those hu-man beings she would be called upon to save when she finished medical school. Perhaps one day she would invent a cure for his disease. But today what Sonny needed was a remedy from the mythical past. Some functionary in the kingdom of the sick had moved her father to the kingdom of the well and replaced him with Sonny. There must be a new magic, perhaps a heavenly one. Maybe the changeable, demanding God of the *Legends* would let Sonny live if Louie bought him a robe edged with em-broidered pomegranates. Or perhaps her mother would redeem the boy by sacrificing one of her daughters, the way Hannah devotedly sacrificed Samuel to Eli, the way Beauty's father un-wittingly sacrificed his girl to the beast. The selected daughter— Mindy?—would marry Sonny, and on their wedding night he'd be transformed from a turnip into a prince; Mindy would be-come a princess. Talia would be rid of her.

On Saturday afternoon Mindy and Tem were playing gin rummy. Their father had been kibitzing but he had gone upstairs for a nap. Mindy revealed the latest news.

"Children don't die," Tem countered. "Sometimes they drown, that's all."

How innocent a twelve-year-old could be. "They die of diseases too."

"In books. Not here. Stop talking. Gin."

The bested Mindy exited through the archway to the dining room just as their father descended the stairs into the hall. Tem was treated to the back view of her sister, all grace and angora, and to the front view of her parent—what a tiny nap he'd taken, how could it have been restful. Her hand itched for a pencil; she'd use the side of the graphite for those grooves on the cheeks, crosshatches for the area under the pursed lips. *Dr. Margolis, Restored to Health?* No: *Dr. Margolis, Pretending Not to Hurt.* His restoration had been so brief. She felt cruelly teased. But she smiled at him, and he managed to smile at her. He sat down on the recliner. Tem was wearing work overalls that Aunt Cecile had bought for her at a secondhand store, and she knew she resembled a construction worker, and she was sorry for that, for her father was an old-fashioned man who preferred women to look like women. "I'll be right back, Daddy," she said, and ran upstairs and put on one of those pleated skirts that hung in her closet and a white blouse that her mother had ironed. Now she was in costume—in drag, Talia had explained: she was a boy impersonating a girl. She ran back down and dropped onto the floor beside his shins and put her hand on his knee, and he took it. She placed his palm next to her cheek. Tomorrow, back in overalls, she would make him a present—an Arcimboldo-like portrait, created not out of vegetables but out of articles from his kit bag: bandages for hair, a swab for a nose, Mercurochrome-soaked cotton for a mustache, and, for eyes, cod-liver oil capsules.

*   *   *

The funeral took place in an unfamiliar, dimly lit shul, the plaster walls shredding. This congregation occupied a low rung on the ladder. Mrs. Louie was undiscoverable within a knot of her family. Louie was shrunken and wrinkled like a forgotten cucumber. A red-bearded rabbi tried in vain to talk sense. Roz remembered the funeral of Cassie Mae, who had worked for the Margolises. The congregation there stood up and wailed and shook its hundreds of black arms. Why couldn't this bunch of underprivileged Jews let themselves go, become unseemly fools; what a relief that would be. They could storm up to the bimah and kill the robed representative of an incompetent God.

Roz saw tears slide from beneath Talia's glasses. Mindy sobbed. Tem was stony, as if reserving her grief. Dr. Margolis had stayed home. Cecile had come; school was closed for vacation. She sat at the end of their row wearing her suit for occasions—brown, ill-fitting, with a dreadful blouse in a different brown. She looked dowdy and enviable both. She would never have to bury a child. A child's death was the one unsupportable grief; Talia had said so, Aristotle had said it to her—as if anybody had to bother to say it, as if every parent didn't already know. That insupportable grief might be destined for Roz herself, who could tell.

But for her daughters? With lips pressed together and eyes fixed on the comfortless ark, Roz prayed for them. She asked not for lives free of sorrow—what deity would heed that request? No; she made a sensible plea: she prayed that all three would turn out to be barren.

The Descent of Happiness

I was eight—old enough to be taken along on a house call as long as I stayed out of the bedroom or whatever room was to be used for the examination. Little children were sometimes examined on the kitchen table spread with a quilt. In those cases I hid behind an open door or maybe squatted outside the house beneath a window so I could hear the conversation, all sentence fragments as my teacher would have pointed out, that got batted like a shuttlecock between my father and the child's parents. But this morning my father was visiting an adult, Mr. Workman, patient and friend. Mr. Workman had a bad heart, not as bad as he thought it was, my father had told me, but bad enough to be listened to whenever he phoned.

"Can you hear that syncopation on your receiver?" he'd shouted.

"No. Sam. Sam! Take the phone away from your chest..." Pause while Mr. Workman presumably obeyed. "Put it back up to your ear and listen to me. I'm on my way with my stethoscope."

"Good," Mr. Workman said. "And after you listen to my heart with that thing I'll use it to call my aunt Mary."

So he probably wasn't in too much discomfort.

My father was what you might call a country doctor if by that you meant something sociological: a doctor who practiced in both a small town and the rural area surrounding it. Or you might mean something more artistic, more Norman Rockwell–ish—a doctor who drove a car so old that his patients were likely to outlive it, a doctor whose stubby fingers, smelling of cigar overlaid with soap, seemed Velcroed to an old black bag, except this was seventy years ago and Velcro had just been invented and none of us had heard of it. In the trunk of his rattly car he kept a case of medicines, a few of which he always transferred to the house icebox whenever he entered a home and never forgot to remove on departure. Sometimes I thought he never forgot anything. But I have discovered through the years that anyone who restricts his conversational responses to what he knows—what he knows he knows—will always seem to have an extraordinary, well-stocked mind. My father did know a lot but not everything. He knew midcentury medicine and American history and some botany. He knew some chemistry and a lot of anatomy. He didn't know the world of animals or the world of stories—two worlds I considered one, since the only books I read were about horses. He knew my mother. He knew me. He knew Mr. Workman and all his other patients too.

We got into the moribund car that October Saturday and drove over back roads to Mr. Workman's house in the woods. The fall had been relentlessly wet, but the rain had stopped the day before. In the moist clearing where my father parked, yellow leaves seemed pasted to the birches, and brownish leaves fallen from the maples made the path from the clearing slick as oilcloth. An occasional wind shook drops from the branches as if new rain were welcoming us.

We could see glimpses of Mr. Workman's elfish house. I loved that house, with its peaked small windows that resembled its owner's small eyes and the roof over the front door that extended widely like an upper lip. A carpenter's bench stood at one side of the front door and a handmade table on the other. You'd think that Mr. Workman was a Wood Workman, and in fact making furniture was his hobby, but he was a lawyer by profession. He practiced in a one-room office near the courthouse. He was a bachelor, and lived with a dog I did not like—a large noisy hybrid named John Marshall. John Marshall had a pointed snout and black gums. To me he looked like a wolf—no, he looked like a dog who had reverted to wolfdom and then reverted farther back to whatever lupine species had preceded wolves. I knew nothing of Darwin then except what my father had revealed to me: that once nothing on earth was as it is now, that everything we see descended from something else—sycamores from ferns, sparrows from flying dinosaurs, Mr. Workman from a chimpanzee (but Dad didn't say that last). There was something called evolution and something else called natural selection.

John Marshall barked at all Mr. Workman's visitors, strangers or not. He bounded toward them and put his paws up on the newcomer's shoulders and, delicately refraining from licking, gave the visitor a whiff of his dreadful breath. In this way he resembled not the wolves his ancestors had been but the dancers his species might become in a few more centuries of evolution.

"He is saying hello," Mr. Workman often explained to me. "He's overfriendly but harmless." But he frightened me—I sensed that his harmlessness was only a ploy, like my pretending to play outdoors when I was really listening at the window. And so, out of sympathy with my timidity, Mr.

Workman kept John Marshall tethered to a post when I was expected.

But today he had forgotten to tie up John Marshall. Or perhaps John Marshall had learned to undo knots. At any rate, we heard the animal barking as soon as we parked the car, and his barks grew louder as we walked up the path, my father going first with his bag attached to his hand and his box of medicines under his left arm. I knew that if I kept close to him he would protect me from John Marshall; but the increasingly louder barks rattled me—this crescendo had never happened before—and in an access of terror I wheeled, turned my back on my father, and ran in the other direction. I would reach the car before John Marshall; I would leap onto its curved roof, meanwhile transforming myself into a cat; I would arch my back and hiss, I would frighten *him*. But in my hurry to change species I neglected to grow the necessary forelegs. Two-legged, slipping first with one and then with the other, feeling one of my sneakers loosening, I fell on my all-too-human knees and then fell farther forward, ending up prone on the wet path. I slipped ahead an inch or two, wiggling like a primitive fish. Then I lay still. John Marshall yapped at my useless feet.

This was the end. I knew there was an end to everything—I had lost grandparents to old age and a schoolmate to accident, and I had seen diseased vegetation, and I had wept more than once over the death of Black Beauty. But this was the end of me. John Marshall would choose a way—would drag his canines across the back of my neck, severing my head from my body; or hurl his own body on top of mine and gnaw me to extinction; or simply bite me in an available place and infect me with fatal rabies that he himself had caught from a bat.

I was calm. If one of these cruel ends was in store for me,

there was nothing to do. John Marshall had stopped barking. I could hear him panting first behind me and then by my side. He panted into my ear, perhaps singing a doggy lullaby or even a waltz, maybe "The Merry Widow," my parents' favorite, though the three/four beat seemed to be beyond him. Perhaps this was a doggy extreme unction.

Then I stopped considering him or his feelings. I had fallen in such a way that my nose was touching a maple leaf. I followed its periphery, I traveled its veins, I remembered that deciduous plants evolved later than earlier plants, well, naturally later was later than earlier, I was no longer making sense, the rabies was already affecting my brain...

"Emma!" And his strong hands with their soap-and-tobacco fragrance picked me up under the arms and lifted me and turned me at the same time, so my chest was pressed to his, my cheek to his, our two hearts beat as one. I think there was a waltz of that name. "Why did you run, you know John Marshall would never hurt you." And indeed there was John Marshall, my sneaker in his smiling mouth, and Sam Workman, panting a little himself but only slightly; his heart was probably okay this time, as it usually was. I had run because I had to... but I couldn't explain that, so I didn't. I had run because I wanted to be caught, not by John Marshall but by the country doctor who had fathered me, who would always rescue me from danger.

I will never forget that day. I had never been so happy before. I have never been so happy since.

Honeydew

Caldicott Academy, a private day school for girls, had not expelled a student in decades. There were few prohibitions. Drinking and drugging and having sex right there on the campus could supposedly get you kicked out; turning up pregnant likewise; that was the long and short of it. There was a rule against climbing down the ravine on the west side of the school, where a suicide had occurred a century earlier, but the punishment was only a scolding.

Alice Toomey, headmistress, would have welcomed a rule against excessive skinniness. Emily Knapp, all ninety pounds of her, was making Alice feel enraged and, worse yet, incompetent—she, Alice, awarded the prize for Most Effective Director two years in a row by the Association of Private Day Schools. This tall bundle of twigs that called itself a girl— Alice's palms ached to spank her.

Emily: eleventh grade, all As, active member of various extracurricular clubs, excused from sports for obvious reasons. Once a month she visited a psychiatrist, and once a week a nutrition doctor who emptied her pockets of rocks and insisted that she urinate before stepping on the scale. She had been hos-pitalized only twice. But according to her mother, Emily was never more than two milligrams away from an emergency ad-mission.

She displayed other signs of disorder. Hair loss. Skin stretched like a membrane over the bones of the face. A voice as harsh as a saw. But her conversation, unless the subject was her own body mass, was intelligent and reasonable. Alice had endured a series of painful meetings with Dr. Richard Knapp, physician and professor of anatomy, and his wife, Ghiselle. The three met in Alice's dowdy office. The atmosphere was one of helplessness.

On one of those occasions, "I worry about death," Alice dared to say.

"Her death, if it occurs, will be accidental," said Emily's fa-ther evenly.

Ghiselle flew at him. "You are discussing some stranger's case history, yes?" Despite twenty-five years in Massachusetts, she retained a French accent and French syntax, not to mention French chic and French beauty.

Richard said: "It is helpful to keep a physician's distance."

Husband and wife now exchanged a look that the unmarried Alice labeled enmity. Then Richard placed his fingers on Ghiselle's chiffon arm, but it was Alice he looked at. "Emily doesn't want to die," he said.

"That is so?" scoffed Ghiselle.

"She doesn't want a needle fixed to her vein. She doesn't want an IV pole as a companion."

"That is so?"

"She doesn't want to drive us all crazy."

"What *does* she want?" Alice said. And there was a brief

silence as if the heavy questions about Emily's condition and the condition of like sufferers were about to be answered, here, now, in Godolphin, Massachusetts.

"She wants to be very, very, very thin," Richard said. *No shit*, Alice thought. "Achhoopf," snorted Ghiselle, or something like that. She herself was very thin, again in the way of Frenchwomen—shoulders charmingly bony, neck slightly elongated. Her legs under her brief skirt—too brief for fifty? not in this case—were to die for, Caldicott students would unimaginatively have said.

"She wants to become a bug, and live on air," Richard added, "and a drop or two of nectar. She thinks—she sometimes thinks—she was meant to be born an insect."

Alice shuddered within her old-fashioned dress. She wore shirtwaists, very long in order to draw attention away from her Celtic hips and bottom, and always blue: slate, cornflower, the sky before a storm. She wondered if this signature style would become a source of mockery. She was forty-three, and six weeks pregnant—in another few months the shocked trustees would have to ask her to resign. Perhaps it would be more honorable to expel herself. "What can we do?" she asked.

"We can chain her to a bed and ram food down her throat," Ghiselle said, her accent lost in her fury. Alice imagined herself locking the chain to the headboard. Now Richard's fingers slid down the chiffon all the way to Ghiselle's fingers. Five fiery nails waved him off. The two younger Knapp daughters, their weight normal, were good students, though they lacked Emily's brilliance and her devotion to whatever interested her.

"Emily must find her own way to continue to live," Richard said, at last providing something useful and true; but by now neither woman was listening.

*   *   *

Though Caldicott was not a residential school, Emily had been given a room to herself. It was really a closet with a single window looking out on the forbidden ravine. Mr. da Sola, jack-of-all-trades, had lined two of the walls with shelves. Mr. da Sola was a defrocked science teacher from the public schools who had seen fit to teach intelligent design along with evolution and had paid for that sin.

"I don't need another science teacher," Alice had said, wondering where he got the nerve to sit on the corner of her desk. What dark brows he had, and those topaz eyes...

"That's good. I don't want to be a science teacher," he told her. He didn't tell her that no other private school had agreed to interview him. "I want to return to my first loves, carpentry and gardening." So she took him on.

On Mr. da Sola's shelves Emily had placed her specimen collection equipment; the specimens themselves, collected from the ravine and its banks; and some books, including the King James Bible and an atlas of South America. There was also a box of crackers, a box of prunes, and several liters of bottled water.

Emily was permitted to take her meager lunch here and also her study periods, for the study hall nauseated her, redolent as it was of food recently eaten and now being processed, and sometimes of residual gases loosed accidentally or mischievously. She dined among her dead insects, admiring chitinous exoskeletons while she put one of three carrot sticks into her mouth. Chitin was not part of mammal physiology, though she had read that after death and before decomposition, the epidermis of a deceased human develops a leathery hardness—chitinlike, it could be called—which begins to resemble the beetles that gorge on the decaying corpse and defecate at the same time, turning flesh into compost. The uses of shit were many. The most delightful was manna. Emily liked the story of Moses leading the starving Israelites into the desert. Insects came to their rescue. Of course the manna, which Exodus describes as a fine frost on the ground with a taste like honey, was thought to be a miracle from God, but it was really Coccidae excrement. Coccidae feed on the sap of plants. The sugary liquid rushes through the gut and out the anus. A single insect can process and expel many times its own weight every hour. They flick the stuff away with their hind legs, and it floats to the ground. Nomads still eat it—relish it. It is called honeydew.

Ah, Coccidae. She could draw them—she loved to draw her relatives—but unfortunately the mature insect is basically a scaly ball: a gut in a shell. It was more fun to draw the ant—its proboscis, pharynx, two antennae. Sometimes she tried to render its compound eye, but the result looked too much like one of her mother's jet-beaded evening pouches. She could produce a respectable diagram of its body, though: the thorax, the chest area, and the rear segment, segmented itself, which contained the abdomen and, right beside it, the heart.

Richard was pulling his sweater off over his head. The deliberate gesture revealed, one feature at a time, chin, mouth, nose, eyelids closed against the woolen scrape, eyebrows slightly unsettled, broad high brow, and, finally, gray hair raised briefly into a cone.

Alice and two Caldicott teachers lived on the school grounds. Their three little houses fronted on the grassy field where important convocations were held. The backs of the houses overlooked the ravine. In the wet season the ravine held a few inches of water—enough for that determined suicide a century ago. These days it provided a convenient receptacle for an empty beer can and the occasional condom. On the far side of the ravine was a road separating Godolphin from the next town. The Knapps lived in a cul-de-sac off that road. Leaving his house, walking across the road, side-slipping down his side of the ravine and climbing sure-footed up hers—in this athletic manner Richard had been visiting Alice twice and sometimes three times a week, in the late afternoon, for the past few years. Sometimes he picked a little nosegay of wildflowers on his way. Alice popped them into any old glass—today the one on her bureau. She was undressed before his sweater had cleared his head. And so, reclining, naked thighs crossed against her own desire, she watched the rest of the disrobing, the careful folding of clothes. Sometimes crossing her thighs didn't work, and she'd surrender to a first bliss while he busied himself hanging his jacket on the chair. Not today, though. Today she managed to keep herself to herself like the disciplined educator she was, waited until her body was covered by his equally disciplined body; opened her legs; and then spinster teacher and scholarly physician discarded their outer-world selves, joined, rolled, rolled back again, each straining to become incorporated into the other, to be made one, to form a new organism wanting nothing but to make love to itself all day long. Perhaps some afternoon they—it—would molt, grow wings, fly away, and, its time on earth over, die entwined in its own limbs and crumble to dust before midnight.

Emily didn't do drugs often. Her substance of choice—her only substance, in fact—was *bicho de taquara,* a moth grub found in the stems of Brazilian bamboo plants, but only when they are flowering. Mr. da Sola tended bamboo in one corner of Caldicott's glass-covered winter garden. He harvested the grubs, removed their heads, dried them, ground them up, and stored the resulting powder in a jar labeled RAT POISON. Each year he produced about six teaspoons of the stuff; three times a year he and Emily swallowed a spoonful each...

The Malalis, in the province of Minas Gerais, Brazil, had reported an ecstatic sleep similar to but shorter than the unconscious state produced by opium, and full of visual adventures. Emily could attest to that, but she did not share her visions with Mr. da Sola, who enjoyed his own private coma beside her on the floor of her little room. In Emily's repeated dream she was attending a banquet where she was compelled to crawl from table to table, sampling the brilliant food: pink glistening hams, small crispy birds on beds of edible petals, smoked fish of all colors ranging from the deep orange of salmon to the pale yellow of butterfish. And then: salads within whose leaves lurked living oysters recently plucked from their shells, eager to be nibbled by Emily; the mauve feet of pigs, lightly pickled; headcheese, the fragrance of calf still floating from its crock. And vegetables: eggplant stewed with squash blossoms; a pumpkin, its hat off, stuffed with crème fraîche and baked. And desserts: melons the color of peaches, and peaches the size of melons, fig preserves in hazelnut cups; and, at last, a celestial version of Brie *en croûte,* the *croûte* made of moth wings, for Mr. da Sola allowed a few moth grubs to hatch and mature and deposit their larvae before he gently pinched them dead and removed their new wings, and he caught butterflies too, in the outside garden, and sewed wing to wing to make several round fairy quilts and sugared and steamed them and laid them out on the carpenter's table and plopped into each a light cheese faintly curdled;

and then he molded several *croûtes* and baked them. He did all this off-dream. Emily plunged into the pastries. When she awoke there was often white exudate on her teeth, which she removed with her forefinger. Then she rubbed her fingertip dry on the unvarnished floor of the room while watching Mr. da Sola awake from his own glorious adventure, whatever it was. She suspected Alice was its heroine.

The rest of her time in the little room, Emily studied. She had become a master of the ant heart—like the hearts of all insects it was a primitive tube—and now turned her attention to the complicated stomach. She was soon to give a lecture on the ant stomach to the middle school and to anyone else who wanted to listen. Caldicott students were encouraged to share their interests. Wolfie Featherstone had recently talked about utopian societies, and her sidekick, Adele Alba, had analyzed figures of speech and the power of syntax.

And so, one Tuesday, Emily stood on a platform beside an easel where her diagrams were propped. "The abdomen is the segmented tail area of an ant," she rasped, pointing with her father's hiking stick. "It contains the heart and, would you believe it, the reproductive organs too, well, you probably would believe that, and it contains most of the digestive system. It is protected by an exoskeleton. And get this"—she licked her lips and let her pointer hang vertically between her pipe-cleaner legs until it touched the floor, making her look like a starving song-and-dance man—"the ant has not one stomach but two."

"So does the cow," drawled a fat girl.

"The cow's two stomachs only serve the cow."

"Serve the cow only," corrected Adele.

"Whatever. The ant's larger stomach, called the crop, is at the service of all. As an ant collects food and eats it, the nutrient is dissolved into a liquid and stored in the crop. When a fellow ant is hungry, its antennae stroke the food storer's head. Then the two ants put their mouths together, together, together"—she controlled her unseemly excitement with the aid of the soothing smile Mr. da Sola sent from the back of the room—"and the liquid food passes from one to the other. And in addition to the generous crop, each ant has another, smaller stomach, its 'personal belly.'"

Alice, wearing a faded denim dress, said, "Then the larger stomach belongs to the community."

"Yes!" Emily said. "And if philosophers had brains in their heads they would realize that the ant's collective pouch is the most advanced device that evolution, or God if you prefer, has come up with."

"A soup kitchen," interrupted the fat girl.

"And the ant feeding her associates through her mouth out of her own belly is the fundamental act from which the social life, the virtues, the morality, and the politics of the formicary— that's the word for the ant as a society—are derived." Alice saw that Emily used no notes. "Compared to this true collective, Wolfie, Brook Farm is a sandbox."

A few girls were gagging or at least making gagging sounds.

"The ant is being exploited by her pals," said the irritating fatty. Her size-six jeans were big on her and she wore her little sister's tee. A strip of pink flesh showed between the two, like a satin ribbon. "When does *she* eat?"

"She cannot be said to eat as we understand eating," said Emily severely. "She collects and stores and regurgitates. She is the life spring of her world."

"So we evolved, and lost our second stomach," Wolfie said. "We got ourselves brains instead. A good deal."

"What's good about the brain?" Emily said. "*It* evolved to make money and war."

"Zeugma!" Adele shouted.

Perhaps it was because of the only moderate success of her lecture, perhaps because of her binge at the banquet—at any rate, Emily turned up at the nutritionist that week at an unacceptable weight. She was hospitalized. She was not force-fed, but her room's bathroom had no door, and while she consumed one pea at a time she was watched by a nurse's aide with baroque curves.

"Sugar, eat," the aide coaxed.

"Honey, do," Emily mocked. But she acceded to the regimen; her work was calling her. Soon she'd gained enough to be discharged, though she'd have to see the nutritionist twice a week for a while. She was released a day earlier than planned. Her mother drove to the hospital in a downpour. She brought a present: a long, black vinyl raincoat with a hood.

"Thank you," said Emily, unsurprised at the kindness of the gift. Her mother was everything a human was entitled to be: outspoken, attached to her particular children, unacquainted with tact. Ghiselle had no concern for the superorganism—but, after all, ever since the development of the spine, the individual had become paramount, the group disregarded. Ghiselle was only following the downhill path of her species.

"There's a candy bar in the pocket of the raincoat," Ghiselle said.

"Oh."

"Wolfie and Adele can split it. *Veux-tu rentrer?*"

"*Pas encore. Laisse moi à la bibliothèque, s'il te plaît.*" Emily was the only member of the family, Richard included, who had mastered enough French to converse with her mother in her mother's tongue.

Ghiselle parked and Emily got out of the car. The rain had stopped. The new coat concealed Emily's emaciation, and she had raised her hood against the suspended mist that had followed the rain, so her patchy hair was concealed too. She looked, Ghiselle thought, like any serious modern girl—bound for medical school, maybe, or a career in science.

Emily crossed the modest campus and entered the library. Ghiselle blew her nose and drove away.

"Emily is the heroine of the moment," Alice murmured into Richard's shoulder.

"Is she? They all love insects now?"

"No, they envy her monomania—"

"Polymania is more like it. Subway systems, for instance— she can diagram the underground of every major city in the world."

"And they associate it with her lack of appetite, and they associate *that* with free will. 'You can get a lot done if you choose to skip dinner,' Wolfie Featherstone told me. Richard, not eating will become a fad and then a craze and then a cult."

"Well, bulk the girls up ahead of time. Have the cook serve creamed casseroles instead of those stingy salads."

Alice groaned. "You are undermining Caldicott's famed nutrition."

"Screw nutrition. The body tends to take care of itself unless it's abused. All the girls except Emily are strong enough to beat carpets."

"Beat carpets? The maids do that once a year."

"Ghiselle does it more often."

"Ghiselle? I don't believe you. Ghiselle is a grande dame."

"On the surface. She's a peasant inside." He withdrew his arm gently from beneath Alice's shoulder, clasped his hands under his head. The watery light from the uncurtained window shone on him—on them both, Alice supposed, but she had lost all sense of herself except as a receptacle with grasping muscles and a hungry mouth. Only her lover was illuminated. His pewter hair swept his forehead, sprouted from his underarms, curled around his nipples, provided a restful nest for his penis, too restful maybe...she leaned over and blew on the nest and got things going again.

And afterward...well, this woman had come late to passion and had not yet learned restraint.

"Do you love Ghiselle the grand dame or Ghiselle the peasant?"

"I love you, Alice."

"You *do?*"

"I do." He loved Ghiselle too, but he didn't burden Alice with that information. He had come to believe that monogamy was unnatural. He would like to practice polygamy, bigamy at least, but Ghiselle would run off to Paris, taking the girls...

"Oh, Richard," Alice was lovingly sighing. Then there was silence, and the room that had seemed so steamy grew cool like a forest brook, and she was as happy as she had ever been. They lay side by side in that silence.

"So you'll leave her," Alice ventured after a while.

"...No."

"No!" She sat up. "You are going to stay with the bitch."

"She is not a bitch. We're a bit of a misalliance, that's all, fire and steel, you might say."

"Misalliance? A disaster!"

He kissed her left nipple, and the right, and the navel; and if she'd had any sense she would have dropped the argument and lain down again. Instead, "You're going to stay with her for the sake of the children instead of divorcing her for the sake of yourself. And for the sake of me," she cried. "But, Richard, children survive this sort of thing. Sometimes I think they expect it. I've noticed at the bat mitzvahs I get invited to, and I get invited to them all, the girls with two sets of parents and a colony of half sibs—they're the snappiest. Richard, come live with me, come live with me and be my—" He covered her mouth with his. "We belong together," she said when she got her breath, and he did it again. "You are practicing probity," she said, and this time he didn't interrupt her. "You are a prig!" She began to sob in earnest. He held her until the sobs grew less frequent, and they lay down again, and she fell asleep, and he held her for some time after that.

At five o'clock he woke her. Bleakly they dressed, back to back. Richard put on the clothes he'd folded earlier; Alice pulled on jeans and a Wedgwood sweater. Then they turned. Her cheekbone touched his jaw. *We'll meet again.* Richard left by the back door, walking carefully because the rain had made the earth slick. The air was cold now. Alice, standing at the doorway, crossed her arms in front of her waist and cupped her elbows in her hands. Women have worried in that position for centuries. She watched her lover make his slippery way toward the bottom of the ravine. Maybe Paolo da Sola would marry her. She could raise his salary.

Emily was now standing on Alice's side of the ravine, not far from Alice's house. She leaned against a birch. She had just left the library, where she had been reading about ants' circles of death. Sometimes ants, for no apparent reason, form a spiral and run in it continuously until they die of exhaustion. What kind of behavior was that from so evolved a creature? Oh, she had much to figure out. But at the moment all she wanted to do was watch her father behaving like a boy. If he sprained an ankle it would put a crimp in his love life. Too bad he didn't have six ankles. But with only two he did manage to leap over the little creek at the bottom of the ravine, land without incident, and start to climb the far side. He did not look up over his right shoulder or he would have seen Alice standing in her doorway, and he did not look up over his left shoulder or he would have seen Emily and her tree; he looked straight ahead through those binocular eyes embedded in his skull. Emily herself had compound eyes, at least some of the time—the images she saw were combined from numerous ommatidia, eye units, located on the surface of the orb. These eye units, when things were working right, all pointed in slightly different directions. In a mirror she saw multiple Emilys, all of them bulging, all of them gross.

Alice wrenched her gaze from Richard's climbing form and looked sideways and saw Emily, aslant against a white tree, spying on her father. She was covered in a black, helmeted carapace. She looked as if she had attached herself to the tree for nourishment. She was a mutant, she was a sport of nature, she should be sprayed, crushed underfoot, gathered up, and laid in a coffin...Then rage loosened and shriveled, and Alice, in a new, motherly way, began to move toward the half sister of her child-to-be. She couldn't keep her footing in the mud so she had to use her hands too. She would bring Emily to her house. She would offer her a weed. She would not mention food. She would whisper to the misguided girl that life could be moderately satisfying even if you were born into the wrong order.

Having safely ascended the opposite bank of the ravine, Richard turned and squinted at the artful bit of nature below: two banks of trees slanting inward as if trying to reach each other, some with pale yellow leaves, some brown, some leafless; more leaves thick at their roots; and mist everywhere. It was a view Ghiselle would appreciate, she loved pointillism, though she had decorated their house in bright abstractions for no apparent reason. For no apparent reason one of his two promising younger daughters spent her evenings in front of a television screen and the other seemed to have sewn her thumb to her BlackBerry. Perhaps it was in the nature of people to defy their own best interests. Why, look, as if to validate his insight, there was his beloved Emily, oh Lord, let her live, make her live, there was Emily, plastered lengthwise to a tree like a colony of parasitic grubs; and there was his Alice, intruding like the headmistress she couldn't help being, undertaking to crawl toward Emily, not on hands and knees but on toes and fingertips, her limbs as long as those of a katydid nymph. And above her body, her busybody you might say, swayed that magnificent blue rump.

Some of what Alice wished for came about. She and Emily developed a cautious alliance. Emily's weight went up a bit, though her future remained worrisome. Paolo da Sola said "Sure!" to Alice's proposal of marriage. "And I don't want to know the circumstances. I've been mad about you since we met."

Richard eventually replaced Alice with an undemanding pathologist who already had a husband and children. The baby born to Alice had Paolo's dark brows and golden eyes— surprising, maybe, until you remember that all humans look pretty much alike. And when Caldicott's old-fashioned housekeeper discovered Wolfie and Adele embracing naked in Emily's little room, and failed to keep her ancient mouth shut, Alice summoned the trustees for a meeting and told them that this expression of devoted friendship was not in contravention of any rule she knew of. She adjusted her yawning infant on her pale blue shoulder. Anyway, she reminded them and herself, Caldicott's most important rules even if they weren't written down were tolerance and discretion. All the others were honeydew.

These stories originally appeared, sometimes in different form, in the following publications: "Cul-de-sac" and "Stone" in *Agni*; "Castle 4" and "The Golden Swan" in *Alaska Quarterly Review*; "Wait and See" in the *American Scholar*; "Assisted Living," "Conveniences," "Deliverance," and "Puck" in *Ascent*; "Flowers" (as "Hearts and Flowers") and "Hat Trick" in *Cincinnati Review*; "What the Ax Forgets the Tree Remembers" in *Ecotone*; "The Descent of Happiness" in *Epiphany*; "Sonny" in *Fifth Wednesday*; "Blessed Harry" in *Harvard Review*; "Tenderfoot" in *Idaho Review*; "Honeydew" in *Orion*; "Fishwater" in *Ploughshares*; "Dream Children" in *Post Road*; "Her Cousin Jamie" in *Salamander*.

"Honeydew" was reprinted in *The Best American Short Stories 2012*. "Conveniences" was reprinted in *Prize Stories: The O. Henry Awards 1984*. "Wait and See" was reprinted in the anthology *xo Orpheus*, edited by Kate Bernheimer. "Dream Children" also appeared in the anthology *No Near Exit*.

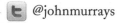
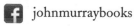